Also available from Jayce Ellis
and Carina Press

High Rise Series

Jeremiah
André

Higher Education Series

Learned Behaviors
Learned Reactions

IF YOU LOVE SOMETHING

Jayce Ellis

carina
press

carina
press®

Recycling programs
for this product may
not exist in your area.

ISBN-13: 978-1-335-51715-9

If You Love Something

Copyright © 2021 by Jayce Ellis

This edition published by arrangement with Harlequin Books S.A.

For questions and comments about the quality of this book, please contact us at
CustomerService@Harlequin.com.

Carina Press
22 Adelaide St. West, 40th Floor
Toronto, Ontario M5H 4E3, Canada
www.CarinaPress.com

Printed in U.S.A.

To my parents, for their continual support on this journey.

IF YOU LOVE SOMETHING

Chapter One

DeShawn

The faint strains of a familiar tune wafting in from the front of the restaurant made me pause my usual hurried pace to my office. Was the pianist playing… I tiptoed down the hall, keeping as quiet as possible, and listened.

Yep. That was definitely the Divinyls' "I Touch Myself." Wow, he was on one tonight, and I bet the esteemed patrons of this starred establishment, one of only two in DC, had no clue.

I covered my mouth to muffle a snicker and snuck back to my office before someone found me and made me perform. I wish I could flout propriety like the pianist but—I paused, looking down at my arms, covered in tattoos that always peeked out of my coat—I guess I got away with enough.

I slipped out of my over-expensive, toe-pinching loafers, into the far more comfortable clogs I wore while working. My butt had just hit the seat when Maribel, our head chef, burst through the door, her normally light tan skin flush with exertion.

"Janice is sick," she said, referring to our first line cook. "Or, rather, her wife is, so she's gone home to take care of their kid."

Whatever joy I'd taken in the pianist's subversive musical selections faded, and I was left with nothing but a nervous energy I couldn't parse. One of our other line cooks was on paternity leave, and rather than get someone to fill in, the CFO had decided we could make do. We had, but we were on the rails, and as executive chef, that was always my fault.

Bel cleared her throat and stepped toward me. "I'll work her station, and you can play head chef for the night," she began, but I waved her off.

"No. I'll handle her job; you keep doing what you're doing." Yes, that was a better idea, one I liked. It might even be fun.

"DeShawn, the line cooks are scared of you."

I snorted and fixed her with a withering look that she knew was all jokes. "They are not. I'm friendly with all of them."

"Friendly, but you're still *the* DeShawn Franklin, god of the kitchen, and we are but mere peons." She fluttered her lashes and kissed the air, and for a brief moment in time, I wished I had those godawful loafers back on, because clogs didn't give me the satisfying clunking sound as I tapped my foot.

"Hush, you." I grabbed my black chef's jacket and cap, smoothed it over my locs, and followed her out the door and to the kitchen. "You go on and be the big bad boss, and I'm gonna be one of the guys."

She huffed and mimed flipping her hair, except it was pulled back into a tight bun with a white cap over it, so not a strand moved. "We'll see about that."

I laughed, the banter with her just what I needed to loosen up. I loved this job, being an executive chef at one of the hottest restaurants in town, but I'd be lying if I said I didn't miss actually getting to cook every now and then. That was dead last on my list of responsibilities, and while I understood, it still grated. I missed the simplicity of chilling in the kitchen all night, shooting the shit and joking with the other line cooks and sous chefs, even when we were slammed. I wasn't nearly as fond of being bogged down by glad-handing patrons who barely touched their plates.

I slid into Janice's station next to Graham, an absolute lumberjack of a guy who made my already short five-six look positively tiny, and he started to grin, then gulped and his body went fainting-goat stiff. "Oh, Chef, I didn't know it was you."

Good Lord, was Bel right? Were people actually afraid of me? Impossible. I refused to accept it.

I elbow-nudged him and gave him a grin, the one that made folks love me or whatever. "You know I don't like being called Chef. Call me DeShawn and let's get to work."

Graham, eyes still saucer-round, nodded, then swallowed so hard his jaw clicked. He gripped his knife *way* too hard and I tried to muffle my small squeak of alarm. Apparently, that was enough to make him take a deep breath, loosen his grip, and begin cutting.

I waited for a few beats, then pulled Janice's card and went to work chopping onions. So many onions. Diced for the mirepoix, sliced for salads and a few of the entrees. Next to me, Graham's shoulders finally relaxed, and I watched him from the corner of my eye. He was a beast with the scallions, slicing with an efficiency I'd never been able to master. Huh, maybe he should give classes.

The door banged open, not an unusual sound, but the loud, nasally "Chef DeShawn" made my heart sink. Mine, and probably more than one person around me.

Still, I tried for a halfway decent grin as I turned and smiled tightly at Christopher. "Yes?"

Christopher—my agent slash publicist slash general pain in the ass—stomped over to me, his warm, slightly sweet cologne a sharp contrast to the pungent onions we were cutting. "We have multiple VIPs waiting to meet you. Powerful, influential. I need you out there ASAP." He paused and frowned, like he'd just realized where he was, or rather where *I* was. "What are you doing here anyway?"

"Helping," I said. "Janice is out. We're short."

"Your job does not involve chopping onions," he hissed.

I straightened and turned. Christopher looked on the verge of tears. He wasn't supposed to be in the kitchen anyway. Served him right that his eyes were watering. Because I'm a G, I didn't smile. "My job always involves service. If they'll wait a few minutes, I'll be right out."

"These are VIPs," Christopher protested.

"And?" I ignored him and chopped half an onion while he stood there. "Every patron wants the same thing, right? The best food, the kind that got us a star, as quickly as possible. In fact, I think they'd appreciate I'm not above jumping on line and helping out."

Christopher didn't answer, but I felt his eyes narrow on my back. We were supposed to work together for things that benefited my career, and his by association, but that glare made me feel like a recalcitrant schoolchild. He waited until I finished before muttering, "Are you ready now?" and turning away before I could answer.

He sounded every ounce the sullen little boy, and I groaned internally. I shouldn't goad my agent, no matter how much he irritated me. After conferring with Graham that he'd be fine on his own, and getting a squeaked "yes" in response, I followed Christopher out, slowing my step to get myself together. I ignored the knowing glance and tiny smirk Maribel gave when I passed, flicking her off as I walked out. By the time I pushed through the door, I was ready, my smile fixed in place. Christopher led me to a series of raised tables, where people who were there to be seen more than to eat sat around the table.

"Took you long enough," one man grumbled, his face

flushed, both a half-full tumbler and a full glass of wine in front of him. I smiled, the smile that made me so popular in the city, and stared at him until he dropped his eyes and coughed slightly, then mumbled he was just joking. Of course he was.

I took my eyes off him and beamed at the rest of the table, then gave a slight bow. "My sincerest apologies for keeping you waiting. We're somewhat short-staffed and I'm a cook at heart."

"I'd think you had better things to do than that," one woman commented, adjusting her posture so I couldn't help but notice the deep scoop neckline of her spaghetti-strap dress. For reasons forever unknown, I got that a lot. My being openly gay hadn't changed it a bit.

So I smiled and even gave her a little wink, making her blush. "I hope to never be so big in my britches that I'm above helping out the line cooks who bring my fantastical ideas to life and make your excellent meals possible."

That got a series of coos from her and the other women there, and even begrudgingly respectful nods from the men. I inquired about their meal—what, if anything, they particularly enjoyed—and, as usual, the restaurant comped their desserts. Throughout it all, Christopher stood next to me, his smile so wide and fixed it bordered on Jack Nicholson's Joker.

After another quick bow, I decided to take one quick circuit through the main room to speak to our other patrons. Once I made it back to the kitchen, it was unlikely I'd have a chance to come back out before the night was over.

Christopher wasn't interested in that, his face drooping the minute we were out of sight of the Very Important People. "We have to get back," he insisted, swiping at my sleeve.

I ignored him and shook hands with the "regular" customers at another table, spending time with them, listening to their stories and answering questions, before moving to the next one. Ten minutes later, Christopher scowling at my side, I headed back to the kitchen.

"I brought you out here to meet VIPs," he hissed in my ear.

"I did. What? You didn't want me to make anyone else feel like a VIP, too, Chris?"

"Christopher."

"My bad." As much as I thought he was a pretentious douchebag on the best of days, I wasn't an asshole about names. Given the number of times my own had been butchered over the past forty years, I was better than that. "What else do you want, Christopher? As you can see, I have work to do. You saw how short-staffed we are, and I made this round because I won't make it back on the floor tonight. What can I do for you?"

"We have a series of events lined up, some television gigs you'll need to be at in the next few days."

I crinkled my nose, well past trying to hide my distaste. "Christopher, why can't Bel do these instead of me? She's as photogenic as y'all say I am, and she actually likes that stuff."

He was shaking his head before I finished speaking, even though her agent worked for Christopher's agency and they usually swapped us in and out like playing cards. "Perhaps, but she's not..." He waved his arm vaguely at me. "You," he finished.

In someone's world, that was a compliment. In mine, it was a pain in the butt. I did not want, actually had no interest in, doing television segments. My desire to be on TV had evaporated after an early and disastrous pitch session, but Christopher was convinced my opinion would change once we found the right opportunity, my protests that I was over it notwithstanding. But Maribel and I had agreed with Criteria's owners to do regular segments with DCFoodie, a local food station.

I rolled my shoulders, knowing I wouldn't win this argument. Nothing to it but to do it.

"All right. Fine," I said. "We'll work it out. Let's schedule a time later this week."

For once, Christopher just nodded, and I pushed into the kitchen, intent on making my way back to my temporary station. Bel caught me as soon as I entered.

"DeShawn, I didn't want to come out and tell you, but your grandmother called while you were out. She says you need to come home."

Coming home didn't happen for two more days, until Janice got back and I finally put my foot down and forced the CFO to get a temp line cook. I'd called Grandma to explain, but she'd always been asleep, per her BFF Miss Maxine. She'd assured me it wasn't critical, that Grandma just needed to talk to me. Cryptic might as well have been both of their middle names.

I made the drive to Baltimore and pulled up to the small, single-story house, located smack in the middle of the block, and climbed out, taking a deep breath to let the calm wash over me. Here, I was just Lil D, Grandma's baby, the sorry one whose mama had passed having me. It'd taken me a long time to not feel guilty, but I'd been loved beyond measure. That knowledge led to a different kind of regret. While it was common for me to talk to Grandma a few times a week, it was rare she beckoned me home, and I hadn't made the drive up for close to six months.

I climbed the front steps and fished my key out of my pocket, leaning against a post I needed to have fixed for her. Which was just one of the many reasons I should've made time to get here before now. She was getting up in age, and I didn't know how much time we had left.

I opened the door and called out immediately, "Grandma? It's me."

The door shut behind me, and I took a moment to hang up my jacket on the coat tree. I turned at the sound of footsteps. Miss Maxine stood in the hallway, her arms open. I wasted no time crossing the distance and engulfing her in a hug.

"Hey, Auntie," I said.

She pressed a kiss to my forehead and patted my cheeks. "Hey, baby. Larry's in there with her now."

I walked in and smiled at Miss Maxine's son. We'd grown up together, but he'd become an adult and gone into law while I played in the kitchen for a living. He sat next to Grandma, who was reclined comfortably in her bed, the adjustable-frame mattress I'd bought her apparently being put to good use, and grinned at me. "Hey, D. What's good?"

"Not much, man. Always looking for a reason to escape the city." I leaned over and kissed Grandma on the cheek. "Hey, pretty lady, how's it going?"

"Good, baby. Take a seat, because we have some things to discuss."

No lie, that sounded pretty ominous, and I paused in front of the chair I'd been about to plop down in. "What's up?"

She wasted no time. "The cancer has metastasized and I'm not doing no more treatment."

If I'd been holding something, I would've dropped it. I sucked in a big gulp of air, but it wasn't enough. My hands tingled, like ants had taken up residence, and my shoulders ached with the sudden weight.

Not this. Jesus Christ, *not this.* She'd been in remission ten years, and I still remembered the fear in Grandpa's eyes when he thought he might lose her. When the doctors told us she was cancer free, Grandpa'd cried. Broke down on the hospital floor, thanking the Lord for saving his wife. I could've handled just about anything she told me. I wasn't sure if I could handle this.

I gripped the top of the chair and fought to stay upright. "Grandma, what?" Someone had taken a meat mallet to my voice, and I barely got the words out.

"I'm tired, I've done what I set out to do, and I'm ready to go when the good Lord is ready to bring me home. Now sit down, because I'm not finished."

I'm glad my legs obeyed her, because they sure as hell didn't listen to me. Or maybe it was the combined efforts of Larry and Miss Maxine pushing me into Grandma's old sitting chair. My fingers fumbled for the little patch of threadbare fabric on the arm that I'd been picking at since I was six. It was harder to pluck at it now than then, but way easier than to accept what I'd just heard.

Larry retook his seat, cleared his throat, and spoke. "Your grandmother has redone her will and wants you to know what's in it."

I nodded, still a little too numb to speak. That made sense, I guess. I knew she'd done one during her first bout with cancer and chemo, but once she'd gone into remission, I'd stopped thinking about it.

Grandma speared Larry with a look, but he just smiled indulgently at her before turning to me. He was a super bigwig at a downtown DC firm. He'd come into the restaurant a few times during lunch and always left huge tips. The servers adored him. "Grandma has left the house to you. She wanted you to have a place to, and I quote, 'get away from the madness of the city.'"

I blinked at him, then at Grandma, who gave me a quick smile. I adored this home, the quiet comfort it always brought me when the world got to be too much, but I'd assumed she'd leave it to my uncle Robert. He'd sell it immediately, because he was all about cash, and maybe that was part of her decision.

I reached out to grab her hands. "Thank you," I said, ignoring the slight warble in my voice. "Corey will love it."

"That dog loves anything. But I want you to love it, too." She sniffed, but she doted on my bulldog as much as, if not more, than I did.

"We will. But he'll especially love having this entire place to himself."

She cupped my cheek and I placed my hand over hers, tears springing up and a few strays spilling over. She wiped them with her thumb and I sat back, then shook myself and let out a hoarse cry, the reality of the situation overwhelming. Grandma, telling me her final wishes. I wasn't ready. Internally, I berated myself to get it the hell together, but it still took a few more deep breaths before I could face them.

Larry waited until I was done, his eyes warm with brotherly concern, before continuing. "Now, the actual cash, savings accounts, checking accounts, those liquid assets?"

I raised a brow. Me and Robert were the only family Grandma had, so if I got the house, he had to get the cash. He'd blow through it, like he'd blown through every bit of money he'd ever gotten his hands on, but it was kind of what he did. I'd long ago given up on Grandma saying no to him. Of course, she could also give it to charity. She was big into her church, and…

"Those are all going to Malik Franklin."

I paused. Closed my eyes, swallowed hard, fought to keep the name from thunking around my eardrums. Fought to keep the memories from swallowing me whole. "Malik? My ex-husband Malik?"

My throat closed all the way up, and I hacked hard enough

that Larry scrunched his nose at me and sat back. Miss Maxine came over and rubbed my back until I found my voice. "I...sure. I mean, it's your money. Do with it what you want."

Honestly, I don't even know why I was pretending. No one in the room believed a word out of my mouth. I didn't have to perform for them, and with that in mind, I blew out a deep breath and focused on what she had to say.

"So," Grandma started, drawing the word out, "that's really why I needed to talk to you. To tell you what we found."

My confusion? Sky high. "What, Grandma? What did you find?" *And why is my gut performing Kegels?*

She cleared her throat, and that really didn't help. "So. You and Malik's divorce..."

My nostrils flared at the word, and I had to take a moment before I could respond. "What about it?"

"Well, there was a problem with it."

"Okay. What problem?"

"Honestly, I'm not really sure."

Not. Helping. "Grandma, what are you telling me?"

"That you guys did something wrong and aren't divorced."

"What!" I leapt off the chair and stared at Larry, then at Grandma, then back to Larry. "What are you talking about, we aren't divorced? We've been divorced for years." Seven of them, to be exact. Seven years, three months, and eighteen days. Give or take. Maybe nineteen.

Larry winced but shook his head. "No, you're not. You were already out of the country when they sent the rejection notice. Not that it mattered, because we didn't see it. They sent a second notice a few years later closing out the case when a new divorce wasn't submitted. If you want one, you'll have to refile the entire thing."

I collapsed back in my seat and closed my eyes, pinching

the bridge of my nose. "How long have you known about this?" I asked Grandma, and felt like shit when her eyes got big and she shook her head rapidly. Hell, I hadn't meant to accuse her of anything.

"Not long, baby, I swear. They sent the paperwork here, but your grandfather had just died when the second letter came and I—"

I couldn't get to her fast enough, to sit on the bed and pull her close. She didn't need to explain. Grandpa's passing had been sudden, had shaken our whole world to its very core. I'd been in Barcelona and had broken down at least three times on the flight home. If I'd been here, there's a good chance I would've missed the paperwork, too.

Miss Maxine picked up where Grandma left off. "We found it when we were cleaning. We didn't want you to have to go through all her stuff the way she did Cornelius's, so we were trying to get that done now, and…"

She trailed off, and my mind circled all the way back around to losing Grandma. To her deciding to let go and let god. And as much as I wanted to plead with her to fight, not to give in, I also thought that her making this decision and doing it on her own terms was pretty badass. Which was Grandma in a nutshell.

"So now what?" I asked, trying to keep my voice light. "You telling me I don't get the house and he doesn't get the money unless we reunite and are remarried within six months or something?"

She laughed, long and loud, and it was music to my ears. And I wondered if this was the last time I'd hear it. I clenched my fists, digging my stubby nails into my palms to keep the tears at bay.

"No, nothing like that. Besides, I asked, and Larry says I

can't do it." She winked at him, and he chuckled, his unbridled affection for her evident.

"No," she said again, settling her gaze back on me. "There's no ultimatum. I'm telling you this so you're prepared. Robert's going to fight it tooth and nail, and you need to be ready. And you need to be there for Malik when Robert goes after him, too."

I frowned, thinking about the terms she'd laid out. "Grandma, are you cutting Uncle Robert out?"

"Yes." She punctuated it with a sharp nod. "I've given him more than enough, and I know he waits for my death with bated breath to get the rest. But I've assisted him enough in this life, and it's time for him to make his own way."

Wow. I had no words, couldn't think of when I'd heard her this passionate. I mean, except for her extremely vocal disapproval of my apparent non-divorce. But yeah, Uncle Robert was going to come out swinging to challenge this.

I looked up at her. "I don't know how to reach Malik. I don't have his number—we haven't spoken since the divorce."

Grandma smiled at me gently, like she was dealing with a toddler and not a forty-year-old man, then glanced at Larry. He cleared his throat and leaned across the bed to hand me a folded sheet of paper. I opened it to find Malik's name and number, and couldn't help but chuckle.

"Why do you have this?" I asked her, though I didn't know why I was surprised.

She snorted. "You two may have divorced, or tried to, but I didn't. That boy's been my grandbaby as much as you since the moment you brought him home."

God, Malik had loved her. Had adored her almost as much as he had me. And as happy as I was that he still spoke to her, hadn't let that die when we had, the sour tinge of bittersweet recriminations would haunt me tonight.

"Yeah, okay," I said, staring down at the paper in my hands. Wondering what I could possibly say. "I'll reach out to him."

"Don't dillydally, DeShawn." Grandma's voice was gentle, but she was serious. "This is important, and you need to reach out to him soon."

"I will, Grandma. I promise."

Chapter Two

Malik

Franklin's Homestyle Restaurant was too quiet when I walked in, and that wasn't a good sign. If I looked in the kitchen, I knew I'd find my baby sister, Sheila, putting her foot in whatever she was making, and I hated how often the food went to waste.

I nodded at the few patrons—regulars, too stubborn to move on, and bless them for it—before walking down the narrow hallway to my office. I hadn't even shrugged my coat off when the door flew open, my younger but significantly more imposing brother, James, filling the frame.

"Malik," he started, waving a sheet of paper in his hand, "we've got to do something about this."

The *this*, I knew, was our family restaurant's finances, and he didn't have to tell me. I was the accountant, after all. I'd been ringing that alarm bell for over a year now. But James was CEO, a title he'd given himself when Mom and Dad left him in charge of day-to-day operations. I could go purple in the face screaming about finances, and until it hit him, I might as well have done some private journaling and moved on.

Still, I nodded instead of giving him a play-by-play of all the times I'd tried to have this conversation with him. It was the truth, after all. "Yes, and I have thoughts. Ideas."

"Yeah?" He almost sounded excited as he stepped in and shut the door behind him, then sank into my spare chair. An old, too-large monstrosity from my old life. Every time I looked at my over-cramped office, I swore I'd get rid of the darn thing. But someone would inevitably come by, make themselves comfortable in it, and act like I didn't have anything to do but talk to them. At some point, I'd stopped fighting. Besides, I had a sentimental attachment to it, and letting it go felt…wrong. And if James was comfortable, this was my opportunity to finally get him onboard.

I shoved the chair out of my mind and finally sat down. "I know things have been slow, but this has become a business neighborhood. Lunches are shorter and people don't have time for a sit-down meal like they used to. Let's take advantage of that."

James sighed, like he knew where this was going. "Please say you're not going to suggest signing on with one of those delivery app companies again. We already went over that."

I rolled my eyes, even though I kept my mouth shut. Perks of being family—I didn't care if he got mad. And from the slight furrow between his brows, he did. Tough. I was just as exasperated as he was.

"Why are we open for lunch if we can't serve them quickly enough for them to eat? By the time most of our patrons order and we get the food out, we're doggy bagging it anyway. Why don't we make it easy for them to come here? We can do just online ordering with pickup only if you want to test it, but I really think we either need to get drivers to deliver or we need to look into an app."

James's face never changed, even as I got more excited.

Yeah, over better ways to serve customers. Sexy.

"Malik," he said, scrubbing a hand over his eyes, "how

many times do I have to tell you we don't have the money for that?"

"James, how many times do I have to tell you I'm the accountant? I know how much money we have." Maybe I shouldn't have matched his pseudo-mocking tone. Because Baby Brother's face pinched, and if we were kids, he'd be running to tell Mom I was being mean to him.

"I don't know. I still think it seems like a long shot. With as far in the hole as we are, it's not going to make enough of a dent."

I hated to admit it, but by itself, my idea was potentially helpful but not life changing. Our parents had taken out a loan three years ago to renovate the restaurant: new awning, facade, floors, the whole thing. The area had turned into a business district, and they needed to try to keep up. But the customers changed even faster, and we went from being one restaurant on a block of family-owned businesses and eateries in a working-class neighborhood to being the dinosaur of the newly named Greenwood Villages, surrounded by chains and franchises.

Everyone else had taken a buyout, from stores to residents, and with a new, young, hard-working business clientele always on the go, our income dropped precipitously without the dinner revenue that'd been our lifeblood. We'd ended up taking that loan money and using it to pay salaries and vendors, and were nearly tapped out. Worse, all the buildings around us were new shiny sparklies—primarily because they were new, shiny, hipper businesses—and we looked decidedly dowdy. Not only did we need to bring in new customers, but we needed to not be the dingy hole in the wall. That worked for some locations. Ours wasn't one of them.

"James," I pressed, determined to make my point, "the customers have changed. We have to change with them. They need good, fast service. An easy pickup or, better yet, not leaving their desks at all. Let's turn lunch into our biggest moneymaker."

The way he cut his eyes showed me what he thought of that idea. Still, he ignored me in favor of grabbing the remote to the mounted TV I perpetually forgot was even there, and flipping it on and over to DCFoodie, which had been James's favorite station for more years than I could remember. I heard a familiar voice, one that even seven years later had the same mouth-drying, heart-racing, body-craving effect it'd always had, and forced myself to stay immobile.

"See? That. That's what we need," James said, pointing at the screen, his eyes lighting up. "Something big, bold, flashy. DeShawn Franklin would bring in so many people. His presence alone would turn this place around."

"How?" I sounded suitably droll, and mentally patted myself on the back for it.

"He could spotlight us on DCFoodie, or even do a guest appearance here. Remember when he used to do those blind taste tests, trying to pick out the seasonings restaurants used for their specialty meals? That would kick ass."

Unfortunately, I remembered the taste testing all too well. DeShawn and I'd played that game when we were young and showing off for each other. It'd always, without fail, ended up in sex. On the bed, or the couch, against the counter, sometimes on the kitchen floor.

I closed my eyes and massaged them for a few seconds before letting my hand fall. "For how long?" I asked, somehow managing to sound as unimpressed by James's suggestion as he did by mine.

James crinkled his nose. "Long enough to give us a big boost in sales, after which we might have enough cash flow to consider one of your little penny-ante ideas."

"The ones you just said were too expensive?"

"They are. Too much money for what good they'll do. Like I said, penny-ante."

I tried not to bristle at his dismissiveness. My ideas were good, goddammit. "Yeah? And how much would we have to pay to bring him here? What's our ROI after he gets his cut?"

Air left James like an exploded balloon, and now I felt bad. "I know, it's a pipe dream. A guy like that would never bother with a small-time operation like ours."

I swallowed the words that threatened to spill out. A guy like that? Would do this for free. Not as any favor to me, of course, but he'd do anything to make his grandmother happy.

I winced and smoothed my face over before he noticed. My family didn't know about DeShawn. That I knew him. That I *knew* him. As far as they were concerned, our all having the same last name was a happy coincidence.

Now that I thought about it, I hadn't spoken to Grandma for a few days, and I needed to give her a call. She got touchy if I didn't reach out at least twice a month. Besides, I missed her. Hell, I missed him, too, but I couldn't do anything about that. He'd chosen his path, and it wasn't me. The past seven years proved he'd definitely made the right call.

"You got any other bright ideas?" James asked, his voice soft, a mix of panicked and desperate. "You look like you zoned out."

I swallowed. "I think we should take up some of the companies on their catering requests. We could do that during the day, for office meetings and parties. It's another way to take advantage of the shift in clientele."

James sighed, like the very thought exhausted him. "Haven't we gone over this before?"

"James, these people are offering us good money to do this. We know our food is top-notch, and if nothing else, they like the idea of patronizing the little restaurant that stayed. Heck, me and Sheila could do it and put it in the company's name if it meant helping with finances without the expense."

The snort James let out was not helping. "You can't cook, so what you really mean is Sheila could do it. But if you screw up, it's also in the company's name, and that's not a risk I can take."

I ignored the remark about my cooking, same as I had for thirty years. "But I can, and I'm the accountant."

"And I'm the CEO, and I say no."

I opened my mouth to argue, but what was the use? We'd been over this before, had these same discussions for years now. Before Mom and Dad took out the loan, before the neighborhood and our customer base changed so fast we couldn't keep up, before James had taken on the mantle of CEO. I'd had these same arguments with Dad, and it'd gone nowhere then, too. I'd hoped James would be better, but he was maybe more conservative about new ideas, if that was possible.

"Don't worry, old man, we'll think of something," James said, trying for a spark of levity, and I managed a smile.

"We don't have much time." I hated sounding ominous, but the reality? The situation had moved past worrying and was full speed ahead toward dire.

"Trust me, I'm aware." He knocked on the desk a few times and stood. "Check you later."

He slipped out the door and I blew out a breath, closing my eyes. DeShawn's voice was a melody in the background, crisp and clean and downright infectious. That was the thing about him. He always sounded excited, like he was thrilled to death with what he did. I knew it wasn't the reality, but I envied his ability to pretend. Always had.

Once upon a time, I'd been his comfort when he'd peopled too much for too long. But he no longer needed me, and I couldn't look at him. Hearing him was bad enough, but seeing him? Was more than my poor soul could take. My dumb heart didn't understand why we couldn't just track him down, and my body had been nearly vibrating from the moment James turned the TV on.

I fumbled across the desk for the remote, and squeezed my eyes shut as I flicked off the power. Yes, it was pathetic. No, I didn't care.

Maybe James was right. Maybe I should call Grandma tonight, shove my pride into my pocket, and ask for DeShawn's help. Even if he came—and he would if she asked—without a longer, global plan, it'd all be for naught. We needed to do something real to save this restaurant, and fast.

There was nothing I wanted more when I got inside than to collapse on my couch and sleep till tomorrow. But Bruno, my mastiff, who had free run of the house and the backyard all day, sat patiently in the foyer, leash in his mouth. Sometimes I hated how well I'd trained him.

I reached down and rubbed his head, and he nuzzled into my thigh. "All right, boy, give me a few moments to change, and we'll go out."

A solitary bark was my answer, and I jogged up the stairs of my home and into the bedroom.

James's idea that DeShawn could help us? It had stayed with me the rest of the day. I hated to think he might have a point, but it wasn't the worst idea on the planet. It wasn't enough, and even if DeShawn did it for free, we'd need some way of sustaining it, but it *would* be a huge boost. No one in their right mind could deny that. And maybe he could talk James into some of my other ideas, too. Lord knew he'd listen to DeShawn before he did me.

I changed out of my slacks and shirt into a pair of track pants and a T-shirt with a reflective stripe, then walked back downstairs and hooked the leash to Bruno's collar so we could head out. Bruno wasn't one of those dogs who strained and pulled at me. He liked a nice, long, leisurely walk. One where he could pause, mark over all the territory, and basically peruse his neighborhood. At this time of the year, just tipping from spring into summer, the weather warm but not sweltering, I was fine with it. Come winter, it'd be the bane of my existence.

My phone rang while we ambled along, and I knew from the ring tone who it was. I tapped my earpiece. "Hey, Grandma. I was going to call you when I got back inside."

"Taking that big baby of yours out for a walk?"

The laugh in her voice never failed to soothe something in me. "You know it. Can't bear to listen to his whining if I don't. How are you? I've been meaning to call."

"You're busy, I know that. I just enjoy hearing your voice. Lord knows I hear from you more than my child."

Years ago, me and DeShawn lived just a few miles away from Grandma. I'd had the...pleasure of meeting her son, Robert, and let's just say it'd left a lot to be desired. How she was so kind and caring, and DeShawn so loving, when that greedy man sat in the middle? Blew my mind.

"Well, you know I love talking to you," I offered.

"Speaking of talking to, has that wayward grandson of mine reached out?"

"DeShawn?"

"Only one I got, last I checked."

I snorted, but my chest tightened. This must be Throw-DeShawn-in-Malik's-Face Day. "No," I said, trying to keep my voice neutral, "DeShawn hasn't reached out. Is there a reason he should?"

She hummed. "I spoke to that boy a few weeks ago. Told

him he needed to call you ASAP. Don't know why he's so stubborn."

Anyone coming up on me and Bruno right now would probably scurry across the street, because I'm sure the frown on my face made me anything but approachable. "Grandma, what are you talking about? What do me and DeShawn need to discuss?"

"That's between you and DeShawn."

I sighed. Most of the time she was straight up, but occasionally she preferred to be enigmatic. It was a little unhelpful and a lot of anxiety inducing.

Bruno tugged, and I let myself get back to walking before I answered. "Grandma, we haven't spoken in years."

"Fools, the both of you. You know how I feel about all that." I could practically see her pounding the bedcovers in frustration.

Bruno paused in front of a patch of grass to do his business and I took the moment to breathe. Grandma had called us fools when we'd told her we were divorcing, too. She'd thought, even though I wasn't out to my family then and DeShawn had been offered the opportunity of a lifetime—working alongside a restaurateur who saw his potential and wanted to make him the head chef of a new venture in Rome—that we should've shoved that aside and made things work. That's what marriage is, she'd said. Making those hard decisions, figuring it out together.

What me and DeShawn had known even then was that, as much as we'd loved each other, our paths had irreparably diverged. That saying "if you love something, let it go?" Yeah, I'd done that. And watched from afar as DeShawn thrived without me. He may have been willing to stay, but after his successes, no way he'd consider coming back.

That reality hit me square in the chest. I couldn't ask her for DeShawn's help. There had to be another way.

I coughed a few times before speaking. "Grandma, I'm sure DeShawn is super busy, and he'll contact me when he has time. Right now, I want to talk to *you.*"

She snorted. "Boy acts like we've got all the time in the world, and we don't. Let me give you his number."

Me, have DeShawn's number? Bad idea. It was hard enough not to watch him on TV every chance I got. Keeping myself from calling him, from dialing those ten digits just to hear his voice on a machine? More than a man should be forced to take.

"Grandma," I interrupted, "I'm out with Bruno. I don't even have a pen on me."

She laughed. "Like you couldn't just type it into your phone." She had me there. Damn technological proficiency. "I might be some dumb, but I'm not plum dumb. That's okay. I'll just text you his card."

There was no way I could talk her out of it, but I'd delete it as soon as possible. I didn't need that kind of access to De-Shawn. I hurried to change the subject. "Seriously, though, Grandma, how are you? How have you been?"

She went quiet for a beat, then, "You know I don't like giving less than positive news."

I stopped walking, causing Bruno to jerk and whine. *Sorry,* I mouthed to him. "What do you mean, less than positive news?"

"Well, we're preparing for hospice care. So it won't be long now."

"What? No! Grandma, why didn't you say anything? What's happening? I'll be there ASAP." Words tumbled out of my mouth faster than my brain could keep up. This wasn't happening. Couldn't be happening.

"You'll do no such thing." Her voice, clear and sharp,

snapped me back to reality. "I didn't say anything because I knew you'd react like this, which is not what I want. Everyone's time comes, baby, and I'm happy with what I've done. But I need you and DeShawn to make sure things go the way they're supposed to."

I didn't know what that meant, and it didn't matter. I was losing her. She sounded too strong, too sure of her decision, and I hated it. Hated that I wanted more time with her, wanted *her* to want more time with me. Hated knowing the biggest decision of my life had been the biggest disappointment of hers. Especially hated accepting that, if I could do it over, I'd let DeShawn go again. Because he needed more than I could give him then, and deserved more than I could give him now. And god, what must DeShawn be feeling? I was all in my own feelings, but DeShawn revered his grandmother. He had to be going crazy with this news…but surely he had people he could call on, right? He wouldn't appreciate hearing from me. Otherwise, he would've already reached out. Boy, could I wind myself in circles justifying actions, or the lack thereof.

A big, weary breath left me, and I looked up with amazement. We were back at the house. I hadn't even noticed Bruno, his tongue hanging out, leading us back here, ready to rest. Same, boy, same.

"Grandma," I said, remembering I was still on the phone, "I want to see you."

"Absolutely not. I'm old and frail and I don't want you seeing me like this. I want you to remember me as young, vibrant, full of life and energy."

I laughed, but it was an ugly, snot-filled thing. "You mean exactly how you sound right now?"

"Exactly that. But I'm sending you this boy's information. The two of you need to get over whatever bullshit tore you apart all those years ago and make this work."

That'd never happen, but I wasn't arguing. "Sure, Grandma. We'll do it."

"I know when you're lying to me, boy."

Now my laugh was real. "I'm calling you again in a few days. You hear me? And you better pick up."

She laughed again and her voice softened. "I will, baby. I will."

We clicked off, and my phone buzzed almost immediately after. I opened it and saw DeShawn's contact info. I deleted it within seconds, but the number was already burned in my memory.

Chapter Three

DeShawn

On god, if one more person interrupted me, my cheerful persona was going to crack like a poorly installed induction cooktop.

All I wanted to do was get through this day. I was off tomorrow, but I wasn't even waiting till then to get to Grandma. Me and Corey were going up there tonight. The knot at the pit of my gut had been building since I'd last seen her, and was now the size of a small boulder. I kept saying I'd call, but the past week had been full of sixteen-plus-hour days, and by the time I got to my apartment at night, I was barely capable of rational thought, let alone serious conversations. Thank god for dog walkers, because at least Corey was good.

"Chef DeShawn, I need your opinion on this sauce." The sous chef who'd made it looked apprehensive, and that was never a good thing. He gave me a clean spoon and I tasted it.

"I understand this is a lower sodium meal, but we need to increase the flavor. What herbs did you put in?"

"The usual: parsley, thyme, sage, and a bit of rosemary."

"Fresh or dried?"

He looked nearly offended by the question. Must be a newbie here, because I had a love/love relationship with dried herbs. "Fresh, of course."

"Add some dried to it. Stronger concentration of flavor. Let it steep. I'll be back to check on it soon." Once the shock wore off his face, he nodded and went back to it.

I made my way over to Maribel, standing at the front with a clipboard, her eyes seeing everything and checking things off. "How's it going here?" I asked.

Her snort mirrored my feelings. "I'm through with just about everybody, to be honest."

I chuckled softly. "You don't have to tell me."

Bel's face softened as she looked me over. "I know you know. Have you done whatever your grandmother asked?"

She was the only person who had even a hint of what was going on, the only person who actually cared about me outside the restaurant. After all these years, it didn't sting the way it had when I first started. But even then, I hadn't talked about my life pre-Criteria. I'd been single when I met her, and had spent years deflecting questions and jabs from other cooks about my love life. Trying to explain now that I'd been divorced, but somehow now wasn't, was more than I could take. It didn't even sound real to my own ears.

To her, I shook my head. "I haven't, and before you chastise me, I know I need to."

"DeShawn," she said, her voice dropping that polite facade we normally maintained in earshot of other people, "she called you to her house to tell you about her will. She told you she wasn't getting more treatment. Why are you acting like this isn't happening?"

"Because I don't want to lose her." My voice broke on the last word, and Bel sighed, her face creased with sympathy, before she placed a hand on my elbow.

"I know you don't," she said, her voice gentling, "and I understand. But we need to prepare, to game plan for when you're gone for a few days, few weeks, whatever, so things don't fall through the cracks."

She was right, and I was damn lucky to have her on my team. I ran a hand over my face, but before I could say anything else, Christopher barged in. There was little I hated more than non-cooks in my kitchen, but getting that through to him was like having a deep and meaningful conversation with a steel door.

He found me and his nose twitched, and for a second I wished we were by the onions again. "DeShawn," he began without preamble, "I'm sure your attention could be better utilized elsewhere, correct?"

For him, better utilized was typically code for schmoozing the patrons. Which I did regularly, and wasn't a reason for him to come to the kitchen. So there had to be something else. "Once we get this prep settled, I'll be out to do rounds. Might be the last time for a while, because I need to head home."

"Excellent. We need you to do a segment for the show."

But it was Tuesday evening, and I taped segments on Thursday mornings. "I...what?"

"Now, if you can," he went on as if I hadn't interrupted. "Shouldn't be long, only fifteen or twenty minutes."

I blinked, then closed my eyes to keep my expression neutral. Christopher was singularly focused; I had to give him that. Right now, all that attention was on the weekly segment I did for DCFoodie, and everything funneled into that, while I was still stuck wondering what the hell "excellent" had been referring to.

I raised a brow and shared a look with Maribel. She understood me. When I'd first been named executive chef of Criteria, I'd been thrilled about being on TV. It was a spotlight, but it was controlled. I thought it'd be my jam, and my real struggle would come with the nightly interactions with customers. It wasn't. Quite the opposite.

I loved meeting the patrons who truly enjoyed the meals we prepared. I loved interacting with people on a real and genuine basis. I'd wanted to do that on television, too, but the network heads had balked at my ideas. They were much more interested in playing off the tattoos and locs and piercings, and not in building legit connections with local businesses. Not that Christopher cared about such things. I was the "pretty, bad boy" executive chef, and viewers loved it. As long as I kept my tongue and my face in check, he could care less what I did or did not like.

"The sooner we get this done, the sooner you can get back to"—Christopher paused and looked around—"whatever it is you do here."

I bristled, and Maribel stiffened next to me. This, of course, was why I didn't like him in my space. He didn't know anything about how kitchens ran, and honestly, he didn't care. As long as it—scratch that—*I* was popular and made money, he got his cut, and that was the entirety of his focus.

"You got this?" I asked Bel, and she gave me a curt nod, back to being her usual reserved self.

I looked at Christopher and straightened, then grabbed the double-breasted white chef coat that I only wore to do the segments. Apparently the white was more approachable, especially to older audiences. I draped it over my arm and nodded at him. "Let's get this over with."

The studio was a few blocks away, and we walked at a quick clip down the block. As was becoming familiar, though no less disconcerting, people who recognized me stopped to point and smile, and I immediately returned their waves.

"Chef DeShawn! We love you!" one young lady called out, surrounded by friends nodding their agreement.

I waved and gave them a slight bow, slowing but not stopping. "And I love you guys, too." I'd never gotten used to being recognizable, but I preferred meeting people organically rather than at formal events. It didn't feel as staged, wasn't as intrusive, and didn't last as long. Win-win-win, as far as I was concerned.

They squealed and bent their heads together, then one sprinted down the block and tapped me on my shoulder. "Can you sign this?"

"DeShawn, we have somewhere to be." The rapid *thudthudthud* of Christopher's shoes on the pavement made the woman shift closer to me and away from him. I ignored him and signed four sheets of paper, one for her and each of her friends, posed for a selfie, then kissed the back of her hand before she ran off.

"You never listen to me, and one day it's going to get you in trouble," Christopher whispered tightly once she was gone and we'd started walking.

I didn't break stride. "If getting in trouble means I don't have to do any more TV spots, I'm here for it."

Christopher narrowed his eyes but didn't respond. He knew I wasn't lying. If I never saw myself on television again it would be too soon.

Before long we'd wound our way through the front lobby into the studio, all bright lights and pristine white kitchen with that aggravating herringbone subway tile backsplash and stainless steel everything. Christopher left to do whatever he did while I worked, and the makeup artist hurried over to me.

"Just a bit of blotting and powder, then you're ready to go," he said, pressing blotting papers to my T-zone.

I grinned at him and his cheeks pinkened. Or that could be blush. Whatever it was, it looked good on him. "You flatter me."

"Never." He brushed my forehead and nose with the tiniest bit of powder—more would make me ashy, he said—then popped me on the arm and pointed. "Go."

My phone buzzed as I walked to the kitchen. I normally kept it on silent during the day, and I almost ignored it. I should've ignored it. When I pulled it out of my pocket, I saw a message from Larry.

LJ: It's go time. Robert's filed suit.

I stumbled to a stop and almost fell, then reached out to grasp the side of the producer's chair.

"You okay?" she whispered. I shook my head, my throat too clogged to speak.

"DeShawn! Places." That wasn't even the director, that was Christopher, and I cringed at his strident tone. My heart raced too fast for me to respond.

Was Grandma gone? She had to be, right? Robert wouldn't be filing for anything if she was still here, and Larry wouldn't tell me she passed in an email. Or maybe she'd taken a turn for the worse and needed a power of attorney? That could be what Larry meant. I needed more information. I stared at the message again, but the words didn't change, didn't shift into something that made sense, and I was spiraling.

The producer leaned in toward me again. "Do we need to find someone else?"

Boy, I was tempted to say yes, but I shook my head. Right now, I needed the distraction. These segments were short, and it'd keep me from mentally cycling into ever more grim scenarios. Christopher was by my side and in my ear in a flash. "We have work to do. Why are you dillydallying?"

He was truly on my last nerve, but his complete obliviousness to my distress was the push I needed to keep going.

"What are we doing today?" I asked the producer, pulling on my classic, devil-may-care persona as I slipped into my coat and fastened it, then donned a white toque saucier.

She launched into their segment plan with the director and host, and I worked through a short segment about ensuring a steak's proper doneness without cutting into it and losing the flavor. We went over various types of meat thermometers to check temperature, and I pulled the steak off to a perfect, medium-rare doneness, to finish it off. The host's moan of pleasure was not faked, and I smiled. I did make a pretty bomb-ass steak.

The minute cameras cut off, I removed my cap, peeled out of my jacket, and sprinted toward the exit.

"Where're you going?" Christopher demanded as he maneuvered through people to reach me.

"I'm leaving, I have to go back home. I'll be in touch with Maribel shortly. She knows how to handle things."

"Handle things?" Christopher leaned over and grabbed my elbow, but at the pointed look I gave him, dropped it and herded me into the corner. "You can't just up and leave."

"I have a family emergency. Which I tried to tell you earlier, but you weren't listening." That I wasn't quite sure on the exact nature of the emergency wasn't his business. "Maribel and I were planning for it when you came in today, and I'll follow up with her when I get home."

"I expect you back here in three days."

Wasn't going to happen. "No. If that's your expectation, prepare to be disappointed." I walked off, not caring what else he had to say. I needed to call Malik. He'd for sure be mentioned in the suit, maybe even made a defendant. God, Grandma was going to kill me. It'd been about a month since she'd told me to call him, and his number had branded itself on my brain.

What did I say, though? *Hey Malik, remember how we thought we were divorced? Surprise, we're not!* I still didn't believe it myself, and no matter how many times I repeated the words, they sounded ridiculous. Never mind that Malik made me tongue-tied, enough that I choked on my spit the first time I tried to approach him. We'd dated for one year, been engaged for another, and I'd still been awestruck at our wedding that he'd picked me. I'd be less than surprised if I acted the same way when I spoke to him again.

I shot Bel a text, telling her I'd reach out soon, then hurried to my office, grabbed my stuff, and left. I needed my dog, and then I had to deal with the fact that my world seemed to be crumbling all around me.

Malik

No matter how hard I tried, I couldn't focus on the spreadsheet in front of me. It wasn't that there was a discrepancy, or the numbers were off somehow, or anything that made sense. But my mind was somewhere else. I'd called Grandma last night, and she sounded more tired than usual. Longer pauses and deeper breaths between answers, and her voice was softer and slightly strained when she spoke. She assured me nothing was wrong, but I didn't believe it. I didn't care what she said: Bruno and I were going up there this weekend and parking our butts on her couch.

Someone knocked on the door, and I knew it had to be Sheila. She was the only one who knocked. "Come in," I called out.

She poked her head through, then stepped inside. "How's it going?" she asked.

"It's going. I'm here," was about all I could say.

"I don't even know why. No one's here but family."

I nodded. This wasn't the first time lunch service had consisted of family and no one else. Our regulars would show up later, closer to the dinner service we'd once been known for. This was too bustling a neighborhood for that, and James refused to take advantage of it. And our parents, having turned over the reins, refused to intervene. I wondered if, watching people hurry up and down the streets, ignoring our door, they could finally see what I'd been trying to say about shifting our focus. Not that it'd do much good if they insisted on remaining hands-off.

"We could be doing so much, but James doesn't listen to me," I told her, and she plopped in the chair and nodded.

"Same. We've never had to really advertise before, and now we do. It's a tough reality, but that's where we are. Else we're not going to make it another year. Stubborn ain't doing us a stitch of good."

Despite being the youngest sibling, James was probably the most old-fashioned. He wasn't interested in expanding or branching out into new directions. With our parents, that had been sustainable, but we'd passed that stage years ago. And despite both my and Sheila's efforts, James so far refused to acknowledge, accept, or prepare for that eventuality, other than his "big name" suggestion, which I'd ruthlessly shoved in the back of my mind.

"What should we do?" I asked, and wanted to smack myself for not talking with her sooner. She had a business degree, too, but loved cooking enough that it was easy to forget. Hell, Sheila was bar none the sharpest of us. Together, maybe we could come up with a plan James couldn't ignore.

She sat back and draped her arms over the chair. "Ideally, we'd have a mix. Indoor dining, patio service when the weather's nice, online ordering for pickup, and delivery options. Our goal should be to meet our customers where they are and"—she straightened and pointed her finger at me—

"if they trust us, that puts us at the top of the list for holiday parties, special events, all that."

I huffed at the last suggestion. "I already talked to James about catering, and he's flat-out against it."

"He's a fool, then." Her nose crinkled in disgust, even as her bottom lip jutted out.

"James's idea is to bring in a big name and use that to give the place a boost."

"Like what? To do some showcase of the food and get people in because so-and-so mentioned it?"

My snicker slipped out. "That's pretty much what he said, actually. It's what comes after the celebrity endorsement he stalled on."

Sheila waved her hand. "I love that boy, but I don't understand how he became CEO. All he thinks about is short-term, huge immediate profit, and then the tail drops off the map."

"Probably because he was the only one who wanted the job," I said, fixing her with a pointed look.

She handed that look right back at me, then stuck her tongue out for good measure. "You would have been just as good a CEO as him."

I shook my head. "Nope. You would've been superior, plus you actually like talking to people."

"But I like cooking more."

"And that's why no one fought you about it."

I closed my eyes. Maybe I should've fought harder but, outside of Christmas cards, I hadn't spoken to my family for years before I popped back up out of the blue. Vying for the CEO job had felt like cutting James off at the knees, because that was the only thing he really wanted to do at the restaurant. I hadn't pressed, which seemed to be a running theme for my life.

I looked up to find Sheila watching me, her eyes narrowed,

her elbows on her knees. "What's going on with you, Malik? You're down about something, and I can't figure it out."

The answer fumbled on my tongue, but another knock came. That was odd. I stood and crossed to open the door, and an unfamiliar man stood in the doorframe. "You Malik Franklin?" he asked.

"Yeah." I raised a brow and folded my arms across my chest, which didn't seem to faze him in the least.

He thrust an envelope at me. I took it with wary hands. "Consider yourself served." He walked down the hall and out the restaurant without a backward glance.

"Served? The hell is he talking about?" Sheila asked as soon as I shut the door.

"No clue. Let's find out." I flicked up an edge of the envelope and ripped it open. "Robert Moore versus Malik Franklin. Fraud in the Inducement of the Will of Anna Mae Belle Moore." I flipped through the rest of the pages, not seeing a single word, before letting them fall to the ground. Sheila scooped them up, and then walked me back to my chair and pushed me into the seat.

It was quiet while I let her read the document. A dull thud started in my ears and steadily increased, and I dropped my head back to suck in a few breaths. Grandma knew this was coming. *This* had to be why she'd been insistent on me and DeShawn talking. I'd deleted the text with his number, but it had fused itself to my heart and whispered across the edges of my brain for weeks now. The numbers weren't whispering anymore; now they were screaming.

"Malik," Sheila said, and I couldn't tell if she was whispering or if I just couldn't hear her over the roar in my head. "Honey, what's all this about?"

"Grandma."

The family knew about Grandma, that she was the grandmother of one of my friends from when I was in school, but no one knew the full story. Grandma got a special kind of kick out of that. Mom, Dad, Sheila, and James had all spoken to her at least once, and they all knew how special she was to me. Sometimes I felt bad about obscuring my relationship with DeShawn, but Grandma had no such compunctions. She was a wily one, to be honest.

Sheila took her seat, the papers still in her hand. "It says here that you tricked her into cutting off her son and naming you as a beneficiary?"

"Which I damn well didn't do." Then her words hit me. I was a beneficiary? Holy mother of god.

Sheila's face softened. "Of course not. But why would he even say that?"

Because Robert was an ass who thought the world owed him. What, exactly, I didn't know, but I remembered the disdainful way he glared whenever our paths crossed. Like me and DeShawn were scrubs for going to school and getting jobs instead of "hustling," which he had the nerve to put on a business card. Robert Moore, Professional Hustler.

I didn't know how to encapsulate all that, so I just shrugged and said, "That's who he is." And I was more worried than ever about Grandma. Robert was an asshole, but he could be charming as hell when he wanted. No doubt he'd try to sweet-talk her into making modifications, and if that's what she wanted, great. But I had to make sure.

"I need to get up there. I need to see her and spend time with her. She made these vague references about things I have to do, but wouldn't tell me what they are, and I don't know if I'm more concerned or irritated right now."

"Concerned," Sheila said without hesitation. "Definitely concerned."

I blew out a noisy breath. "You're right."

We fell silent, and I tilted my head to the ceiling and closed my eyes. Once again, I'd refrained from mentioning De-Shawn's name. But there was no way I was getting through this without spilling the beans on that relationship.

Our divorce had been amicable—on the surface at least. Underneath, fears and frustrations had nearly swallowed us whole, and we'd put duct tape and Flex Paste and Gorilla Glue on years' worth of hurt. The idea of picking up the phone and facing those fears again nearly made me nauseous.

I needed to read the paperwork. I needed to pick up my big boy pants and call DeShawn, like Grandma had implored me to do. This wasn't to catch up or shoot the shit. No, this was business only. Surely we could handle that.

I cleared my throat and sat up straight. Sheila still sat there, nibbling her lower lip and watching me with worried eyes. She'd set the document on the desk. I grabbed the pages and started to read, but was startled by a yell. We stared at each other, then I rounded the desk and we sprinted to the front of the restaurant.

The entire family was circled around a stranger, and when his eyes darted up and he saw me, the faintest smile graced his lips. And my body jolted in a way I didn't have a chance in hell of hiding.

"Malik. Malik!" James yelled, waving me over, excitement pouring off him in waves. "Do you know who this is? This is *the* DeShawn Franklin. This is—"

I finished the sentence for him, imagining the beans spilling all around me. "My ex-husband."

Chapter Four

DeShawn

Two things were immediately obvious. One, Malik had come out to his family, given the casual way he described our relationship. Good for him. Two, Grandma hadn't yet shared the little nugget about our marriage with him.

Oh, and three, Malik had aged like fine wine. I mean, good *goddamn*. The specks of gray around his temples really gave him that whole distinguished gentleman look, and as I let my gaze travel over his body, across those broad pecs, those thick arms barely constrained by the plain white button-down he wore, to the gray slacks and simple black loafers, he was every ounce as delectable now as he'd been ten years ago. He had the slightest paunch in his belly now, and honestly, I loved it. I wanted to nuzzle it before I went on to…other things.

My eyes met his and he fidgeted, taking a step back, the sheaf of papers he held in front of him fluttering. Malik crossed his hands in front of his waist and glared at me. Huh. That was sexy, too. I raised a brow at him, wondering what he was trying to hide.

"Wayment, wayment, wayment." The guy who'd yelled when I walked in, the spitting image of Malik a decade younger, pointed at me, his eyes wide and mouth hanging open. "DeShawn Franklin is your ex-husband? How in the hell did you not tell us you were married to *the* DeShawn Franklin?"

Malik's frown deepened, his spine went poker straight, and he took a deep breath before blowing it out and looking out the window.

"Our relationship wasn't something we were all that open about," I said, giving him a chance to gather himself.

"You were married, but not open about it?" the woman who'd run down the hall with him asked. Her voice was careful, considering, like she was putting together pieces of a jigsaw puzzle.

I shrugged. "I mean, my family knew."

She hissed, and the guy went silent. Yeah, I'd said what I said, and as we stood there in a wretchedly uncomfortable silence, I knew they got my meaning. Maybe I should have kept my mouth shut, but the stiffness with which Malik was holding himself made me hyper-protective, a now foreign emotion.

The woman, who looked enough like Malik that I hazarded a guess was his sister Sheila, cleared her throat. "I see." Then she tilted her head to the side and smiled at me. "It's ironic, really."

My eyebrow raised on its own. Really. I fought to keep my posture loose, purposely not crossing my arms as I looked up at her. "What's that, ma'am?"

Her nose crinkled at the *ma'am*. "That my brother married someone with the same last name."

I laughed, long and loud. This *definitely* had to be Sheila. And Malik had told me enough about her—namely that she was the smartest woman he knew—that I knew she didn't believe what she'd just said for a minute. Something that thawed my inherent defensiveness. "Not quite. My former name is Moore."

"Oh, for chrissakes," Malik muttered, the first words he'd

uttered since his original declaration, then stomped off down the hall, slamming the door shut behind him. I took a step in that direction, but the younger version of him stopped me. I racked my brain for a minute. James, the baby of the family.

"Are you telling me that Franklin is *our* family name?" He bounced like an excited puppy, and I vaguely wondered if I'd ever seen Malik with that look on his face. Memories of our time dating and the early years of our marriage swamped me, and I had to suck in a harsh gulp of air so I wouldn't drown in them. Yes. The answer was yes.

I smiled at him and laid a hand on his shoulder, looking him square in the eyes. "I married your brother, I took his name, and when we separated"—*not* divorced—"I kept it."

"Holy mother of god," he whispered. "We're related to DeShawn Franklin."

"Were," Sheila spat out. "We *were* related to DeShawn Franklin, and we didn't know because Malik didn't trust us enough to come out. If we're going to tell the story, we need to tell the whole story."

I turned to her. "That's pretty much the whole story." I stuck my hand out. "DeShawn."

"Sheila," she said, confirming my suspicions. I couldn't stop my smile. Malik had crowed about her. Young, vibrant, an absolute beast in the kitchen who would be an amazing CEO. I wondered if she'd taken up that mantle.

"I would love to get to know you," I said, dropping her hand and looking at James, "but I'm actually here on some business."

Sheila's eyes widened and she nodded, like she knew exactly what I was talking about. "Grandma. Moore. That's your grandmother, isn't it?"

I huffed. "Yes, she is."

"Malik just got some paperwork. Why don't you go talk to him?"

Dammit. Malik had been served before I'd manned up and gotten here, and Grandma was going to have my ass when she found out. I thanked Sheila, nodded at James, then took off in the direction of the closed door I'd seen.

I knocked on it, waited a beat, then poked my head in. Malik sat behind a big mahogany desk, his elbows on the table, his head in his hands. I stepped in and clicked the door shut, then frowned. The big, grotesque, overstuffed chair I'd bought him as a gag gift when we were first married sat opposite the desk. For reasons I'd never been able to figure out, he'd wanted to keep the damn thing when we divorced. I'd assumed it was so he could burn it in effigy, so seeing it here? Now? All these years later? I honestly didn't know what to make of that, but something inside me unfurled. Probably my common sense taking flight.

I sank into the seat across from him and cleared my throat. "Your sister told me you got served."

Without looking up, Malik took one hand and shoved the paperwork across the table, then went back to holding his head.

I scanned the paperwork and scowled. Uncle Robert was a piece of fucking work. He'd hated Malik, and for a long time I thought it was because of our relationship. Even back then, though, that hadn't made a ton of sense, because Robert had known I was gay since I was thirteen and had never cared. Multiple boyfriends had come and gone in high school and college, and he'd treated them like any other kid in the neighborhood. Hell, he'd gotten along better with some of them than I had. And in the beginning, now that I was really thinking about it, he'd been like that with Malik, even though Malik had always been cautious around him. I'd chalked it up to his issues with his family, but in retrospect, maybe he'd seen something in Robert early, because the closer we got, the more withdrawn, distant, and frankly hostile Robert'd become. He'd skipped the engagement party and we'd joked that he might object at the wedding. He'd no-showed instead.

Now, however many years later, the reason hit me like that gif of the boombox smacking someone upside the head. Robert had known, way before me or Malik or probably even Grandma had figured it out. Malik was a replacement, the son Grandma always wanted. I knew she loved Robert despite his flaws, but she *had* pulled back from giving him money hand over fist. That's probably why he'd barely been able to contain his glee when I'd confessed Malik and I were divorcing, and while our relationship had never recovered from how he'd treated Malik, it had gotten more cordial over time.

Well, this nipped that shit in the bud. I read the pleading, then threw the pages on the table. "I'm sorry, Malik."

At that, he dropped his hands and sat back in his chair. From here, I could see crow's feet around his eyes, and crease lines around his mouth. I loved those lines, because they were proof of him employing that nearly infectious laughter. But the lines around his eyes? Sure, they may have been from crinkling while smiling at people not named DeShawn, but there was a weariness in them, and in the lines on his forehead. Like he was tired and worn down about something beyond the bombshell Robert had dropped on us.

"Sorry about what?" he asked, his voice so quiet I had to strain to hear it.

"I was supposed to reach out to you sooner. I should've, but…" I trailed off, not knowing what to say.

He shook his head just a fraction. "Don't be. Grandma gave me your number, too."

"Yeah?"

"I deleted it."

At a different point in time, I'd have been offended by that. But that action was so Malik, so indicative of how hard he'd tried to sever our ties, that I couldn't help but laugh. "Well, that's one way of handling it."

"Nah. I'd memorized the damn thing by then."

And with that, I sobered, my grin fading. "Yeah. I get that. I—" How the hell did I bring up the real issue? How did I explain that, somewhere along the way, we'd screwed up the paperwork?

I ran a hand over my face, then gripped my knee to keep from bouncing it. "Malik, there's something else I need to tell you."

"I assumed it was this," he said, gesturing vaguely to the paperwork.

I dropped my head and massaged my closed eyelids with my thumbs. "That's not all, unfortunately."

Malik inhaled deeply, his chest expanding, before he blew out a breath so deep his shoulders hunched over. What was one more straw on his back, when he clearly already carried the weight of the world? "What is it, DeShawn?"

Damn. He sounded so much like he had when we were married. Not those happy times, but at the end when we were trying, flailing, *failing*, to save what we had. I hated it. I hated feeling I couldn't do anything right, and since I was the one who'd submitted the paperwork, this would just be one more in a long list of things I fucked up with this man.

"The divorce paperwork didn't go through."

Malik cut his eyes to me. "What do you mean?"

"There was an error in it. I don't even know what. And we didn't catch it and the file is closed and—"

"DeShawn, what are you saying?"

I sucked in a breath, closed my eyes, then let it all out in a rush. "I'm saying we're still married."

Malik

The beautiful thing about being an adult was having options. Option one, I could sit on my ass and drink until I erased the memory of everything I'd learned this afternoon. Option two, I could gorge myself on sweets until my stomach cramped, *then* go for the alcohol.

But I was a professional. So I naturally went for option three: stress baking alcohol-infused desserts that I would then gorge. Best of both worlds.

Chocolate raspberry whiskey truffles? Tell me they didn't sound divine. Lemon vodka cream tarts? Who could say no? Grand Marnier vanilla cream cake pops? Who would deny themselves? Certainly not me. I baked two batches of Bruno's favorite biscuits first, though, so we could indulge ourselves together.

So there I was, after taking Bruno for his nightly walk, forcing myself not to call Grandma and ask how she could have kept something so important from me, baking my ass off instead. And when the doorbell rang, I jumped like hares did when they spotted Bruno.

Now, Grandma might be pushy, but she had boundaries, so I knew it wasn't DeShawn. I wiped my hands down the front of my apron as I walked to the front and glanced through the peephole. See, I was right. Sheila.

"I come bearing gifts," she said as I opened the door.

No, Sheila looked like she'd gone to our distributors to stock up on liquor for the restaurant. "Dear god, what are you doing with all that?"

"You looked like you needed it." She winked, then nudged me aside. She set it on the floor next to the island and looked around, hands on her hips. "What in the world is all this?"

I shut the door behind her and squared my shoulders. *This* was my dirty secret revealed. "I bake, okay?" I said, ignoring the way she followed me with her eyes. "And right now, I'm stress baking. You going to help me, or you going to gawk?"

"A little bit of both, I think."

I was the non-cook in the family. Sheila put her entire foot in everything she made, and when it came to the dead of summer? No one, and I do mean no one, could fuck up a grill the way James did.

I was more than passable, and in a family of non-cooks, I would reign supreme. In this one? They kept me out of the kitchen and in the back office handling money. So my fascination with baking? Yeah, I'd kept that shit under wraps the same way I had with my DeShawn. And dammit all to hell, I was thinking of him as mine already. That was a dangerous path to go down.

I stepped back and shook my head. "If you're here, you're working. Check and see if the dough is ready to roll out so I can make these crusts."

After a beat of silence, I heard Sheila's feet move toward the fridge. "Yeah, it's ready to go."

"Great." I reached underneath the cabinet and pulled out a bunch of mini tart pans. "You want to make the crust?"

"Egg glaze?"

I nodded.

She went to work, and we were silent for a few beats. "You really weren't going to tell us about DeShawn?"

I shrugged, trying to feign nonchalance. "Wasn't much to tell. We were divorced before I came back home."

"Didn't look like he much cared about that, the way he was watching you."

I'd noticed that, too. It'd been like being twenty-three again, the way his eyes roamed over me like he wanted to devour me, and no one had looked at me like that since, well, DeShawn. Oh, I'm sure there'd been some mutual attraction with other men, but not enough to do anything about it. After DeShawn, where everything was so easy and comfortable—until it wasn't—I just hadn't had the energy to try again.

"So," Sheila went on, ignoring that I hadn't responded, "DeShawn confirmed that Grandma is his grandmother."

"Yep."

"And...you weren't going to explain that relationship?"

I braced my hands on the counter and rocked back slightly while I put my words into place. "If I'd explained who Grandma was, you guys would want to know how I knew him, why I spoke to her, everything. James would have been relentless."

"Ugh." Sheila shook her head. "You should have seen him after you left. He was already making plans."

Of course he was. James didn't care about people. James cared about profits. "I was not using my ex"—*not* my ex, and boy, I wasn't touching that with a thirty-nine-and-a-half-foot pole—"that way. Or our connection. Or anything."

Her smile was soft, sweet. Sympathetic. "I get it, I do. You don't have to explain it to me. Except..."

When she trailed off, I glanced at her. "Except what?"

"Malik. You. Were. *Married*. How could you not tell us you'd been *married*?"

Should've known she'd dropped the matter too quickly for it to be truly over. I stuffed a truffle in my mouth while I figured out how to string together words that made sense. Finally I sighed and said the hell with it.

"The only thing worse than coming home with your tail tucked between your legs, having to finally explain why you've been gone so long, completely incommunicado except for the annual Christmas cards, is to explain that, not only did you get married—and divorced—in the interim, but the guy you left is ballin' out of control as a result. It was bad enough dealing with the fallout from being gay and not trusting Mom and Dad enough to tell them sooner. Adding that I'd been married, to someone they'd never meet, and that a big—huge—part of why we got divorced was because I wasn't ready to come out?" My stomach twisted on itself at the memories of how screwed up I'd been then.

Across the island, Sheila frowned, scrunched up her nose, and started chewing on her lower lip. Mom never could break her of that habit. I sighed. "What is it?"

"I mean," she started, then paused. "Why would you have had to come out? I guess that's the part I'm missing." When I opened my mouth, she hurried to add, "Don't get me wrong, I'm glad you did. But..." She trailed off and rolled that lip in.

I grabbed a stool and one of the mini tarts, then waited while Sheila got one for herself. "D was a sous chef at a hotel restaurant. Nothing big, just getting his foot in the door. He liked to fool around and make concoctions after hours, and the head honchos didn't care as long as it didn't mess with their supplies for the next day. A group of them were eating at the bar when some guy came up and asked for a plate, and it was love at first sight. Turned out the guy was a restaurateur, and was opening restaurants in Spain and Italy."

"And he wants DeShawn."

"Yep." Even that one word sounded bitter to my ears. "He was so fucking excited. This was it, his big break. And that guy was the real deal. Wanted him to head up the damn restaurant from jump. Wanted magazine spreads and home interviews and shit."

"And naturally they'd mention his husband and home life and boom, you're out."

"The first magazine that wanted to do an interview was *Family Restaurant Enterprises*."

Her eyes widened and I didn't have to say more. We'd had

a subscription to that magazine since it'd been founded. Mom read it cover to cover every month like clockwork. Put a Black man on the cover of that magazine? Hell, Mom would've bought multiple copies of it. And she would've learned that her oldest son was gay by reading it. That I wasn't in contact with them? Would have meant diddly squat. I would have been bombarded with calls and conversations I couldn't handle, and I'd had my first and only panic attack at the thought.

I'd been terrified. So damn scared I hadn't been able to muster up an ounce of enthusiasm. It'd gotten so bad D had said he'd turn the guy down, and that was even worse. Giving up his dream because I was scared to come out? Absolutely not. Divorcing had been the lesser of two evils, and I'd spent seven years convincing myself of it. "Yeah. Grandma hated it, us divorcing, especially over something she felt we could overcome. She called the day after he submitted the paperwork, and we've talked weekly since then."

"About everything except DeShawn, I'm guessing."

"We were divorced. There was nothing to say, and even mentioning his name was a surefire way to make me defensive. She hadn't mentioned him in years, until a few weeks ago, when she said I needed to call him."

"She say why?"

"Of course not," I grumbled. Sheila huffed and I rolled my eyes. "She just said we needed to talk. Never thought I'd actually see him, and I wasn't ready."

"Which explains why you skipped out. You're usually pretty stalwart. I was kinda surprised."

Yeah, Bruno had been, too. When I'd come home, hours earlier than normal, I'd almost had no choice but to take my baby for a walk. And when I'd come back, taken a quick shower, then collapsed on my bed, that had apparently been so unusual that Bruno hopped on with me, a big no-no, and fell asleep right there next to me. Trust me, waking up next to doggy breath? Hadn't been on my agenda.

I didn't have much of an explanation for Sheila, so I just shrugged and we went back to work. The silence was comfortable and gave me time to think. Which, to be honest, wasn't my brightest idea.

But dear god, one look at DeShawn today proved the cameras didn't hold a candle to his beauty. He always looked taller on camera, which was probably why they often paired him with women. But DeShawn was five-six, five-seven on a good day, and looked like he still worked out regularly. His body was slender, the kind that stayed naturally slim but showed impressive muscle definition. Two full-arm sleeves now, something he'd been working on when we were together. I'd tried valiantly not to stare, not to try to see if our initials had been covered up. His locs were longer, nearly to his waist, whereas when we'd divorced, they had just passed his shoulders. The bottom half were blond, but the top were his gorgeous naturally dark brown color. Not black, very obviously brown, and I'd started baking years ago trying to create something sweet that matched his color.

When I'd seen him in the doorway, that hair pulled back into a long braid, that little filthy grin on his face, one that looked almost like he couldn't help it, my first instinct had been to wrap my hands around that braid and hold him in place while I took him the way he'd always liked. That same desire made me scurry like a rat back to the sanctuary of my office.

"So," she asked, after putting the tarts in the oven to bake, "what are you going to do about the lawsuit?"

That was another excellent question. One I hadn't even considered yet. The attorney we kept on retainer was a business one, not...whatever this was. And Lord knew I didn't have enough money to afford the big guns I'd need to fight this. Never mind that I still needed to call Grandma and ask her what in the heck she'd been thinking, making me a beneficiary. Yeah, that was high on my list of things to do.

"Malik. Earth to Malik."

Sheila snapped her fingers in my face. I swatted at them, then shoved a truffle at her. She accepted it, sniffed it like Bruno did the trees on our walks, then took a bite. "Holy crikeys," she garbled, her hand in front of her mouth, "what is this? This is delicious."

I smiled. "Chocolate raspberry bourbon."

"Oh, I'm down to get fucked up off these."

I laughed and rolled my eyes. We were definitely family. She finished that truffle, then snagged another one and shoved it into her mouth as well. When she finished, though, she looked at me with those same worried eyes. "Malik, you know you have to talk to him again, right? You guys have to figure out how you're going to fight this."

I pulled out one of the stools behind the counter and sank onto it. "That's the thing, Sheila. I don't know if I want to fight it. Maybe it's better just to let Robert have the money. I don't want him and DeShawn fighting."

Sheila sat on the other stool and leaned forward. "You can't do anything about that. Robert knew what he was doing. He had to know DeShawn would find out. And, whatever happened with you two, that *was* your husband."

"Is."

She frowned, like she was replaying our conversation, then looked at me with wary eyes. "What do you mean, is?"

I groaned, arching my neck up toward the ceiling to avoid her stare. "That was the other thing DeShawn told me. Our divorce didn't go through."

"You're still married?"

"I'm still married."

"You're married to DeShawn Franklin?"

"I'm married to DeShawn Franklin."

"Want to trade?"

I snickered, then bust up laughing. "You're sickeningly in love with Bryan, and while he and I are cool, I'm pretty sure he'd veto the suggestion."

Sheila fluttered her lashes. "I can't imagine what you mean. You're an accountant. He's an accountant. You two would be as interesting as watching paint dry."

I appreciated her attempts to keep me from withdrawing back into my own head. "It'll be fine," I said, getting us back on track. "It's just one more thing we have to get resolved. I'll decide if I want to contest this at all, then resubmit whatever paperwork we need to get this divorce finalized."

I was sure DeShawn thought I was angry with him about it, since he'd been the one to submit the final paperwork. But DeShawn was meticulous. He reviewed things two, three, four times. I did the same as an accountant, but when it had come to the divorce, I'd made the decision, then put the onus of it all in his hands. I couldn't be upset with him now for missing something when neither of us had wanted to hire attorneys. If anything, I felt a nagging guilt that I'd made the decision and left him to do the work.

"Are you sure you want to do all that? Why don't you talk to DeShawn first? I mean, you really *have* to talk to Grandma. Figure out why she did this, before you make these grandiose plans."

She made an excellent point. I shrugged. "I'm going to need a real drink to have this phone call."

The timer dinged then, and Sheila hopped up from her seat. "That's what I'm talking about." She pulled the tarts from the oven and set them on the cooling rack, then pointed at them. "And this? You're going to explain how you've been hiding all this from us and the store. These, sir, could be a game changer."

Any other time, that would have been exactly what I wanted to hear. Right now, it was just one more secret I'd have to come clean about.

Chapter Five

DeShawn

"You cutting them carrots up like they did something to you."

I chuckled at Miss Maxine's chiding and put the knife down. "Guess I'm not used to Grandma resting like this. She's always up and about and all that."

She hummed. She couldn't argue that seeing Anna Mae Belle Moore resting midday wasn't a common occurrence, but I should've known she wouldn't just accept that excuse.

"You're right. It's hard to see Annie this way. But you're a fool if you don't think I see through you."

Because Malik was on his way over. Grandma said she wanted to rest before her baby—that was him, not me—got here, so she'd gone to sleep not long after I arrived. Corey was resting with her, his gentle doggy snores occasionally filtering under the door to the small, U-shaped kitchen I'd grown up in.

"Have you spoken to him since the restaurant?"

"Nope." Not that I'd tried. Seeing him had thrown me for a loop. Grandma's words were real then in a way I hadn't been ready for. I wasn't looking at a remnant from my past. I was looking at my *husband*, and I still didn't know what to make of it.

"Y'all were such a cute couple. I don't know why you divorced to begin with."

Ugh. I'd spent years asking myself that same question. I had my readymade answer, but it felt as false and carefully rehearsed now as it had then. Hell, maybe the better question was why we'd married in the first place.

I'd fallen for Malik nearly from jump. He was so big and broad and reserved, preferring to spend his time buried in books rather than social butterflying. He left that to me, but was never jealous I went out without him, and never tried to force me to stay home. He'd trusted me, implicitly, and I'd done everything possible to honor that faith.

He'd worried even then about not being out to his family. I hadn't much cared, because he rarely contacted them anyway, and I figured he'd deal with it in time. When he said he was waiting for the other shoe to drop, for me to decide I was tired of him and his hiding, I proposed. He'd said yes, like he didn't believe me. Until I introduced him as my fiancé to Grandma, and she'd been over the moon.

Just like she was now, knowing he was on his way. In fact, I could hear the stirring from the room, and wasn't surprised when the door opened and she padded into the kitchen. "Y'all getting food ready for my baby?"

Corey's soft chuff behind her made clear who he thought "baby" was, and she bent down—with more effort than I liked—to scritch his head.

"I'm making dinner for the family," I said, and yes, my words sounded stiff even to my own ears, "not for anyone in particular."

"Roast beef, rosemary potatoes and root vegetables, and a balsamic glaze? Yes, yes, of course that's not for anyone in particular."

Dammit to hell. I honestly hadn't been thinking about it,

but Grandma hadn't forgotten Malik's favorite meal. And subconsciously, I guess I hadn't either.

Grandma came up and palmed my cheek, and Miss Maxine left the kitchen, coaxing Corey with her. "It's okay to still have feelings for him, you know."

But was it? It's not like he'd been thrilled to see me, not like he'd wanted to jump into my arms or anything like that. It wasn't his fault my stupid heart had spotted him and been like a four-year-old seeing his favorite candy in the store and deciding nothing else would do. We'd severed those ties, or tried, and Malik was only coming here for answers, nothing more. If I tried to explain that to Grandma, she'd get that glint in her eye and surely start plotting our reunion. Besides, those feelings could just be a fond heart after seven years of absence.

I pressed into her touch for a brief moment, then pulled away with a shrug. "He's a good man. He doesn't deserve what's happening to him. If I can help him through it, I will."

Her gaze was a combination of soft and shrewd, and just like every time in the past forty years, I withered under it. She opened her mouth to speak when the doorbell rang and Corey went into guard-dog mode.

I'd love to say I was saved by the bell, but the look on Grandma's face told me to get that fantasy out my mind, because she wasn't done with me yet.

Corey's barks turned to pants, and I hung my towel up before stepping into the hallway. Malik was crouched on one knee, wearing a pristine pair of khakis and a plain white shirt, and Corey was doing his absolute best to ruin the whole thing with doggy slobber.

"Jesus, Malik, I'm sorry," I said, hurrying to pull Corey away. "He loves people and pretends not to understand the word *no*."

Malik smiled, and I would give my left arm to put that

smile on his face every day for the rest of my life. "It's no problem. My Bruno is the same way." He stood and faced Grandma, opening his arms wide, and engulfing her when she crossed the short distance to him. He didn't try to keep the tears away, and I wanted to soothe him, to take away the pain I felt just as acutely.

"Now you stop that," Grandma said, wiping his tears brusquely with her thumbs. She sniffled once, then straightened as best she could and tossed her head back, as though she was quite through with heavy emotion for the night.

Miss Maxine hugged Malik as well, kissed me and Grandma on the cheeks, and left us. Which somehow made everything awkward immediately. Grandma watched us like she wanted to force our faces together and make us kiss. My heart and body were onboard with that even if my brain hadn't quite caught up. And Malik? He looked like he wished he was anywhere but here.

I stepped back and cleared my throat. "You hungry?"

He frowned, sniffed, then groaned. "Is that…"

"Your favorite," Grandma confirmed. "I think DeShawn's perfected the recipe by now." She patted me on the shoulder and grinned.

I refused to respond, instead escaping to the kitchen while Grandma led Malik to the small dining room table she'd long stopped using unless she had company. One wall of the kitchen was open, and I watched Malik set the table like he'd been doing it for years. I wondered how many times he'd come here since we'd separated, and my chest seized at the thought.

Dinner was delicious, if I said so myself, and I contented myself with staying quiet while Malik and Grandma caught up. Once the plates were empty, Malik laid a hand over Grandma's. "Grandma, what were you thinking?"

She huffed, like the question was silly. "About what? Not

wanting to see everything I've worked so hard for be frittered away inside a year? Why would I possibly do anything to prevent that?"

Her sarcasm was on another level. Malik smiled even through his sigh, like this was a conversation they'd had more than once. "Grandma, Robert is your son, and you know, he might be more cautious with it knowing that's all he'll get."

I fought not to snort. Even though Malik kept his voice perfectly level, I knew damn good and well he didn't believe that. No one who knew Uncle Robert thought he'd be circumspect with even a dime of Grandma's money.

But Grandma wavered, grabbing her napkin and fiddling with it. "You've always been honest with me, and you've never asked me for anything. I know the restaurant's been struggling," she said, her voice softening, "and I thought this would help."

Malik cut his eyes to me, and I knew that was information he hadn't wanted me to know. I looked away. When I'd gone to his family's restaurant and seen it so empty, I'd assumed they were only open for dinner. Not uncommon. But maybe it was more than that?

"Grandma, you don't need to do that. We'll make do."

"With you at the helm, baby, I have no doubt. Still..." She paused and her shoulders sagged. I scooted my chair closer to her on one side and was grateful when Malik matched my move opposite her. She grabbed both our hands, and I ran my thumb over the back of hers. "I know things didn't work out with you two, but you're my babies. Both of you. And I want to take care of you."

Malik caught my eyes over the top of her head, and I tried for a smile. He gave me a half grin, then wrapped an arm around her and pulled her close, kissing the top of her head.

"I love you, Grandma. You know that. I just don't want to be the cause of a rift in your family."

Her laugh was soft and a little warbled. "Don't you worry about that. Robert would cause a rift with or without you."

"And I'm sorry for it."

"Boy didn't even have the decency to wait until I was dead. He nearly sounds like he wants a guardian appointed for me. A damn fool."

I rolled my lips in to stifle my laughter. Only two things made Grandma curse: her wayward son, and me and Malik's non-divorce. Malik just held her tighter and rested his cheek on the top of her head.

"What do we need to do to make sure your will goes through the way you want it?" I asked after a few beats of silence.

"You need to talk to Larry." She made no move to extricate herself from Malik's hold, and was I jealous? Yes. Yes, I was.

"We'll do that." Malik kissed her head again and sat up, staring at me. "We can find a time to meet with him, right?"

I nodded. "Of course."

"He can take care of everything. Your will and finalizing the divorce."

And...there went the relatively comfortable silence we'd created. Back to the massively large elephant looming over us.

I didn't have words, and Grandma sighed. "Yes, Larry can take care of everything. Including the divorce. If that's what y'all really want."

Malik

If that's what y'all really want. Those words stayed with me for the next three nights, until we were able to squeeze on to Larry's schedule. I'd met him a few times, and he was a distressingly pretty drink of water. A little aloof, calm, charming as hell when he wanted to be, but the liquid nitrogen that ran through his veins? Fucking scary. He was protective of De-Shawn, treated him like a little brother, and I'd known immediately I didn't want to be on his bad side. For this, I was glad he was on ours.

I pulled up to the underground parking lot a few blocks away from his firm, Carter Andrews LLP. They occupied a few floors of a downtown K Street building, the same as plenty of national law firms around here.

When I'd met Larry, he was fresh out of school and just starting. By now he had to be a partner or something. And DeShawn was the goddamn executive chef of a starred restaurant. While I toiled along as the accountant of a failing family restaurant. God, DeShawn had made the right call letting go of my sorry behind.

I walked across the marble floors at the lobby and signed in at the security desk, noting DeShawn's elegant scrawl just a few spots above mine. I inhaled deeply while I waited for the elevator. I could do this. I might not be these guys' peers, or anywhere on their level, but Grandma saw something in me. Enough to make me a beneficiary. And once upon a time, DeShawn had, too. I kept those thoughts in my back pocket as I approached the sixth floor.

I spotted DeShawn immediately when I got off. His eyes roved over me, taking his time looking me up and down before returning his attention to the magazine in his hand. I gave my name to the receptionist and took a seat a few chairs away, then grabbed whatever magazine was on top. A parenting one. Another reminder of conversations we'd started and stopped, letting those dreams die along with everything else.

The side door opened and a man walked out, looking like he belonged on a gay magazine rather than in the office. Rich brown hair, so carelessly styled it had to be intentional, brown eyes with flecks of gold in it. His light blue button-down and gray slacks were the definition of business casual, but they moved on him like they'd been tailored to his frame. "You must be Malik Franklin?" He looked at me and I nodded, then he turned. "And you're DeShawn Franklin. I recognize you."

DeShawn smiled, that bad boy one that made me flip channels with lightning speed. Sure, it was practiced and only for effect. But the first time he'd come on to me, all those years ago—because my dumb ass would've never considered someone that fine would spare me a first glance, let alone a second—he'd given me a version of that smile. An almost shy one, like he was waiting to be rejected. And I hadn't been able to dissuade him of that notion fast enough.

The guy was still talking, and I forced myself to pay attention. "I'm Collin, Mr. Jackson's secretary, and he's asked me to bring you back and get some preliminary questions started. He's meeting with his protégé now."

DeShawn and I stood and followed him back, and DeShawn launched into an easy conversation. "Protégé?"

Collin laughed. "Yes. Ms. Chang, one of our senior associates. I'm her secretary, too, and they're like a wrecking ball together."

"You sound like you enjoy your job," I cut in. Did my voice sound a little wistful? What was that all about?

He paused midstep, then nodded and kept walking. "I guess I do. It's been a journey to get here, but I'm happy where I am."

We rounded a corner and he led us into the biggest office I'd ever seen. Next to me, DeShawn whistled low. "Good gracious."

"That's what I said." Collin pointed to a circular table on the opposite side of the room from the desk and two guest chairs. "Have a seat."

We did, and the table wasn't big enough for me and De-Shawn to not sit side by side. And unfortunately DeShawn sat on my right side. Which wasn't a problem, except he was left-handed and it kept brushing against my arm. He muttered, "Sorry," and moved away, and dammit, I didn't like that either.

Collin ran through a list of questions and had just finished when someone rapped lightly on the doorframe and Larry entered.

"Malik, good to see you again." He stuck his hand out and I scrambled to stand and shake it.

"Larry, how's it going?"

"Pretty good, thanks. Not to sound like a complete ass, but I go by Lawrence in the office." He inclined his head toward Collin. "This one would never take me seriously if he could call me Larry."

DeShawn snorted, then stood and hugged him. When he sat, Larry ruffled the top of DeShawn's head. He smiled at me. "Collin take care of you guys?"

My head bobbed automatically. "He was great, thank you."

Larry looked around me at Collin. "Close your mouth. You'll get flies with it hanging open like that."

Collin shook his head. "You're just so…human," he finished. "It's weird."

He immediately blanched, but DeShawn bust out laughing and Larry rolled his eyes and glanced at me. "Why does everyone think I'm not human?" Before I could think of a response, he faced Collin again. "Check with Gwen and make sure she doesn't need anything, then you can leave."

Collin's face lit up and he hurried to gather his things. "Will do."

"Tell Jeremiah hello for me."

Collin beamed at the mention of the other man's name, waved at us, and disappeared, closing the door behind him.

Larry sank into the vacated seat, his face morphing from friendly to all business. This was the Larry—Lawrence—I knew better than to fuck with. I retook my seat, DeShawn following my lead.

"So, this lawsuit," he began. "Robert really has no legal standing. But it's not going to be as cut and dry as a summary dismissal."

"Why not?" DeShawn asked, his voice soft.

"The courts are taking more interest in making sure adults aren't being taken advantage of in their final wills, as opposed to simply assuming everyone's of sound mind unless proven otherwise. Since Robert is specifically alleging Ms. Moore is not of sound mind, the judge is going to at least hear evidence. He didn't specifically seek being named power of attorney, but I'd be surprised if he didn't ask."

I swallowed. I'd been afraid of that. "What if I just relinquish my claim?" I asked. "Would that make it go away?"

Larry looked at me, his expression inscrutable. I swallowed hard enough I was sure they all heard it, though no one said anything. After a moment, his face went carefully blank.

"There are, in my opinion, two reasons it wouldn't work. One"—he ticked off with a finger—"if you relent, he'll just go after DeShawn next. He's testing the waters with you to see how far he can go. Two"—and now Larry's face morphed into that charming one I'd first met over fifteen years ago—"Miss Annie Moore would whoop your ass."

DeShawn snickered, and even I had to laugh. Because wasn't that the damn truth? Grandma would find a switch and use the last of her strength on my behind if I rejected her bequest. "I know," I said, admitting defeat. "So we need to win, and that's your forte. What do we do?"

Larry sighed and tapped a pen against the table. "Here's your big problem. Robert says you aren't family, because you divorced years ago. That lends credence—an infinitesimal amount, but some—to an abuse allegation. But..."

"But the divorce didn't go through, so we could use that in our favor. Say we filed the paperwork but when it was rejected, we saw that as fate and decided to try again?"

DeShawn's words warmed me like a hot torch over crème brûlée. I couldn't even explain why, but Larry shook his head and sat back, which brought me back to the present. "That might work, but you haven't exactly been celibate, D. And you haven't exactly been shy about it."

I hated the way DeShawn's face flamed, and I ached to touch him. To assure him it wasn't his fault. His job as the hottie bad boy head chef meant he was always attending events, and he rarely went alone. If we'd decided to give our marriage another go, he wouldn't have had so many men hanging on him.

"Hey, it's okay," I whispered, and the look DeShawn gave me was soft. Soft and sweet and so damn tender I wanted to bottle it. "You were single and enjoying it. Nothing to be ashamed of."

He winced, a tiny thing, and I wanted to apologize. "I'm not saying it's bad," I rushed to add. "Just that..."

"It's okay," he muttered, sliding farther down in his seat and crossing his arms. "It's complicated, but I definitely had a hoe phase after you left. I admit it." He shrugged. "Can't take it back now."

God, how had this conversation gotten so off track? Larry patted DeShawn's hand, and cut his eyes to me, like DeShawn's remorse was my fault. In a way, I guess he was right, and I felt distinctly out of place. I coughed to clear my throat and straightened.

"So what's our plan?" I asked. "How do we keep Robert's hands off Grandma's will and prove to the judge that I didn't unduly coerce the functional equivalent of my mother-in-law to sign something over to me?"

Larry sighed and ran a hand over his face, but didn't answer, and DeShawn was probably still beating himself up for acting like a single man when he thought he was one.

But the wheels in my head were turning. Divorces were public record, so anyone could see we filed for one. But what if DeShawn was on the right track? What if we pretended like we'd taken news of the second notice as a sign we'd been hasty, that maybe we needed to give our…whatever the hell we'd had…a second chance?

That type of reconciliation didn't happen immediately, or easily. Folks would understand. They would cheer it, especially for DeShawn. The bad boy happily married, tamed as some people would call it? That could play really well. And people would want to be a part of it. It could bring business to Franklin's, people wanting to catch a glimpse of the man DeShawn had loved and lost and found again, and when we beat Robert, it'd cement Grandma's wishes.

"There's only one thing to do," I said, firming the decision in my mind, satisfied with the fantasy I'd just played out in my head.

"What's that?" DeShawn looked wary, like he was afraid I'd suggest he'd yeet himself into the sun.

"We're still technically married? Maybe it's time we act like it."

Chapter Six

Malik

It was wrong for a grown man to sneak into his office, let alone for him to even remotely consider working with the lights off. Not because of migraines or sensitivity or anything like that, but because he didn't want to deal with his family. Yet that was me come Monday morning.

Unfortunately my family knew me, and knew that, come hell or high water, I'd be behind that desk. So I shouldn't have been surprised when James walked in without knocking. "We need to talk."

I was *so* sick of hearing him say that, especially when it meant shoveling the same shit and getting nowhere. Somehow, I didn't think that was the case this time. I sat back and laid my hands on my stomach. "If it's about DeShawn, not now."

"Malik, I've been trying to call you all weekend."

I knew this. No way I could have missed those messages and voice mails. I'd needed time to think. About seeing DeShawn again, about the reality of our marital situation, about the decision we'd—I'd—made at Larry's office.

"This is something that involves the entire family," James insisted, and I frowned. Because that was bullshit.

"No, it doesn't. It involves me. It involves DeShawn. You're no more involved than we are with you and your wife."

James straightened, his shoulders stiffening and his arms hanging low at his sides. I saw the tightness in them, though, the way he flexed his fingers wide before fisting them again. He hated to be reminded about his slightly more-than-estranged relationship with his wife, and he'd put his foot down on anyone asking questions about it. Goose, meet gander.

"I agree we need to talk about DeShawn," I said, trying to soften the admittedly low blow, "but not now. Now, I'm at work. I have work hours, and I don't talk about my personal life during said work hours."

James glared at me for another moment, then turned and walked out. At least he had the sense not to slam my door. I sank into the chair and ran my hands over my face. DeShawn and I hadn't spoken since Larry's office, other than to schedule a time to meet. He was coming to the house—tonight. With his dog, who would meet my dog, and we were going to figure out the bounds of this "reunion."

That had been enough to keep me awake the whole damn weekend, and I hadn't thought of a single thing other than the idea of DeShawn in my home for however many weeks we had before trial. James's protests over not returning his calls? Subbasement level on my list of concerns.

I spent the next however many minutes doing all the deep breathing and meditating I could, and finally had enough wits about me to get some work done. It was hard. For every two or three or four items I checked off my list, a memory of DeShawn—his smile, his appreciative gaze—flashed in my head. Another three or four or five items, and I heard his voice in my ear. What would he say about the state of our restaurant? Would he say I'd screwed things up? Would he agree with James that my ideas were worthless?

"Arrgghhhh!" I flicked my pen down across the desk and pushed my chair back. I couldn't think, I couldn't focus, and

I damn sure couldn't do my job. A quick glance at my watch showed it wasn't even ten, and no way in hell was I getting two more hours of work done.

I left the office and walked up front, hoping to at least talk to Sheila a bit while she prepped for lunch, and found James sitting there. Which was a surprise, because James typically came in like a whirlwind, bellowed at me, and left just as quickly. He didn't linger.

"Malik," he said, straightening and pasting perhaps the fakest smile I'd ever seen across his face. He seemed to struggle for words, eventually landing on, "Hey."

I raised a brow. James had been pissed with me just a minute ago, so why was he still hanging around here? And why was he playacting at being nice after being his usual assholish self just minutes before?

Sheila came out from the kitchen, a towel thrown over her shoulder, murder in her eyes because someone was fucking up her schedule, and sat next to him. "Mom called. Said to find out how all this happened. Like I don't have better things to do."

"Why didn't you just tell her? You've got the whole story."

I don't even know why I was surprised by the brow raise. "It's not my story to tell."

Of course not. Just mine to repeat ad nauseam. I sighed and pulled up a chair. Might as well get this over with. "Okay, let's do this," I said. "What do you want to know?"

"Well," James started, then coughed. "I guess…everything."

I ran a hand over my face. This was a part of my life I'd thought would stay dead and buried. I did *not* relish reliving it with an irritated sister and pissed-off brother. "I honestly don't know how much there is to say. We were married, and we divorced. Years ago."

"Oh, bullshit." James pushed his chair back, and I watched it wobble for a second before righting itself. "How the hell didn't you tell us you were married to DeShawn fucking Franklin?"

Sheila groaned and threw her head back. "James, please."

"He kept the biggest news on the planet away from us. Do you know what having DeShawn in our back pocket could have done for this restaurant?"

"See, that?" I pointed at him and he looked at my finger like he wanted to break it. "That right there? That's why I never said anything to you. DeShawn is not a fucking piece of meat. DeShawn was my *husband*. I *loved* him. Before he went to culinary school, when he was a sous chef at a tiny hole-in-the-wall restaurant who liked to use me as his goddamn guinea pig. You are *not* going to use him as a slab of meat to lure people in. And fuck you for even considering it."

"Okay, enough!" Sheila's sharp words were enough to shut me up and make me suck in a deep breath.

I sat, focusing my attention on her and ignoring the asshole still pacing the table. "I wasn't out. I couldn't even come home to you, introduce you to him, because I didn't know how to tell you I was gay. And D? He got that. He never tried to force me, he honestly never cared if I told you or not. But he was such a good cook. And he started getting all these opportunities. Ones that having a closeted husband didn't work with." I shook my head, trying to put together the words in a way that made sense. "I wanted him to have all of his dreams. I wanted him to *do* everything. Have the *best* of everything. And I was a yoke around his neck."

"So he divorced you?"

Sheila looked almost offended, like she didn't give a damn who he was, how *dare* he divorce her big brother? I loved the protectiveness, and needed to quash it. "No. I divorced him."

A lump stuck in the base of my throat every time I thought about that conversation, about telling him it was time for us to move on, about the tears we'd both shared at that brutal realization. He told me he didn't care, that I was more important than the opportunity.

I looked up and tried to smile, but only halfway made it. "I couldn't let him give up his future to deal with my present. He deserved so much more. And the only way I could give it to him was to let him go."

Both of them fell silent. Sheila set her elbows on the table and let her head fall in her hands. James? It was harder to read him, and I didn't have the energy to try. He collapsed into his chair, his eyes searching me like he didn't know me anymore, and in some ways, I guess that was true.

We sat there, the three of us, in the most uncomfortable silence I could remember.

DeShawn

I tried to ignore the increasing butterflies in my stomach as I pulled off 495 and wound through the streets of suburban Maryland. I'd never been all that interested in having a home in the 'burbs, but it had always been Malik's thing, and I drove down the streets of named development complexes, past the recreational center, leasing office, and horses grazing in a pasture, before pulling up near the end of a cul-de-sac. Not at the circular portion, but only two or three spots down.

Next to me, Corey whined softly, and I ran my hand over his head. "It's going to be okay, boy. Malik and his dog will love you."

I hoped like hell that was true. I climbed out and walked around, unfastening Corey from his doggy seatbelt before leashing and walking him up the front steps of the house.

This was just a meet and greet. A chance for the dogs to get to know one another, and for me and Malik to have a real conversation about what we were doing without prying eyes watching our every move. It was one thing to play reunited lovers for the cameras, for the courts, but I knew without a doubt that Malik would be pushing this divorce through as soon as he had the opportunity.

What I also knew, what had become abundantly clear between receiving Grandma's news, having dinner with her, and the meeting at Larry's office? This, this right here? Was what I'd been missing.

Oh, sure, I'd acknowledged for years that I missed Malik with the fire of a thousand suns. That didn't hold a candle in the face of actually being near him again, actually being able to touch him, to feel him. One look and I'd been ready to risk it all. Ready to say the hell with this entire career, if it meant I got to see that face every day for the rest of my life again.

But if I told Malik that? He'd probably laugh his ass off, not because he thought I was serious, but because he'd assume I was making a joke at his expense. It was his defense mechanism.

I took a deep breath, then rang the doorbell. The loud, deep barking from inside had Corey giving it back in spades, and I heard Malik's exasperated sigh. "Calm down, Bruno. It's okay, boy."

Bruno did not calm down, and neither did Corey. He matched the growls on the other side of the door, his body going stiff and taut on my leash, warning Malik's dog of his impending doom.

Malik unfastened the locks, and I could tell he was struggling to keep Bruno in line, only opening the door a crack before an absolutely huge mastiff nosed it open all the way. His position immediately changed, and the big lug sat down, panting.

I waited a few seconds, then unleashed Corey. He sniffed Bruno, who suddenly seemed more than willing to allow it. And when he was done, Corey let out a short bark, and Bruno took off toward what I assumed was the kitchen, my dog on his heels.

"Just like that, the best of friends," Malik muttered.

I snorted. "All things considered, I think that's a good sign."

Malik's eyes drifted to me, across my cheeks, lingering on my lips, down my neck. Then he closed his eyes, gave his head a little shake, and stepped back. "Come on in."

It was nice to know I still affected him. I wanted to still affect him. I wanted him to want me as much as I had him the minute he'd walked down that dingy hallway and into the light. If the physical desire was still there, it meant I could work on everything else. Right?

I followed Malik through the open-concept layout and into the kitchen, pulling up a stool at the beautifully appointed island. A light gray granite countertop, white cabinets, all stainless steel appliances. An absolute bitch to clean, but for just Malik and the dog? Well worth it.

"Your home is beautiful," I said, taking in the hardwood floors, the outside patio just a few steps away, the fireplace that I wanted to cozy up in front of, weather be damned.

How lovely would it be, to come home and recline on the couch with him, let him lean against me and read his favorite book while I thumbed through recipes? To have the dogs lying next to each other in front of the fireplace, or outside, or wherever.

A whole host of things I never thought I wanted rushed through me. And I blew out a breath to stop the tidal wave of sensation from overwhelming me.

I turned to face Malik, who was staring at me. "Thank you," he whispered, almost like he didn't want to break me out of my trance.

I smiled again, then nodded toward his hand, which was holding a square plastic container. "What's that?"

He looked down, like he'd forgotten all about it, then shrugged. "Brownies."

I held my hand out, and he cracked a fraction of a smile before plucking one out of the container and handing it to me. Malik had been trying to perfect his brownie recipe when we'd separated. I took a bite and—yeah, he'd nailed it.

"This is exceptional," I said, shoving the rest of it in my mouth and then holding my hand out for another one.

Malik laughed, which had been my hope, but damn, I still wasn't ready for what that sound did to me. How much it warmed me. How much it calmed me. How much it made me want to lay across the nearest surface and take everything he had to give me.

"So," I said, forcing that thought out my head and focusing on Malik. "How do we want to do this?"

"I guess, I mean—" Malik stopped, closed his eyes and gripped the counter, then blew out a breath and looked at me. "At the end of the day, this isn't about you or me. It's about honoring Grandma and her wishes, and not let that lying sack of shit uncle of yours keep her from that. Right?"

"Right." And it *was* right. Never mind that I'd nearly forgotten about it in the rush of pleasure that shot through me at seeing Malik again. But he was right, painfully so, and I needed to remember that.

Although, to be fair, it looked like Malik was having a hard time staying on task, too, but I refused to think about what that meant. "The dogs get along, and that's half the battle." He grinned and I nodded. Truth, and praise Jesus for it. "So I guess it's just a matter of setting public and private boundaries."

I raised a brow. "Are they going to be different?"

His eyes flashed. His nostrils flared, and his tongue darted out to wet his lips. I mirrored his movement and leaned a fraction forward, wanting to chase his tongue with mine. Malik cleared his throat, straightened, and stepped back. Fuck. Hadn't meant to do that.

His voice sharpened. "Yes. When we're in public, I'll follow your lead. You know what plays well with the cameras. Whatever it takes to make us look like a happily married, happily reunited couple. But here?"

After a beat of silence, I prodded him. "Here?"

He frowned, then bracketed his hands on his hips and nodded. "Here, we're roommates. Nothing more. You stay in your bed, you take care of your dog, you fix your meals. You don't worry about what I'm doing, you don't worry about how I'm eating, you don't worry about Bruno."

"Barely passing acquaintances."

He raised a brow at me, then gave what I'm sure he hoped was a nonchalant shrug, but it was far too stiff. "Exactly that. That's what we are while we're here."

I wanted to argue, to trample over every word he said. But that wasn't the way I'd won Malik's heart in the first place, and if I wanted another chance, disregarding his needs wasn't the way to go now. I'd had a few weeks to accept that we were still married. I could afford to give Malik time to catch up.

But if he thought I was letting him go again, he had another think coming.

Chapter Seven

DeShawn

Coming into the office at the beginning of the day was infinitely more boring and more adult than showing up to prep for dinner service. But my mind had been burning with new recipe ideas, desserts in particular. Sure, people came to the restaurant for an entire experience, but after tasting Malik's brownies, I wanted to do an "elevated" play on them. Something with the same brownie crust, but lighter in texture. Something that melted on the tongue like dissolving sugar crystals.

My mouth watered at the thought, and I shut the door behind me, intent on spending a few hours brainstorming. This was what got us that star. The time we took to think about what we wanted, how we wanted the entire meal to come together, testing and retesting and re-retesting, refusing to be rushed, much to the chagrin of absolutely everyone involved, before I deemed something available for circulation.

Excitement zinged through me, until I noticed an envelope, my name handwritten by someone who was clearly a lettering master. I closed my eyes and tried to think happy thoughts. But I knew inside would be an invitation to another event Christopher would pester me to attend, a place where

I'd spend hours shaking hands and smiling and fielding more questions about my sex life than about my cooking.

Cooking, I could talk someone's ears off. The rest was no one's business, except it was unusual to have a Black executive chef, and unusual to have a *starred* Black chef, and gay as a cherry-topper. Recipes and cooking techniques were definitely not as interesting as my general existence. Years ago, I'd sworn I wanted this, but the reality was, most people were far too concerned about what I did in the privacy of my bedroom, and not nearly concerned enough about my actual work.

I thumbed open the envelope and pulled the card out. The same gorgeous hand lettering greeted me, and it was almost enough for me to ignore the words. No surprise, a gala in three weeks' time. But this was a big one. They were bringing in chefs from all over the mid-Atlantic region, culminating in "a friendly cooking competition with the best chefs in the area." That was interesting. An opportunity to actually cook. For the second time in a month. It might even be fun, but I set the card down for the moment, determined to get back to brownies.

Someone knocked on the door, then Maribel poked her head through. "I thought I saw a light on here. What are you doing here so early?"

"Playing," I said. "I have a new dessert idea brewing, and I wanted some quiet time to think about it."

"What, Corey not letting you get any rest at home?"

Corey was working my last nerve. All that dog did was sit and whine for Bruno. I hadn't moved us in yet, both me and Malik deciding we needed a few days before starting on that journey, but god, Corey was all in on the larger dog. It was like he'd lost his best friend.

"Corey is being a pain in my butt," I told her. "The dog

walker came and that was frankly the highlight of both of our days."

Maribel laughed and took a seat. "I see you got the invite, too?"

"Yeah. You and Jesus coming?"

"He hates that stuff, but I'm gonna try to drag him out with me. Depends on if we can get a babysitter." She waggled her brows and leaned forward. "But who are you going to bring?"

I laughed, because Bel was the only one who knew my different dates had almost all been escorts. No sex, just dates. Christopher had been the one to arrange it, and it had fueled that bad-boy image he so loved. Then I closed my eyes and groaned. "Fuck."

I'd tried to keep my voice low, but it wasn't enough. She sat up, her face creasing in alarm. "What's wrong, DeShawn?"

"I know who I have to bring, and I also know he's gonna kick my ass for it."

"DeShawn Franklin, what are you talking about?"

I massaged my closed eyes with my thumb and forefinger, then let my hand fall and stared at her. "You remember when Grandma called?"

"Yes," she started warily. I took a breath, then told her the entire story, ending with the decision Malik and I had made.

Maribel whistled when I was done, then leaned forward and propped her elbows on the desk. "DeShawn, are you trying to tell me you're married? As in, legally?"

I nodded. "Apparently so. And with everything going on, we've agreed to act like we've reunited, but I know he hates being in the limelight." Hate might be an understatement. What was a stronger word? Despise? Had been willing to divorce his husband in part because of it?

"You think he'll come?"

I shrugged. "I mean, I guess he could just stay home and I'd come solo, but—"

She cut me off. "But that won't work, because you have a reputation and he won't risk it. If you show up alone, it'll look worse for your case."

The ways that Maribel just got it, understood what I was trying to say and trying to do? Was one of the reasons our friendship was so strong. Her being an absolutely bomb-ass chef didn't hurt either.

"I know, but I'll still have to convince him."

There went that little mischievous grin again. "And just how do you plan to do that?"

I laughed and shook my head. "Not going there. Suffice it to say, I'll figure something out."

If anything, that smile brightened before her face grew more serious. "Okay, but be real with me. How're you holding up? With Grandma? Your uncle? Your ex who's not an ex?"

In the weeks that'd passed since Grandma had given me her news, since I'd found Malik again, since we'd agreed to this plan? No one had asked how I was, and it took me a moment to catalog my feelings.

"Some are pretty simple," I said. "I'm furious with Robert, angry that he's so selfish and so entitled that he thinks Grandma is supposed to support him from beyond the grave. That pisses me off." I leaned forward and blew out a breath. "With Grandma, I'm..." I shook my head and huffed. "Both impressed and terrified."

"Give me more."

"Impressed that she's made the decision, that she's decided how she wants to live out her days, that she accepts the inevitable outcome. Terrified because I don't know what to do in a world without her."

"Oh, DeShawn." Maribel reached across the table and

squeezed my hand, and I used the other one to swipe away the tears that had started to fall unbidden. "And Malik? Your husband?"

God, that word. It was the first time I'd heard it from someone else in reference to Malik, as opposed to me whispering to myself. I straightened, gave her hand another squeeze, then pulled mine away. "Maribel, he's so beautiful. So pretty and quiet and comforting. And…"

I paused, then laughed and shrugged. "He's everything I forgot I missed. The minute I saw him, I thought about all those late nights, when I'd come home dead on my feet. He was studying for his CPA exam, and he'd put his book down and drag me to bed and massage my back and my arms and my hands and my feet until I passed out. He'd wash the clothes two, sometimes three times to get the smell out, and have everything ready for the next day."

Maribel smiled. "It sounds like he really took care of you."

"He did." At the time, I hadn't appreciated it for what it was. He loved me through actions, and I was more a words type of man. I hadn't thought about it until now, how deeply we'd cared for each other in our own ways.

"What do you want?" Maribel's soft words drew me out of my reverie. "When this is all said and done, what do you want?"

"Him." The words held no hesitation. "I want him, back in my arms. Back in my bed. Back in my life."

Maribel smiled, then sat back and crossed her arms. "That's what I hoped you'd say. So, what are we going to do?"

Malik

The more I looked at the numbers, the worse they got. Our lunchtime traffic had slowed to—what's worse than a trickle? A complete standstill? And with James's stubborn refusal to either expand access for lunch or close altogether, we were compounding an already shit situation.

Hell, maybe I needed to think about taking over as CEO, even though that would bring a shitstorm on the family. James wasn't giving up that position without a fight, but he damn sure didn't seem to know what to do with it.

My phone buzzed, and I swiped it off the desk, grateful for the interruption.

DeShawn: Hey, I'm heading up your way now. Meet you at the house?

Dear god, this was happening. DeShawn, and his dog, were on their way to move in with me. Not permanently, I reminded myself, ignoring the way my heart had no intention of listening. This was *not* permanent. This was a temporary situation until we got this case resolved, then DeShawn and I were going our separate ways.

Me: I'm stuck at the office for a bit. Swing by here? You can come through the back.

DeShawn: Sounds good.

I swallowed in air, then blew it out loud enough that I startled my damn self. DeShawn was on his way here. I checked my watch, determined to get some work done before he arrived. Closing my eyes, I shook myself, gave myself a stern talking to, then went to work. I inputted all the sales figures, reviewed all the contracts. I'd already contacted the vendors and renegotiated as many prices as I could. We were as low as we could go and still make things profitable for them, so we had to find another way.

I don't know how long I sat there before I heard a soft knock on the door.

"Come in."

DeShawn stepped through, Corey hot on his heels. Corey came to me immediately, and I laughed as I bent over to rub him.

"Sorry, but he gets hot in the car fast, even with the windows down and the air on, and I didn't know how long you'd be."

I shook my head. "No, this is perfect."

"He misses Bruno," DeShawn said, sitting in the overstuffed chair. Yes, he'd bought the chair as a gag gift, but he looked so comfortable in it, I couldn't help but remember the shenanigans we'd gotten up to in it. I clenched my jaw and forced myself to pay attention. DeShawn had the smallest grin on his face as he continued. "The minute I said *you want to go see Bruno again*, Corey nearly ran me over to get out the house."

That shouldn't have been as cute as it was, but there was no denying that it was adorable.

I gave Corey a last scratch before I sat back. "Bruno's missed you, too, boy."

He barked, those happy, butt-wiggling barks, then padded over to plop himself in front of DeShawn.

"So," he began, and I nodded.

"So."

We stared at each other for a moment before he started laughing. "Are you as nervous about this as I am?"

I wanted to ask what he could possibly have to be nervous about, but my door slammed open and a furious James stood in the doorway. "You know damn good and well pets aren't allowed," he started, then noticed who was sitting in front of him, and nearly tripped over himself. "Chef DeShawn. I didn't know it was you. I'm so sorry. Is this your dog?"

Oh, so now James was a dog lover? He hated Bruno. Now, Bruno was a big boy, so I wasn't going to beat him up for that, but still.

DeShawn raised a brow at me before returning his attention to James. "Sorry about that. This is Corey, and I didn't want to leave him in the car. Wasn't sure how long we'd be."

If James nodded any harder, his head would crack the fuck off. "Totally understand. Totally." He looked back and forth between us. "So, what are you doing here?"

DeShawn glanced at me, then smiled, before returning his attention to James. "We had a few things to talk about."

"Yeah?"

"Yeah. You might see a bit more of me over the next couple of weeks. I hope that's okay."

James's face lit up like a hot air balloon on fire. "That would be amazing. You know, I'd been telling Malik that we really needed to get a big presence here to help boost business. And you are exactly that. If you could come, do some events, do some shows—"

"James."

The scowl on his face was not to be fucked with. "What, Malik? You want to protect this guy, wax poetic about how you loved him and all that, but he just said he's going to be here for a while. Why shouldn't I ask him to help when you won't, and all you can come up with are those silly lunch ideas?"

Dear god. DeShawn's brow rose clear to his hairline, and would have kept going if it could. But James wasn't done. "You said we couldn't ask him, but he's here, and he said he'd be around for a while, so why not?"

"Did it ever occur to you that he's here for me, not you? That he's here because we have business to take care of, not to save a restaurant that wouldn't be in such dire straits if the

CEO had considered any semblance of renovation and expansion with the times?"

James squared his shoulders, and DeShawn chuckled. A soft, light one, just enough to remind James he was there.

"I have no problem doing a few appearances here at the restaurant," DeShawn started, and I felt my back stiffen, "but I'd love to hear more about the other suggestions that have been put on the table." And there it went, loosening again.

James nodded, then looked around the office, like a spare seat would miraculously appear. In his haste, he accidentally nudged Corey, who let out a low growl.

"Sorry. Sorry, sorry, sorry," James said, holding his hands out in front of him and backing away.

DeShawn rubbed Corey, drawing him closer, then smiled. "Don't worry. You're still a stranger. I accidentally bump him all the time."

James's laugh was nervous, probably the first time I'd seen that emotion out of him.

"So, tell me about these lunch ideas you've been brainstorming."

I kept quiet, not sure I could handle my suggestions being shot down by DeShawn with the same vigor they were shot down by James. James snorted, then made himself comfortable against my file cabinet, crossing his arms and ankles.

"Malik wants to expand beyond the sit-down," James said, and boy, the derision in his voice was strong. "He wants to have delivery, takeout or carryout or whatever. Things that fly in the face of what Franklin's has always been, which is a restaurant for people to sit down, relax, and take their time with their meal."

DeShawn nodded slowly. "I understand the sentiment. I like my patrons to come, sit, enjoy themselves, too. Criteria is meant to be a full experience as well."

If James's smile could get any more smug, I didn't know how.

Then DeShawn shrugged. "But the ability to sit down, make time, enjoy themselves? That assumes they *have* that time. For some people, what they have is thirty minutes. And I'd assume you'd want them to be able to take that full thirty minutes being able to sit down and enjoy themselves, right?"

"Of course." James managed to look almost offended, but schooled his response again when he realized who he was talking to.

"Of course," DeShawn repeated. "But those thirty minutes? That doesn't have to be here, does it? Why can't they spend those thirty minutes at their office? Why can't they order the food fifteen minutes before their lunch break starts, know that someone will drop it off directly to them, and then use what little time they have really being able to sit and savor and enjoy their meal?"

The way James stared at him, you'd have thought DeShawn was speaking in Yoruba. "So, you think it's a good idea?"

"Honestly? I think it's an excellent one. This is a business district. People here are on the go, go, go, and they don't have time for sit-down meals. They want good food, they want it fast, and then they want to get back to their jobs. I'm assuming the restaurants around here that are doing the best understand that."

"So, what you're saying is, I should do what Malik says?" And James was right back to sounding like the petulant little child, chef god to the stars be damned.

DeShawn smiled, that practiced one that had made him a household name. The one he'd never turned on me. "I think I would be willing to do more than one appearance here. But only if you implement at least one of Malik's suggestions. I'll provide the boost, you do the rest of the legwork, and we'll give it a month to see how it goes. If it does well, I'll do another appearance, and you try another idea. If that sounds good, I'll get my agent on it."

James looked like he'd sucked on the worst lemon, but he was getting what he wanted. He just hated that I was, too. He stuck his hand out. "It's a deal."

DeShawn smiled, shook, then turned to me. "Is it time?"

To go home. To start playing pretend.

For a second I faltered, then I sucked in a breath, and all my courage, and smiled. "Yeah. It's time."

Chapter Eight

DeShawn

I'm not sure I'd ever been as frustrated with someone as I was with Malik's brother, James. A more pompous, arrogant, insecure man, I'd never met. And it said a lot about how much James had worn down on Malik's confidence that he would even remotely think I was siding with James over him.

But even though he hadn't said the words, I hadn't missed the way his body stiffened when I agreed to do the appearances, the way his jaw tightened, and I just *knew* he was waiting for me to reiterate what his asshole of a brother had said. I'd been sorely tempted to give James the brushoff, but this was technically my...brother-in-law? And for my grand plan, it'd help to get in good with the family, even if I wanted to dropkick him into the sun.

Relief had been evident on Malik's face when I'd asked if he was ready to go, and now I was pulling up to the sidewalk in front of that same gorgeous single-family home I'd been at before. I followed Malik, then parked on the street while he backed into one side of his two-car garage. I started to get out the car, but he waved a hand at me to stop, then jogged over.

"I cleared off the other side so you can park there," he said.

I gulped and nodded. "Oh. Okay. I don't want to put you out. I'm cool to park right here."

He shook his head. "It's no bother. Just back on in, then we can go in through the garage."

I gave him a too-tight grin and, when he moved out of the way, reversed into the second space. And no, I wouldn't dwell on how much like home it felt to do it. I stayed in the car long enough to send Christopher a text. He could make sure doing an appearance at Franklin's didn't interfere with my other obligations.

Malik followed me in, waited for me to get Corey out, then leaned into the backseat.

"Oh," I said, "you don't have to do that."

Malik paused with a handful of items, pretty much toys for Corey. "You're a guest. Of course I do."

I'd never had a problem with the word *guest* before now, but I murmured my thanks and followed him in. Bruno sat there in the foyer, leash in his mouth, and dropped it when he laid eyes on Corey. The dogs bounced around each other, barking and sniffing and doing whatever form of dog greeting they needed to. Then, just like last time, Bruno took off with Corey right behind him.

I chuckled at the sight. "Corey loves dogs."

Malik gave a little half smile. "Bruno too, though a lot of dogs are afraid of him. Corey's not, which means Corey will probably be in charge."

"Probably so." Alone now, our conversation about the dogs having come to its natural conclusion, we seemed to both find parts of the wood floor fascinating. Eventually, I broke the silence and hefted my bag on my shoulder. "Where should I put this?"

Malik stared, then shook his head. "My bad, I'm being so rude. Let me show you to your room."

I nodded and followed him to the stairs separating the front room from the rest of the living area. A few steps behind him,

I couldn't help but notice the way his ass filled out those slacks, the fluid movement in his shoulders. I couldn't help my small moan of pleasure either, and Malik stopped on the second to last step and turned.

I should have been embarrassed by the way I had to drag my eyes up to his face at his slight cough, and I was. Not just because Malik caught me staring, but because I was helpless to hide how utterly enthralled I was with his body. Seven years away hadn't changed some things.

This time this smile he gave me was a little wider, and I followed him down the hallway to a room on the back right.

"Here you go. I hope it's okay."

I walked in, frowning, my mouth hanging open. "Who am I kicking out to sleep here?"

Malik chuckled, but it was almost sheepish. "No one. This is the largest guest room."

"This is fucking nice. Way better than my bedroom."

I wasn't being facetious. My bedroom downtown was an eight by eight box. I could fit my queen size and very little else. This room was nearly twice the size, because the bed, a king situated smack in the center of the room, was nearly dwarfed by everything surrounding it. It even had the nerve to have a little sitting area over in the corner, a small walk-in closet, and its own bathroom.

"You sure this isn't the master suite?"

Malik's smile continue to grow, like he was proud of his house. As damn well he should be. "Nah, I'm down the hall to the right."

"Well, shit, if this isn't the master, I'm almost afraid to know what that looks like."

"I'm glad you like it."

"I do."

And just like with the dogs, the conversation had reached its natural conclusion, so we stood there. Because this wasn't like being roommates, no matter what Malik claimed he wanted. We weren't two strangers who might sit down, have dinner, get to know each other. We were two strangers who had known each other, loved each other, *married* each other. Wanted to spend their lives with each other, and now there was nothing but tension between us.

"You hungry?" I asked him, desperate to think about anything else.

He nodded. "I could eat."

I laughed. "One day I'm going to figure out if that means yes or no. Why don't you get comfortable, and I'll fix you something?"

"That sounds like a—" He stepped back, cutting off the words with a near scowl. "No. No," he said again. "That's not what we agreed to."

I held my hands up and took a step back, giving him even more space. "I'm sorry, I didn't mean it. I just—I just thought it made more sense for us to eat, get something in our system. Whatever. I wasn't trying to disregard your rules."

He ran a hand over his face and nodded, but his expression had shuttered. It had gone to that blank, pleasant look I'm sure he'd perfected when dealing with his brother, and I hated it.

"Why don't you do…" I paused, then flailed my hands a little, probably looking as hopeless as I felt. "Do whatever it is you do, and me and Corey will just get settled. How does that sound?"

"Good. Good," he repeated, but the second time was softer, almost like he was trying to convince himself as much if not more than me.

He backed out of the room, then shut the door behind him. I sank on to the bed, a plush, soft, cottony masterpiece, and buried my head in my hands. Not thirty minutes in, and I was already fucking things up. I sat there, waiting, until I heard a beeping sound. That had to be Malik leaving the house. I took a chance and wandered downstairs, and found Corey sitting by the entrance to the garage, whining.

"Hey, bud, what's wrong?" He trotted over to me, held still for a few head pats, then went right back to the garage door. A quick glance around and I realized Bruno wasn't there.

"Oh, I see. Bruno's master took him for his walk and left you behind?"

Corey's high whine told me everything I needed to know.

He had already had his walk, else I would've been tempted to take him out for a second time. Even though I didn't have a key, and I didn't have the code to the garage door, and I didn't want to make Malik feel bad when he realized he hadn't given me either of those things.

"Come on, boy, let me get you something to eat. Then maybe we can play out back, until your boy gets home, before we go to sleep."

Reluctantly, Corey followed me into the kitchen. As much as I wanted to create something for Malik, something he could dive into, sink his teeth into and revel in, he wouldn't appreciate that. Not from me, not right now. Disagreeable roommates had nothing on us.

I opened the fridge, pulled out some ciabatta bread, and made myself a sandwich. Corey sat by my feet on the patio, taking nibbles of it from me while he waited for his new friend to get home.

Malik

It had taken me what seemed like forever to fall asleep last night. I'd felt like shit when I got home and watched Bruno pad over to where Corey had been—where I'd left him whining when I leashed up Bruno and ran—knowing I'd been an ass to DeShawn for offering to make dinner. I'd planned to apologize when I returned, but the house was dark and the light under D's room had been off. So I tossed and turned, then tossed some more, then sat up in my bed like I'd just given up on the whole damn thing, before exhaustion claimed me sometime in the middle of the night.

But whenever I'd fallen asleep, I was rejuvenated as hell right now. Which was great, and... I sat up so quickly my head spun for a fraction. Fuck. It was almost 9:00 a.m. I was three hours late getting up. Sheila and James were going to kill me, not to mention Bruno.

That dog was nothing if not regimented, and I was surprised he wasn't leaving gouge marks on my door. I hurried into a set of track pants, slipped on the first pair of decent walking shoes I could find, then practically tripped over myself getting down the stairs.

"Bruno? Hey boy, it's time for your walk."

I heard a deep bark, then not one but two sets of paws scampering toward me. There was Bruno, and his faithful sidekick Corey behind him. Or maybe it was the other way around, which wouldn't surprise me in the least.

I knelt and rubbed them both, then straightened. "I'm sorry, boy," I said to Bruno. "Daddy missed your walk."

He butted my palm but looked like he was in no great rush. In fact, he was remarkably chill for a dog who was off his damn schedule. After a few seconds of rubbing, he pulled away and trotted back into the living room. I followed him and Corey, and found DeShawn, wearing pajama pants and a white undershirt, sitting there with a notepad and his laptop in front of him. The scent of maple syrup drifted from the kitchen, and I followed it to find a plate of French toast, scrambled eggs, and bacon in the warmer.

I was tempted to eat, but I'd be a good host first. I walked around the island to him and tapped him on the shoulder. "Morning."

He jumped and laid a hand over his heart, then pulled out an earbud I hadn't even seen. "I'm sorry, I didn't hear you come in."

I shook my head. "No, I didn't realize you had your earbuds in." Though how I could have forgotten was beyond me. DeShawn wasn't the type of person who needed silence. Silence was, in his words, loud and oppressive. He needed white noise, something to zone out to while he worked.

He gestured to the couch, like I didn't own the place or something. "So," he started. "You were dead to the world asleep this morning. I woke up, tried to wake you a few times, then went on and walked the dogs."

I nodded, then paused. "What do you mean, you walked the dogs? Both of them?"

He shrugged. "Well, yeah, but—"

My stomach squeezed, all thoughts of food forgotten. "I thought we agreed you weren't walking Bruno."

"I'm sorry, Bruno looked fucking pathetic this morning, and I wasn't leaving him for who knows how long before you stirred."

I ran a hand over my face. "You should've gotten me up."

DeShawn frowned, set his notebook down, then leaned forward, his elbows on his knees. "Did you miss the part where I said I tried to wake you and you didn't move?"

"Then you should have tried harder."

He opened his mouth, like he was ready to argue more, then snapped his mouth shut so hard his teeth clicked, and sat back. "I'm not fighting with you about this."

"Of course not," I said, unable to hide the venom in my voice. "Because DeShawn Franklin doesn't need to explain himself to anyone. DeShawn Franklin does whatever he wants, and to hell with the rules, right?"

DeShawn looked at me, his eyes creased, like he'd never seen me before. He shut his computer, shoved his earbuds in his pockets, and stood.

"Come on, Corey," he whispered softly, and the bulldog lumbered over to him. DeShawn knelt, rubbing all over Corey's head before drawing him close and kissing the top of it. "Such a good boy."

Then he stood and looked at me. "I get this is hard for all of us. I'm sorry for stepping on your toes. I guess I just haven't learned how to be as cold blooded as you are. The next time I see Bruno whining because his master isn't awake, I'll leave him with the same ease you left Corey last night. That make you feel better?"

He didn't give me a chance to answer, instead urging Corey away. I heard the garage door open, then his engine start.

Fucking hell. I'd driven the man away, pissed him off so much he left the house in pajamas. What kind of absolute asshole was I?

Not that he'd been wrong. Not at all. Because leaving Corey last night when I went to take Bruno for his walk? Had been a dick move. The poor dog looked so lost, but I'd hardened my heart, and honestly, I was grateful as hell DeShawn wasn't the bastard I was and had done more for my dog than I had for his.

Bruno whined, no doubt looking for his faithful friend, then eventually joined me on the couch. Which was a no-no, but I didn't have it in me to tell him to get off. Right now, I was grateful for the company.

I snatched my phone off the side table and called Sheila.

Her voice was muffled when she answered, a sure sign she wasn't wearing her headset and instead had her phone tucked into the crook of her shoulder. "Hey, what's up? You're not at the office already?"

Because I was always at the office. I woke up early, walked Bruno, then went to work, hours before we opened for any meals. I couldn't even blame it on wanting to keep a nine-to-five schedule, because I was often there from seven to seven.

"I overslept."

"What's sad about that is it's newsworthy. You never oversleep. So, tell baby sis what happened."

"DeShawn is here."

"What you mean by *here*? Here as in he's coming to the restaurant, or…"

"Here as in he's living with me."

"And you were going to tell us about this when, exactly?" I had no fucking clue. "Malik, what happened? If DeShawn is there, why are you calling me?"

"Because I ran him off."

"Already? How long has it been?"

"One night."

"Oh, Malik." Her voice had gone soft, that sympathetic sigh mixed with a healthy dose of exasperation. "Tell me what happened."

So I did, and to be honest, it was hard to get the words out. Because the more I spoke, the more I knew how messed up it was. When I was finished, I waited for her to castigate me, which was only right and fair at this time.

Instead, she asked a very simple question. "Malik, what are you so scared of?"

"What do you mean?" I had a pretty good idea, but I needed her to say it.

"You've created all these rules, basically saying that you want to be perfect strangers, nearly enemies, all that. But I mean, it sounds to me like he did you a favor, right?"

"Yes." I couldn't argue with that.

"Then what's the problem?"

How did I say it in a way that made it make sense? If that were even possible. "It's not that I ever stopped having feelings for him, you know. But whatever we had is gone, and I don't want to get used to him being around. I don't *want* to want him around."

"Is it such a bad thing to want?"

"With him? Yes. Yes it is."

Her laugh was light and made me join her.

"I'm not laughing at you," she said. "Well, I am, but you understand. It's just, you're so adamant you don't want anything with him. This isn't the fact that you're still married to him…doesn't that mean something?"

"Yes. It means we fucked up. It means that somehow we screwed up the paperwork, and now we still got this legality hanging over us that clearly neither of us wants." I did not want it, and I'd be damned if I let him make me wish for something it'd taken every ounce of willpower to walk away from the first time.

"Are you sure about that?"

Jesus Christ, what was it with her and all these damn questions? My sister wasn't the person who grilled you. She was the person who listened, nodded, and was decisive. But she sounded almost like she was on his side. Like she wanted me to give him a chance.

I pulled the phone away from my ear for a moment, then put it back and asked the key question. "If it wasn't DeShawn Franklin, executive chef of starred Criteria restaurant, recognizable face and household name, would you be asking this?"

"My feelings would almost be hurt by the assumption, but I can understand why you're asking it, so I'm not going to rail on you. Yes," she said. "I would still be asking it, because I didn't miss the way you looked at him. I didn't miss the way your eyes widened, the way your mouth fell open, the way you couldn't get out of the restaurant fast enough. And I'm sure there was a reason for that. And I want you to be honest with yourself about why that is."

"You're seeing things. Absolutely a figment of your imagination."

"Bullshit, and you know it."

"You're supposed to be helping me."

"I am. I'm helping you by telling you that you're on some bullshit. And you need to get over it. This guy is back in your life for a reason, and you need to figure out what it is. And you need to not run away from it."

If there was one thing time had proven I was good at, it was running away from something. And seeing DeShawn this morning, how easily he fit in, how well he smoothed things over with everyone and everything, how much he had to give that had nothing to do with me and our small-time restaurant, the more I knew that I would have no part of it.

No way was I telling my sister that, though.

"Well," I said, "I just wanted you to know so you understood if I were in a shitty mood when I show up at work today."

"I understand," she said, "and I'll forgive you for it. But I'm going to get your ass in gear. That man feels something for you, and I'm not going to let you hide and pretend it's a whole bunch of nothing."

I chuckled. Everyone thought that, but it hadn't happened yet.

Chapter Nine

DeShawn

I pulled in front of Grandma's house and heaved out a breath loud enough that Corey whined. I reached behind me to rub his head. "Sorry, boy."

He panted, and I got out the car and let him out. He trotted up the front steps like everything was just fine, like I hadn't royally screwed up on Day One.

Pulling on the facade I used just about every time I set foot in the restaurant, I opened the door and called out. "Knock knock! Your favorite grandson is here."

The laugh from inside Grandma's room was softer and tinnier than before, and I had to brace myself against the door for a moment. The reality of what was happening flooded me. I was losing my lifeline, and instead of me just getting to spend every waking moment with her, I was stuck trying to keep my uncle from ruining what she'd worked her whole damn life for. And with a man who had once been my whole damn world, and now looked like he despised my very presence.

"DeShawn? Baby, get in here."

I scrubbed my face, wiping away the tears that had the gall to pop up, then walked down the hall. Corey's whines were nearly overwhelming.

"D, get that boy up on this bed."

It made me laugh. When I was a kid, animals weren't allowed, and on the bed? Not a chance. She'd softened so much, and my heart gave another stuttering ache at how much I'd miss. I picked Corey up and placed him next to her. He laid his head in her lap and her smile was one of pure joy. Until she looked at me, and a scolding sympathy replaced it.

"Did you drive out here in your pajamas? What on god's green earth?"

I looked down at myself. Yep, pajama pants and a too-thin undershirt, flip flops and socks. "Sorry, I—"

"What did you do?"

I couldn't even be offended. She'd always taken Malik's side, and nine times out of ten, she was right. That tenth time usually wasn't worth mentioning.

I flopped on the other side of the mattress. "Broke his rule."

"Which was?"

"Not to walk Bruno."

Grandma paused midstroke on Corey's head. "Why can't you walk him?"

My exhale was noisy. "Because he's trying to keep things as separate as possible. I do my thing and he does his."

"So why'd you walk his dog?"

I threw my hands up. "Because Malik was asleep and I couldn't wake him, and Bruno looked so damn miserable I couldn't leave him like that when I took Corey out."

Grandma popped me lightly on the back of my head for cursing, then settled against her pillows. "So you did him a favor?"

"Not sure he'd agree with that assessment."

"Of course not. He's trying to guard his heart, and it's the little things that make it impossible to do."

That made a lot of sense, and was far more lucid than the panorama of thoughts that had gone through my head on the drive up. The little things, walking the dogs, making dinner for us both? Those were the things that made houses feel like homes. Now that I was thinking about it like that, it scared me, too. Maybe I was being too hasty?

I sat up against the headboard, and Grandma handed me the remote to elevate my side of the bed. "So what do I do? I can get with not doing a lot of stuff, but making the boys suffer isn't my thing."

Grandma started to speak, but there was a knock on the front door. She frowned. "What in the world?"

I understood. The people who came regularly, like me and Miss Maxine, had keys. Very few people knocked. "I'll get it."

I climbed off the bed and slowed my steps to the front, then peeked out the side window. Of course. Would I never know peace?

I yanked open the door for Malik and Bruno, then turned back down the hall without a word.

"DeShawn, who was—" Grandma didn't get a chance to finish her thought, as Bruno barreled in and hurried to her side. "Oh, you're a big boy, aren't you?"

She leaned over and rubbed Bruno's head, and he wagged his tail for all it was worth. Thank goodness there was nothing to knock over. He stomped his feet in a tap-dancing motion, and Grandma just laughed. "You want up, too? Come on then." She patted the spot I'd vacated and Bruno rushed around the bed to climb on.

A big, happy sigh as the dogs got themselves situated, then Grandma turned to us. "Malik, it's always a pleasure to see you, but I can't lie and say I'm not surprised."

Malik cleared his throat and scuttled around me to approach the bed. "I didn't mean to interrupt."

Grandma shook her head. "You're never an interruption.

But what happened with you boys this morning? My grand-baby drove down here in his pj's, and you don't look no better."

Malik shuffled his feet like a naughty schoolchild, and I was pretty sure I'd never seen him do that. He was always the calm, in-control, take-no-prisoners one. I was the manic one who made a mess of things as often as I got it right, and was used to being called on the carpet.

"I screwed up," he said. First to her, then he turned to me. "You did me a favor and I didn't even have the decency to say thank you. I'm sorry."

The last time Malik had said those words were the last time we had sex, one of those going-away fucks where the emotions were too big for words, and all we could do was hold on for dear life and pray the morning never came. But it had, and I'd started it by filing the signed divorce papers. It'd been the last time I'd seen him.

"DeShawn, what do you say?" Grandma's words had the slightly harder tone of a parent giving their child one last opportunity not to embarrass themselves before they got yanked by their ear.

So naturally, I did what I would've done then. "Why? Sorry you yelled at me, or sorry you made a stupid rule?"

"DeShawn Antonio Moore!"

"Franklin."

She huffed. "So now you're all about having his name."

I crossed my arms, an almost instinctive protective gesture. "I never let it go. I wasn't the one who wanted out."

"Mother of Christ." Malik sank into the chair, my chair, and his hands found the worn patch the same as I did. "Is that what we're doing? Rehashing our ill-fated romance?"

"Fuck you."

Grandma and Malik both stared at me like I'd sprouted horns. I did. Not. Care.

"How dare you reduce our marriage to a romance? How dare you reduce what I felt to a romance? How dare you reduce what I lost to a romance? I didn't care if you were out. I didn't give a damn if you didn't want to come to the bullshit events or galas or whatever I had to do. I wanted you. And you didn't want me enough. So I gave you exactly what you asked for, but I'll be damned if I let you sit here and treat it like it was a soggy tissue destined to disintegrate and not something we ripped to shreds."

Silence. The kind that was so loud I could hear the low hum of electronics from the front room. Even Corey and Bruno were quiet, not a whine or moan or anything. Malik's mouth hung open. Only Grandma looked even remotely pleased. "I should take a switch to your behind for cussing like that. But I won't because I've been waiting seven years for you to do that."

"To act like I have no sense?"

"To act like you cared that he left you."

I cut my eyes to her, then him. His face hadn't changed, but his eyes... They'd gone dark, stormy, but that wasn't the sign of Malik about to pop off. That was the sign of him being in pain, that deep kind he wasn't able to process in the moment.

So it shouldn't have been a surprise when he stood and looked at Grandma, giving me his back. "Would you mind letting Bruno stay with you for a few hours?"

Grandma considered him before shaking her head. "One hour, Malik. You go on and get out your head for an hour, then you come back and get your dog. And then you two fix this."

"Yes, ma'am." He walked to the side of the bed and kissed her cheek, then dropped his head and walked out without looking up.

We waited for the front door to close, then Grandma sighed. "What am I going to do with the two of you?"

I snorted. "Stop saying how we need to be together?"

"Oh no, not that. If anything, I'm more right now than I was then."

I stared at her. Just stared, and dropped my eyes when she stared right back. I'd never been able to win that fight. I sank into the seat, immediately overwhelmed by Malik's scent on it. Warm and comforting and strong. I hated how weak I was for it. How much his words still cut me.

It was that thought that made me focus on Grandma. "What do you mean, more right now than before? Can't you see we wouldn't have made it no matter what?"

She sighed again and pointed to the foot of the bed. I hated to admit it, but I was loath to leave the sanctity of the chair. Of Malik's scent surrounding me when I knew it was the last thing he wanted. Still, I found a spot on the end of the bed. Corey and Bruno looked up, waited until I stopped jostling them, and returned to their rest. Oh, to switch places.

"Malik is always so careful with his words. You know that."

Yeah, I did. It was my job to be the impetuous one.

"He revered the sanctity of marriage. I remember when you said you wanted to take his name. Thought the poor boy would expire on the spot." She chuckled at what was clearly a fond memory for her, then went quiet. "That...whatever he said that set you off? We both know that's not the real him."

"Grandma, I don't know who the real him is anymore."

"Bull." Unlike me, she stopped herself from saying the full word. "Malik now is the same Malik who couldn't stop crying when you separated, who apologized to me for not being good enough for his boy."

I hadn't heard anything about this. And it was the second time someone had made mention of Malik's feelings for me. James had done the same thing, just yesterday, hadn't he? Talked about how Malik loved me and wouldn't let James use me. Now Grandma was reiterating it, and I was having the worst time squaring it with the man who showed me such complete and utter disdain.

"Grandma, what do I do? I get why he has rules, I do, but I don't want to walk on eggshells for weeks on end."

"Then put your foot down. Bend the rules for the dogs, because they're not going to understand why one can go for a walk and the other can't, and keep the rest firmly intact."

"Ugh. I hate those rules."

"I know, baby, but if you're gonna get him back, you need to play this smart. And right now, that means playing it his way."

I shifted on the bed and frowned. I hadn't said anything to her, had I? I know I'd told Maribel, but—

"You're thinking so loud I can hear you from here. How did Grandma know you wanted Malik back?"

I swallowed, but didn't try to deny it. I nodded, and she smiled, that soft one that had gotten me through so many long and lonely nights. "DeShawn, no other man could reduce you to driving in your pajamas. To cursing in front of me like you have no sense. With anyone else, you would have given it back to him as hard as he gave it to you. Walking Bruno meant something to you because *he* means something to you. And"—she paused for a moment before nodding, like she was reaffirming that she wanted to continue—"it meant something to him. Can you really imagine Malik going off like that with anyone else? *Especially* about walking his dog?"

She was making too much damn sense. More than I could really handle dealing with. And she knew it. "Why don't you take the boys down to the dog park? Let them run around and stuff."

"Trying to get rid of me?" I tried for playful, and maybe almost made it.

"Yes," she said without a hint of humor. "I need to talk to Malik when he works whatever out his system, and you don't need to be here for that."

She was right, but I couldn't take the boys to the park in pajamas. I tugged at the pants and arched a brow, but Grandma was unmoved. "You've got a full closet in the other room and you know it."

I chuckled, and called the boys off her. "You gonna be okay?"

She rolled her eyes. "Just put the key under the mat and tell Malik where it is."

Which meant texting him, though I'm sure I was the last person he wanted to hear from. I walked around to her side of the bed and leaned my forehead against hers. "I love you, Grandma."

She patted my cheek and I felt her grin against me. "I love you, too, baby. Now shoo."

Malik

I picked the wrong spot to park my car. Just a few blocks away, just enough to get away from the buzzing in my ears, my lungs, my veins. DeShawn's words, the hurt in them, the hurt I'd spent years pretending he didn't feel? Yeah, I wasn't ready for it. So I did what I'd done as his career skyrocketed and mine looked destined for stagnation. I ran.

Right to Pimlico fucking Race Course, the last place I wanted to see.

I gripped the steering wheel, determined to drive *anywhere* else, but I couldn't make myself move, so I just stared. Home of the Preakness, that hotbed seat of gambling that had entrapped DeShawn's uncle at a young age, and kept him there now, some fifty-plus years later. If not for the debts he'd racked up here, he wouldn't be so desperate for Grandma's money that he was suing me. He wouldn't have destroyed everything she did for him, to the point where she was cutting him off. Me and DeShawn could have found out about the error in our divorce paperwork and handled it without ever having to see each other, something I figured we'd both have found preferable.

The last—the absolute last—thing I needed, was for James to pick that time to call. But my phone buzzed through the stereo Bluetooth, cutting off whatever was on, and I knew that ignoring it was just asking for him to harass me until I gave in. Better to get it over with now.

"Where are you?" he asked as soon as I clicked on.

"Why do you care?" He'd have to excuse me if I wasn't in the mood for his shit today.

"You're not at the office."

"Again, why do you care? I'm the accountant, not a cook. You don't need me there for the restaurant to run."

"I wanted to talk to you about some of those ideas you had."

"So you can set up the appearance with DeShawn, right?"

James was quiet, but I knew my brother. It wasn't because he was in some deep contemplation. He was pissed, and hoping that his grudging acquiescence to my ideas would distract me from the fact that it took DeShawn's quid pro quo to make it happen.

"Does it really matter how we got here? You're getting what you want. Isn't that what matters?"

"I'd love it to take less than a celebrity endorsement for you to see that it's not about brothers arguing, and about what's best for the restaurant. Sometimes it feels like I'm the only one who remembers that."

Wow, I was burning all the damn bridges today, wasn't I? Not giving an inch of space for my brother who was doing his version of apologizing. Which was to say, none at all, but he wasn't reneging, and he wasn't waiting on DeShawn to hold up his end of the bargain before implementing my ideas.

"I'm sorry, James." I sighed and thunked my head against the seat. "I've had a bad day and am being an ass. When did you want to meet?"

We scheduled a time and clicked off, and I closed my eyes. I was still tired from the tossing and turning the night before, still on edge without an outlet for it, and still had to see DeShawn when I went back. To Grandma's house or mine, it didn't matter. He was going to be everywhere I went, and it was going to be impossible to escape from.

My speaker buzzed with another call and I said a quick prayer I didn't blow my top before I answered. "Hello?"

"Hey, sweet boy. You about done?"

God, even in the midst of utter turmoil, Grandma's voice made me smile. "Done with what, Grandma?"

"I know you. You need to blow off steam before you can handle heavy conversations, so I gave that to you. But now it's time for you to come home. I sent DeShawn off with the dogs so it can be just me and you."

She got me, better than really anyone in the family did. "I'll be right there."

"DeShawn left the key under the mat. He was supposed to send you a text, but just in case he didn't."

I'd heard my phone buzz and it was probably him, but I hadn't bothered to check. "Thanks. I'm five minutes out."

We clicked off and I drove the less than two minutes back to Grandma's, then gave myself another three before getting out the car. I found the key and let myself in, then put it back in place for DeShawn's return with the boys. Part of me wanted to stay out front, avoid the necessary convo. But it wouldn't make anything go away, and it wouldn't give me any guidance on how to navigate this. I'd thought the rules would be enough, but...

"Malik Franklin, stop dawdling out there and come talk to me."

I dipped my head and chuckled, then walked down the hall. It was quiet without the boys here, and I wondered how she kept herself from being overwhelmed by it when she was alone. I always had Bruno. My house was too large for one person, but Bruno took up the space of three adults, so I'd never felt alone. But walking downstairs, seeing DeShawn sitting there, the dogs at his feet, like he'd made himself at home, had punched me so damn hard in the gut I hadn't been prepared.

"Malik!"

"Coming." I shook myself again and got ready for the scolding I was sure to receive.

Grandma sat there, the television on low, shaking her head. "You two are as bad now as you were then."

"What do you mean?" I sat back in the seat I'd taken before, and was enveloped in DeShawn's soft scent. A combination of vanilla and amber and maple syrup. Because he'd cooked for me, too, despite my rules.

I leaned back and inhaled deeply, and one of Grandma's brows twitched. She couldn't raise them, but that twitch? Same thing.

"I know you're protecting yourself, Malik, and I can't say I blame you. That divorce and the faux amiability covered up a world of hurt on both your parts, didn't it?"

What did I say to that? Did I deny something we all knew was true? It was far too late for all that, so I nodded.

"This is the first time in all those years I've seen DeShawn go off, and he needed it. What do you need to let go, to move on?"

To bury myself balls deep in him, remind him how good

we were together, prove I could still make his body sing the way I had all those years before.

None of which had a damn thing to do with moving on. All that was about rekindling what we had, which was not what I wanted. Not at all. Not even a little bit.

"I made my will for a reason." Grandma's voice was soft, and I squashed my musings to the back so I could pay attention. "I wanted to help those who had loved me, who had brought such joy to me, especially after Cornelius died. Robert comes to see me once a year." She scrunched her nose with a sigh, and I could take a wild guess it was usually the third weekend in May—the day of the Preakness. "But you and De-Shawn? You kept me sane, gave me such joy with your calls and visits, and that's what I want to remember."

She paused. Closed her eyes. And looked tired. All the reasons I was engaging in this farce roared back, and fuck. What we were doing wasn't about me. Or DeShawn. Or whatever we'd had once upon a marriage.

"I'm sorry, Grandma." My voice cracked and I didn't try to hide it. "I screwed up. I should've thanked him instead of blowing up."

"Yes, you should've."

Despite what I'm sure DeShawn thought, Grandma didn't let me get away with shit either. I winced at the words, but nodded.

"I can understand why you reacted the way you did, though, and I know DeShawn does, too. But you two can't use each other as punching bags for your residual hurt." She blew out a breath and shook her head. "This is why I wanted you to talk before Robert showed his whole behind. So you had time to adjust. You haven't had it and you need it."

But me and DeShawn hadn't listened, because that would've made too much sense. We'd decided we knew better, and were screwing it all the way up one day in. We had to get it together, and fast.

"What do we do?" I finally asked.

"You have to play married, and happily, in public. You have to practice in private." She stared me down when I opened my mouth. "I'm not saying don't have boundaries. I'm saying you have to learn who you are now, not who you remember. You've both grown since then. You don't have to do anything serious, but I'd imagine getting used to kissing each other in public isn't a bad thing. Holding hands. Your neighbors are going to see the news. They're going to know DeShawn Franklin lives there now. They're probably going to be questioned about your relationship. So you have to prepare for all that."

My mouth hung open. She was right, so right. This went further than I'd ever thought to consider. DeShawn was a local celebrity. More than local, with a starred restaurant under his belt. His love life had been the source of more than a little bit of gossip, so the knowledge that he had a husband? That we'd allegedly reunited and were together? It flew in the face of the DeShawn people had grown to love, and they'd be naturally suspicious. I know I would be. Dear Lord, that meant making this stick was going to take some work.

Or not, an almost gleeful voice whispered in my head. *You don't need to pretend at all with him, do you? Throw down those barriers and let nature take its course.*

If only it were that easy.

Chapter Ten

DeShawn

I didn't know what to say when Malik asked me if I could meet him at Franklin's for dinner. I mean, I could've said no, but that was just delaying the inevitable, which we didn't have time for. Typically, I'd prefer someplace quieter, but given how I'd gone off on him this morning, a public place was probably a safer option. So I said yes, talked to myself the entire way home, much to Corey's confusion, then ran upstairs to take a shower and change. All that drama this morning, and I hadn't even bathed.

It was tempting to say the hell with it and crawl into the ridiculously comfortable bed, but Malik lived here. It was his damn house, so avoiding him wasn't a viable option.

I heard the front door beep and waited until I heard it a second time before making my way downstairs. Sure, enough, Bruno and Corey were cuddled up on Corey's too-big-for-his-own-good dog bed, apparently worn out from the day. I understood exactly how they felt. A quick rub over both their heads, and I was out the door.

The drive to Malik's restaurant didn't take nearly long enough, but I'd decided on one thing on the way. I was going to follow Malik's lead, be as easy or rough as him. Given that we were meeting at his restaurant, I figured he'd be on his best behavior, so I'd be on mine.

I pulled up to a spot at the front and climbed out, taking the opportunity to look around. The brick exterior had seen better days, but some patchwork and a coat of paint could help that. The awing was frayed and the sign, *Franklin's*, could use a good power washing. It was out of place with the glass and stainless steel—everything else—surrounding them, but I liked it. It felt homier. Not as rushed. A place for people to come and chill.

With a small grin, I shook my head and went inside. Exactly the same thing James had said, and I really could see where he was coming from. They could absolutely be that in the evening, when people didn't have jobs and responsibilities to get back to. But they needed something more in the daytime. Just like Malik argued. Fancy that. The quarreling brothers both made good points.

"You gonna sit, or you just gonna stand there like a stranded guppy?" Sheila stood on the other side of a bar that looked nearly empty. Did they not serve alcohol here?

I scanned the room quickly and saw that there were only three occupied tables, and one waiter. I walked over to Sheila and pulled up a stool. "I'm meeting Malik here."

"Oh, so that's why he's in his office looking like he's having an asthma attack?"

"He okay?" I straightened, ready to march in there if necessary. Malik's asthma was mostly under control, but when he did have an attack, it was always serious.

"Look at you, so protective. I like it." She didn't cower under my glare. "That look is sexy, not scary. Try again."

A laugh broke free before I could stop myself. "Thanks, I think."

"Gotta say, I didn't know my brother had such good taste. How'd he pull you?"

"He didn't. I chased him like a panting puppy until he gave in and put it on me."

"Eww, okay. TMI."

"I was just answering a question." I winked at her and grinned.

Her smile was glorious. "God, I would've loved seeing the two of you together. I bet he was a totally different person."

Memories rolled through me before I could stop them, and I squeezed my eyes shut to shove them aside. "Yeah. He was."

The change in my tone was impossible to miss, and her smile faded into sympathy. Maybe bordering on pity, and wasn't that a shame? "Take a seat. I'll get Malik for you."

"Thanks." I grabbed a table near the back, where we could talk without being interrupted, and pulled a menu sitting up in the stand while I waited.

The braised short ribs were calling my name. Add some collards, mac and cheese, and some good dessert, and the itis—food coma, whatever phrase people used—already had me in its grip.

"You order something?"

Damn, I hadn't even seen Malik approach, but there he was, standing in front of me, pensiveness scrawled across his weary face. I put the menu down and tried to grin. "The short ribs look good."

"Sides?"

"Collards and mac and cheese."

"Be right back."

He turned around and went to Sheila, then came back with two bottles in his hand. "Cider?"

"God, yes." He chuckled, maybe the first real one I'd heard from him, and I smiled. "Take a seat, Malik."

His eyes narrowed, then he looked at the wall, the ceiling, the door, before sitting down. "Thanks for coming."

"You know I'd do anything for you."

Malik glanced at me, then swallowed so hard I could see the strain in his Adam's apple.

"I didn't actually mean that the way it sounded." Lies. "But you did invite me out, and I think we can both agree we have a lot to discuss."

He nodded, then ran his hands over his face. "I'm sorry about this morning. What you did was really kind, and I appreciate it. I shouldn't have snapped at you like that."

"That's true, you shouldn't have." Malik's shoulders slumped, and damn, I couldn't hold a grudge for shit, because just the look on his face and I was over it. "The dogs can't be part of the rules. They don't get it."

The little half laugh he gave warmed me from the inside out. "You're right. They're not going anywhere without the other, are they?"

"Not a chance."

"There's more." Malik's voice had quieted to a whisper, like he didn't want to acknowledge the reality of what he was about to say.

Which meant I damn sure didn't want to follow up, but I did. "Like what?"

Sheila chose that time to come out with two plates of piping hot food, and the scent of the meat nearly bowled me over. She sat my plate down, then Malik's. Then she hovered.

I looked up. "Everything okay?"

"I just, I mean…" She trailed off and rubbed her hands down her coat.

I got it. Being the "hot" chef in town made eating out kinda difficult. People wanted to know what you thought, but really only if it was good. I'd learned to be super careful with my facial expressions, but I knew Malik would see through anything less than genuine.

I took a bite of the ribs, swirling them around in the jus first, and threw my fork down. "That bitch is delicious."

Sheila half laughed. "You serious? You like it?"

"Fucking hell, yes." I wanted to tip the whole damn plate down my mouth and lick it clean. Sheila could outcook half the chefs I knew, and I didn't mind telling her so.

She twirled, shimmied, and half moonwalked half floated back to the kitchen, and I kept eating.

I looked at Malik, and the expression on his face mirrored ones I'd dreamed about for years after I'd lost him. One I couldn't hold on to, so I focused on my plate. And goddammit, someone had eaten all my food. "I wasn't shitting her."

"I know you weren't. You've just made her year, that's all."

I laughed. "Never that. But…" I sat back in my seat and crossed my arms. "What's the other part we have to keep up?"

"You're a name. You're popular and people know you. My neighbors are going to recognize you. So we have to play at least to the neighborhood crowd."

I closed my eyes and breathed in a deep breath. He was so right. "Yeah, okay, so what does that mean?"

Malik looked as lost and confused as I felt. "I don't know."

I snickered. "I mean, I think we can at least walk the dogs now."

Malik's smile was slightly sheepish, but heartfelt. "At least. But your grandma was right in saying we can't just act like it's a switch we can turn off and on. We have to get comfortable again, learn who we are now."

"That why you invited me out?"

He nodded. "Yeah." He chuckled and looked away for a moment before facing me again. "I'm as boring now as I was then. This is pretty much my life. I guess I wanted you to see what I do, what I'm trying to save."

"It's worth saving."

Malik's not-quite-quarter-grin said more than any words could. His whispered "Thank you," said the rest.

I sat back and sighed, my belly full and ready to sleep for a week. "So how do we do this? Get comfortable and still keep our boundaries?" I added at Malik's slightly perplexed expression.

"I guess… I guess maybe dinner together wouldn't be too bad. We could talk. Get to know each other again. Get comfortable."

I smiled, then a light flashed and popped, making us both squint. Another table was full, one that hadn't been before, and someone had recognized us and snapped a pic. Malik's eyes narrowed and I laid a hand on his to get his attention. He turned to me with a glower.

"Don't worry about that. It was bound to happen."

He didn't speak for a minute, but then closed his eyes and inhaled deep, like he was saying a prayer, before opening them. "I forgot I'm married to a celebrity."

I swallowed the snort that wanted to break free, then leaned across the table. "Let's go get us trending."

Malik

I'm sure, when James said he wanted DeShawn to make a special appearance here, it wasn't like this. He'd expected something formal, a grand announcement during one of DeShawn's TV segments that he could rewind and watch over and over again. Or maybe that was me being uncharitable. Still, baby brother was too old school to want DeShawn's presence here to be announced to the world from a social media post, but that's where we were.

"Chef DeShawn," a woman called out, sitting next to the person who'd snapped the shot, "what are you doing here? Planning to throw some of your special charm on this place?"

DeShawn caught my eyes, gave me that here-we-go look, and pasted that fake-as-fuck smile on his face. The one that made everyone swoon. I'd say I hated it, but it was gorgeous. It just wasn't real.

"This place doesn't need my help in the kitchen," DeShawn said with that low, husky laugh of his. "I just wanted a quiet night out with my husband."

For a brief moment, the silence was almost as loud as it had been at Grandma's; then the front room exploded.

"Husband?"

"But when?"

"Ooh, how? You know I have alerts set up. Dunno how I missed that one."

That last one was a little creepy, but the questions kept coming, melding together, and I couldn't hope to keep up. DeShawn's smile got strained, though to the untrained eye it would look like he found the barrage of questions humorous. He was good at this. I was already over it.

He stood and held his hands up, and the table fell silent. "I think you're scaring him." He turned and extended an arm to me, and what could I do but take it?

This was your idea, Malik. Can't nut up now.

I grabbed his hand like the lifeline it was, put on my best smile, and stood. Together, we approached the table, and the group scooted their chairs around to make room for us. I looked at the other tables, full of regular customers, and even some of them were pointing at DeShawn and nudging each other. Forcing my attention to the table we were standing at, I gave them what I'm sure was an awkward wave. "Hi."

"What's his name?"

"How did you meet?"

"How long have you been married?"

DeShawn tugged me close and slipped his arm around my waist. That small smile, full of what're-you-gonna-do, made my heart flip-flop on itself. He nuzzled my jaw. "I'll make it up to you later."

My body wanted that, and I'm sure what I wanted wasn't what DeShawn had in mind. He turned back to them.

"This is Malik Franklin, and this is his family's restaurant. His baby sister is in the back putting her foot in the food—" He paused and stared at them. "That's a euphemism, just in case this is your first time in a Black spot."

The table laughed, but a few of them *did* look relieved. And DeShawn wanted desperately to roll his eyes, if the way he squeezed my waist was any indication. He was laying it on thick and they were lapping it up.

"So tell me," he started, and plopped into an empty chair, "what brought you guys here tonight?"

I followed suit, settling myself into a seat next to DeShawn's and listening to one woman—Peggy, and yes, that was her legal name, please and thank you—explain how she worked in the area and had stayed late, needed a bite to eat, and was going back to the office when she was done. We were one of the few restaurants still open at this time, and she'd dragged her friends out to join her.

That started gears in my head spinning, about being able to advertise service to folks like her, and it took DeShawn's gentle squeeze on my knee to get me back in the game.

One person at the table, a thin blond with a swoop of hair that fell over his glasses, obscuring that eye, leaned forward. "Your name is Malik Franklin? Did you take Chef DeShawn's name?"

DeShawn's laugh cut me off before I could fumble with a

response. "Didn't you notice the name of the restaurant? It's Franklin's. No, love, I took his name."

He sputtered a bit, the puzzle pieces not quite clicking together. "But...you've been Chef Franklin since forever."

"I have."

DeShawn didn't offer more than that, and there was no way I was giving him the missing links. The door opened and a head popped through. The person frowned before she spotted Peggy, then waved and came in, at least six more people with her.

"We love hitting up new-to-us places," Peggy explained. "I texted some friends to get their heinies down here."

DeShawn beamed. I caught his eyes over the top of the woman's head and his smile widened before he winked at me. I matched his grin with one of my own, then stood to let a man take my chair. I slipped away into the kitchen and grabbed an apron. Someone had to take these orders.

What I didn't expect was for DeShawn to join me a few minutes later. While I was perfunctory, taking orders efficiently if not excitedly, DeShawn was the Energizer Bunny. I hadn't even noticed how he'd maneuvered me toward the people who just wanted to eat, and kept me away from those wanting selfies and discussing appropriate hashtags.

I handed Sheila my orders and started helping make plates. "James is throwing a fit," she whispered.

"Can't imagine why."

"Says it's just going to show how bad things are here."

James *would* worry that people would see how empty it was, that it wasn't as sharp or shiny as the other businesses. I knew, because the same thought had crossed my mind. "He has to know it wasn't intentional. Besides, we keep the place up. It looks good on the inside, and this lady was trying to find a place that was open because so few are. I think those are all points in our favor."

She shrugged. "You think that makes a difference to our favorite pessimist?"

It didn't, but I'd witnessed firsthand DeShawn's ability to spin a narrative to fit what he wanted. I loaded a tray and carried it out, set it down and served two tables. I was on my way back when I heard a squeal, though I couldn't tell who'd done it.

"You shut the restaurant down to spend the evening with your husband? That's so romantic."

I almost tripped over my feet, and it took everything in me to contain the laugh that bubbled up. "I think D's got it in the bag," I told Sheila as I plated the next set of meals. "He knows what he's doing."

"I'm glad someone does, because my arms hurt." She giggled. "Don't know when the last time was I had this many orders at once."

"Don't act like you don't love it."

She looked at me, her eyes shining with a light I hadn't seen in way too long. "I won't."

I spent the next hour playing waiter, and dear god, I was wearing the wrong shoes for this. It had been decades since my forced service as a teen when Dad was still in charge, but apparently some things came back. I got looser, more friendly, and DeShawn's casual touches and glances felt better than I remembered.

"It says here that you two filed for divorce." I spun on my heels to find the same blond guy who'd asked about our last names standing there, a phone in his hand. He must've pulled up the courthouse records, which I knew were available online. "You filed for divorce but there was an issue with the paperwork and a new divorce was never sent in."

DeShawn turned from a few tables over, and the restaurant fell silent. That smile was still there, but his eyes had hardened. And then he clicked his fingers. "Noah Tippin. I thought I recognized you, but I couldn't place it. Tell me you haven't forsaken true journalism for the gossip rags."

Noah didn't even flush. If anything, he straightened, like he was proud of himself.

The side of DeShawn's mouth quirked up and he pointed to Noah's phone. "You see when we filed that divorce? Over seven years ago. Seven years of me trying and failing to find what I had with him, and when I realized the divorce hadn't gone through, it was kismet. It was a greater power telling me I'd already found my one." He walked over to me, stopping just a few inches away. His hand trailed over my cheek, down my jaw, across my lips. "Everything I needed was already there."

He leaned into me and, dear god, were we going to kiss for the first time in seven years right here? In public?

DeShawn breathed into my mouth. I guess we were.

I let my hands find his hips and pull him close, then tilted my head just a fraction and took his lips. DeShawn groaned into my mouth and pressed closer, and that was it. I was a goner.

Time hadn't changed the firm softness of DeShawn's lips, his breathy pants that made my blood soar, the way he pulled me closer like he couldn't get enough.

And time hadn't changed how good he felt in my arms, how my urge to meld us together until not even a sheet of rice paper could get between us never seemed to bank, how I was sure I could live off his taste forever.

"Oh. My." One person's voice was a hoarse whisper. "I didn't actually think kissing was that hot until now."

Yeah, there were people here. Watching us. And I didn't

care. I moved in for more and DeShawn looped his arms around my neck, then turned to the crowd. "All I needed was right here the whole time."

I flexed my fingers against his back. DeShawn turned back to me and brushed his lips against mine, then nibbled along my jaw to my ear. "He's leaving. Just a few more seconds."

And then we could stop playing, but everything about this felt way too damn real. I really hadn't needed the reminder this was fake. The reminder of all the reasons I'd created rules in the first place. How the hell did I go home and sleep in my bed, alone, after this? I didn't know if I was in heaven or in hell, and it didn't matter. DeShawn was front and center of every dream and nightmare. Why the hell couldn't I listen to some Meek Mill when I needed to?

Chapter Eleven

DeShawn

I was practically vibrating with excess energy, and I knew just where I wanted to put it: on Malik.

Because that kiss. Nothing about it had been fake. Nothing stiff or stilted or pretend. I wanted that, in spades, for the rest of my life.

I parked next to him in the driveway, but he was out the car and in the house before I got my engine off. I jogged in behind him, fighting to keep from sprinting, and at least had the foresight to close the garage door.

Malik stood at the counter, gripping the edge. He didn't look up when I came in, but the dogs, who'd been by his side, ran to mine for their necessary welcome. I petted them until they ran off again, then circled the island to stand in front of Malik. I reached out a hand, but he pulled back and straightened.

"What's wrong?" I asked, daring to take another step closer.

"DeShawn, stop. All that at the restaurant was—"

"Amazing. Let's practice more."

"Fake. That's what it was, was fake. You didn't mean any of it."

I wasn't going to comment on how he hadn't included himself in that assessment. Instead, I looked down at my rock-hard dick, then raised my brow at him.

And he rolled his eyes, the turd. "Us getting hard for each other has never been a…hardship," he finished lamely.

I remembered Grandma's words, about Malik protecting himself, and backed off. I wanted to press, god knew I did, but it was still too raw, and too new, and I wanted to remember how good it had felt. Not let Malik bullshit me into thinking it hadn't meant anything, which we both knew was a fucking lie.

I knocked on the counter a few times and turned away without answering. Franklin's didn't serve dessert, which was a goddamn pity, so I opened the fridge and started rummaging.

"What're you doing?" Malik's voice was gruff behind me, and I knew that sound. It was the I'm-still-horny-stop-what-ever-you're-doing-and-let's-go-again sound, and I wanted to shout. I didn't, and I deserved an extra treat for that.

Without turning, I said, "Looking for dessert. Y'all don't serve it."

"Doesn't make sense, does it? Dad was never into sweets like that." He pointed to a smaller fridge in the island. "I keep my desserts in a separate fridge." I turned and raised a brow, and he gave me a little half shrug. "I make a lot. Gotta put it somewhere."

It was a stark reminder how little I knew about this man and this place. He hadn't taken me on a formal tour or anything; I just noticed things as I went along. I probably would've seen it last night had I not been so upset about Malik taking Bruno out and leaving Corey, but reality was I hadn't paid much attention to the house. I'd rectify that later. This house held clues to what Malik thought was important, what he needed to bring him comfort, and I needed every bit of arsenal on my side to get him back in my arms permanently.

For now, though, I walked to the mini fridge built into the island, on the opposite side to the dishwasher. He opened the door and my mouth fell. Mini brownie bites, truffles, little dough balls, probably filled with cream. I wanted ten of all of them.

Malik's low chuckle wasn't doing a thing for my erection, but I could tell he was proud. He definitely had reason to be. I grabbed the dough balls and bit into one. Creamy filling, not too sweet, hit my tongue and the flavors of chocolate, cinnamon, cayenne, and a hint of aged whiskey hit my taste buds.

"Oh yeah," I said, one hand over my still full mouth, "that shit's amazing."

Malik's grin looked so much like Sheila's from earlier tonight that I had no choice but to match it. And we stood like that for maybe a beat or three too long before he cleared his throat and stepped back. "So, now what?"

I made myself a plate of dough balls and leaned against the counter. "Now we figure out how to leverage tonight into real growth for your family." That *your* didn't sit right on my tongue, but I kept my mouth shut. As far as Malik was concerned, this was a fake relationship, and doing anything that might blur those lines would make him put his shields up, which was the last thing we needed.

Malik pinched his forehead and stepped back. "How do we make that happen?"

I took the plate and went for the couch, patting the seat beside me. Malik frowned, and it was my turn to roll my eyes. "We're married, remember? And you could tell from tonight not everyone's gonna just accept it and not dig further. We need an actual game plan now."

Malik paused for an extra beat before nodding and sitting at the far edge of the couch.

"Ooh, so romantic. So in love. Malik, no one's going to believe this if we can't even sit together."

"If tonight's any indication, I'm fairly certain we can make them believe it."

The itch to argue was strong, because Malik was being stubborn for the fuck of it. I popped another delightful dough ball in my mouth instead and let the quiet take over.

It wasn't long before Malik's shoulders slumped and he sighed. "I'm doing it again, aren't I?"

No sense in lying. "Yes."

"I'm sorry." He moved closer, until our thighs were touching, the heat strong enough to melt my pants clear off. Then he reached over and snagged a dough ball off my plate and popped it in my mouth.

"Hey!"

He winked. "Gotta make folks believe it right?"

I sputtered. "That didn't mean you had to actually eat my ball."

Malik paused, and yeah, that wasn't the best phrasing I could have used. "Sorry," I muttered.

Malik gripped me by the chin and pressed a short, almost perfunctory kiss to my lips, then sat back. "I'm gonna be a little hot and cold until I get my feet under me. Be patient, okay?"

I nodded. It reminded me so much of what he'd said when I'd finally worn him down and convinced him to give us a chance. That he'd never been in a real relationship before and I'd need to take my time with him. I'd been willing to give him all the time in the world then, but we didn't have that same luxury now.

"So," I started, clearing my throat and trying not to think about what was at stake, "what's your busiest day of the week?"

Malik startled a bit at the abrupt change in topic but put his game face on. "Receipts show Sundays. We still get a lot of folks who'll come by after church to eat, or folks who want to get a large enough meal for leftovers."

"Sheila definitely makes enough for them."

He snorted. "It wasn't always that way, but bigger portions mean less wasted food."

"What do you do with the extra food?"

"Send it to the shelters. They make it into the next night's meal."

We could work with that. In a way to make it decidedly non-self-serving, since they'd been doing this for some time. But that kind of giving back to the community wasn't something I'd wager the other establishments around them were doing. It was the kind of thing that made communities want to support a place so it didn't die.

"What's the worst day?" I fumbled in my pocket for my phone and pulled up my notes app. Too many years of having outstanding ideas and losing them in an instant had taught me not to forget a thing.

Malik's snort was bitter. "Every other day. We barely get enough to break even, and we're having more and more days when we don't." He got off the couch and started to pace. "James rarely comes by during the day. He doesn't see how dead it can be during the week. So many people are holed up in offices, and sometimes the most people you see are the delivery guys. And we don't have one. I mean—" He threw his arms up before setting them on his hips. "There are a few medical offices in the area. They'll come in sometimes and sit for lunch, sometimes an early dinner, but it's not enough."

Malik's passion for the business was evident. Whoever thought being an accountant meant being mentally removed had never met Malik. "Why is James so big on bringing in a big name?"

"Because he lives for the short term." Malik faced me and shook his head. "That's probably not fair. A couple of the other restaurants around here got some celebrities to pimp them out when they opened, and to him it looks like they've been riding high on that since."

"But he's wrong?"

"Not entirely. It definitely gave them a boost, but if you walk by, their lunch menus are quick, simple, not coma inducing. Our food is a little heartier than a lot of the salads and sandwiches you see around here."

I laughed. "Okay, so let's play with that. You're making meals that'll stick to people's ribs, that will make them truly earn their after-work gym session, but in lunch-size portions that won't leave them with that post-Thanksgiving dinner hangover."

Malik blinked at me. "I kinda love that."

I wanted to fucking cheer. I wanted to fist bump the entire world. I wanted to grab him and salsa our way into the bedroom, because I had a ton of other outstanding ideas.

I didn't. I grinned and shrugged and acted like it was no big deal. "I'm glad you do. You think Sheila would be onboard with it?"

"For sure. She's been pressing to do something with lunch, too, and maybe even have a dedicated brunch menu, so I'm sure she'll be receptive."

"I think, if we have a more formal proposal and not just a general idea, it'll be harder for James to dismiss it."

"You're right." Malik sat back next to me and goddamn, that warmth again. "I hadn't wanted to put that energy into something I was sure he'd reject."

"I get it, truly, but I want to get this going ASAP, so we need to get us all together and make it happen?"

"Tomorrow?"

I paused midnod. "Tomorrow's Saturday. If there's any night I need to be at Criteria, it's Saturday."

Malik's nod was understanding, his eyes full of what looked

almost like pride. "Sunday morning? Sheila will be working because the crowd comes in early, but we can talk then."

And maybe we could do a bit more than that, get Sundays hopping and put everyone to work. A sub-plan was brewing. James wanted to trade on my name? I planned to give him more than he could handle. I hoped he got his comfy shoes and an apron ready, because he was going to need it.

I couldn't remember the last time I hadn't been thrilled to set foot in Criteria. No matter how irritated I occasionally got by my inability to huddle in the kitchen and just cook, this place was my pride and joy. And while having one star was great, I'd be fooling myself if I said I wasn't shooting for two. But right now, even that ongoing pursuit of excellence didn't move me.

I wanted to be at Franklin's, in the kitchen there with Sheila, learning her secrets. I wanted to see Malik wander out front, wink at him and leave him flustered, before Sheila and I were inundated with more customers than we could keep up with.

Not that any of that had happened. But my imagination, what it would be like if Malik and I actually worked together, was enough to send my mind into overdrive. Until I parked in my standard space in the underground lot and walked out. I intended to cut through the side alley to enter through the back like usual, but the front of the restaurant was out-of-control crowded.

"Chef DeShawn!" one journalist called out before I could duck in the back.

I closed my eyes and rolled my shoulders. I had a pretty good idea why they were here, but I'd hoped to have a chance to talk to Maribel and Christopher before they appeared. Still, I planted my smile on and strode down the street like I didn't have a care in the world. I barely got halfway before the crews photographing who-knows-what crowded around me.

"Chef DeShawn," said the journalist who had called out earlier, thrusting her mic in my face, "what can you tell us about Malik Franklin?"

I huffed. "You mean besides the fact that he's my husband?"

"Why'd you file for divorce seven years ago?" someone else asked.

Again, more proof that we should have sucked it up and had that conversation. I just hoped someone played this tonight so I'd remember what I said tomorrow. "We were young and thought we wanted different things. Letting each other go was kinder than breeding resentment."

I wouldn't need to remember that. That was the straight-up truth.

"Why did you guys decide to get back together?"

"How'd you learn the divorce hadn't gone through?"

"Do you feel like you were cheating on him with those other men over the years?"

The words all melded together in my brain, but from the corner of my eye I spotted Christopher. And for the first time in a long while, I couldn't read his expression. But I pointed to him and gave an apologetic smile to the crews. "I'm sorry, guys, duty calls. But Franklin's has a magnificent Sunday brunch. Y'all should check it out."

"Isn't that competition?" someone yelled out behind me.

I turned. "My husband has never been competition, and has always been my biggest supporter. Besides," I said with a wink, "we're not open Sundays anyway."

A round of laughter followed me into the restaurant. I didn't do more than incline my head down the hallway, and Christopher followed, closing the door softly behind him.

"Want to explain to me what that's all about?" He took

off his jacket, paused for a moment, then put it back on. "It's freezing in here."

I huffed. We did this every time he came into the office. He knew I preferred it cooler because between the kitchen and being on the floor, I stayed hot. Christopher, though, treated it like a personal affront.

He waited for a response from me and, when none came, continued. "Not that I'm opposed to the press being here, but they're not here about this restaurant, or specifically here about you. *That* I have a problem with."

"Christopher, we're one of two starred restaurants in the city. I hardly think we need the help. But that," I continued before he could get his dander up, "was not intentional. We were at his restaurant and someone snapped a pic. Things just kind of...snowballed from there."

He folded one leg over the other and stared. "Yeah, I got your texts. Is it true? Are you really married?"

"Yep. We filed for divorce and hadn't known it didn't go through."

"So why not just get the divorce instead of all...this?"

"It's not that easy." If it were, Malik would have been on it in a heartbeat. But after that kiss? His arms around me, holding me close and making me feel safe and, for a moment in time, letting me forget about everything in the world but him? After that, I hoped that maybe a tiny part of him was reconsidering if it was what he really wanted to do.

Thankfully, Christopher seemed, if not content with that answer, smart enough not to press. He paused, then, "So how do we make this work in our favor?"

I swear, he and James should spend time together. Neither of them gave a damn about me or Malik outside of what we could do for them. At least in this, though, I had an answer.

"You want me to give you a rundown of how many dishes were inspired by my time with him?"

Christopher's eyes widened like he'd just struck gold. "You have that? I mean, is that real?"

"For better or for worse, yes." Many nights after Malik was gone had been spent cataloging every scent, every texture, every taste that reminded me of my husband. After a while, all those notes had turned into my first menu. And the second, me turning myself inside out to elevate it until it was as rich and decadent and almost forbidden as my years with Malik had been. Yeah, I could wax poetic about Malik's impact on my menu for hours.

"I love that. I need to set you up with more appearances. You know they'll have a million questions for you about him."

"About the cooking, Christopher. Malik isn't a toy to be used and played with. This thing between us is still new, and I'm not going to let the press screw it up." I'd have plenty of opportunities to screw up myself. I didn't need the help.

Christopher's eyes narrowed, then smoothed out when I raised my brow. "Maybe you should have thought about that before you sucked face with your boyfriend while all the cameras were rolling."

"Sucked face? Boyfriend? What are we, in high school?"

That was maybe mean, and Christopher reddened, then straightened. "The point remains."

It did, and he was right. "We hadn't expected to be interrupted, and I'd hoped to get here earlier to talk to you and Maribel about it. So I'm sorry for that."

That seemed to shock him, and he nodded. "It's no big deal."

I gave him a half grin. "But since we're here and it's happening, let's see what we can do to make it work for both of us. We're not in competition, Christopher. They are straight-up soul food, and they are delicious."

"I checked out their site. I believe it." He shrugged. "I might actually check it out myself. I live not too far from there."

Of course he did, and for a split second I wondered what family had been forced out to make room for him. Then I pushed it aside, because it wasn't his fault, and being angry wouldn't do shit now.

"Let me get some quiet time in," I said. "I have a feeling I'm going to start getting asked questions sooner rather than later."

Christopher chuckled and stood. "I'd say that's a safe bet." He left, and I sank back into the chair, then pulled out my phone.

Me: you doing okay there? There were a ton of people out front when I got here.

Malik: Sheila told me to stay home. She said it's packed, enough that she dragged James in to serve.

I laughed. I'd planned to make him do exactly that tomorrow, but why wait?

Me: good for her. I mentioned you guys to the press tonight. Tomorrow could be interesting.

Malik: Wow. Thanks, but you know you didn't have to do that.

Me: we're on the same team here.

There was a too-long pause before he responded.

Malik: We are. I'll see you at home tonight.

I know he didn't mean it the way it sounded, but I'd be damned if I corrected him. Nope, I was going to let my imagination run wild with those words, let them seep deep into my skin and warm me inside and out.

Me: sounds good. See you at home.

I put the phone away then and reached into my bottom drawer for the worn, nearly decade-old leather-bound journal. My notes, about how I felt about our marriage, our breakup, what reminded me of Malik, both good and bad.

There was…a lot there. I hadn't held back, and memories assailed me. Our first time together, our first I love yous, our last I love yous, the night when we made the decision to separate. All the things I'd wished I told him when I had the chance, that felt flimsy and trite when it was over. Yeah, I had plenty of material.

And thank god for it, because I was inundated with questions from the minute I walked out to the floor. From the VIPs, from the "regular" patrons—hell, from our servers and bartenders. I could only imagine what was being whispered about in the kitchen. I'd check in on them soon.

But boy, if I'd been popular before, finding out about the accidental non-divorce was some juicy restaurant gossip. And, as I should have expected, there were more than a few questions about my regular appearances with folks not named Malik over the years. I needed to warn him, because he'd get the invasive version of it, asking how it felt to see his husband with any manner of person, even though we both thought we were single at the time.

The tables were absolutely packed the entire night, and I must have circulated through the crowds at least five times rather than my usual three. By the time we closed, my feet were sore even in the clogs, my arm hurt from shaking hands, and my throat was hoarse. I asked Maribel to handle the usual end-of-night wind down with the kitchen crew, which was when I usually thanked them for all their hard work and applauded them, but tonight I was intent on getting back home.

To Malik.

Chapter Twelve

Malik

Even with the dogs there, the house was almost disturbingly quiet without DeShawn. He'd left for Criteria early, he said to talk to his head chef and his agent. He was convinced there was going to be blowback, or increased paparazzi, or something. I wasn't so sure, because Lord knew I wasn't that interesting, but since DeShawn actually had more experience with the press, I deferred to his wisdom. Even if I was positive he was overreacting.

That is, until Sheila called me from the kitchen in hushed whispers and told me to stay my ass the fuck home. I normally went in on the weekend more out of boredom than necessity, but she was adamant. The restaurant was more crowded than at any time she could remember, but since we hadn't developed a game plan, my presence could go south quickly.

She'd already roped James into helping her, and I knew I'd hear about that later. I did tell her to snap a few candids of him serving people, though. He'd done his best as a child to weasel out of it, and for the most part succeeded, screwing up enough orders that Mom and Dad had stopped forcing it on him. Now, since he was getting exactly what he wanted—DeShawn's presence to help elevate the locale—he couldn't do that again. And I wanted it recorded for posterity.

So I sat on my butt in the living room while Corey and Bruno alternated between playing tug of war with their toys, and sleeping. I flipped to the local station as a basketball game was ending and transitioning to the news.

"Heartthrob chef DeShawn Franklin and his new boo— his husband! All the details coming up next."

I sprang up in my seat, enough to startle the boys. They padded over to me, and after rather perfunctory head rubs, I forced myself to sit back down. God, I recognized the guy on TV. Reporter Noah Tippin, the "friend" who'd shown up at Franklin's like a bad penny.

"An anonymous call to our station last night brought us to this location." The camera spanned the block, Franklin's and a few of the buildings surrounding it, and boy, did it look out of place. "And what did we find inside but the executive chef of starred restaurant Criteria, DeShawn Franklin, looking mighty cozy, and less than pleased at the interruption."

The story showed a headshot of DeShawn in all his glory, with his standard black chef's jacket, the sleeves rolled up to show his tattoos, his locs half pulled back, the bottom ones falling over his shoulders, that little smirk firmly in place. I had to admit, that photo was killer, had been on the cover of and inside magazines, and I might maybe have cut one or five out to keep in the house. Better looking at an obscenely hot picture than having to hear his voice or see his joy.

The commentary kept going. "But seeing chef DeShawn with a gorgeous man on his arm isn't exactly new." Was he talking about me, calling me gorgeous? He needed his eyes checked, because try as I might have to avoid it, I'd seen some of the guys DeShawn had been out with. I didn't hold a candle to them.

And this sounded way more like gossip TV rather than a serious news story. I wasn't sure if I was surprised or not. They cut to the video from last night, me looking bewildered and beyond out of place in my starched khakis and plain white shirt, while DeShawn looked like, well, him—graphic black tee and faded jeans that looked like they'd molded themselves to his shape. DeShawn's arms wrapped around me, looking at the camera like a man in love. I knew that look. Him nibbling my jaw, running his hands over me. Me forgetting anyone was watching when he kissed me, pulling him close, and drowning myself in the feel of him. Him kissing over to my ear—to tell me we were almost done playing and they'd be leaving soon.

Curse my goddamn memory. Couldn't they have cut the video before that, before I remembered my rules and how much they'd been obliterated? It was bad enough I was rock hard, my dick straining against my loose shorts, precome dampening the front of my underwear. It was bad enough I'd had to jerk off last night and again this morning, and figured I had at least one more session to go before the night was over. It was bad enough that I almost didn't care if it was pretend, because I wanted it so much again.

"Fuck," I whispered in the empty house. Corey didn't move, but Bruno whined plaintively, and I checked my watch. It was time for his walk, and because we'd agreed not to be jerks about the dogs, I was taking Corey, too.

I found my shoes and got their leashes on them, then left the house.

I'd planned to use the time to get my thoughts together, but we barely made it halfway down our usual mile-long hike when we were stopped by the woman who had a small dog, the breed I couldn't place, that was allegedly terrified of Bruno.

"You're… Malik, right? You live up the street from us."

She smiled like we were old friends, and I tightened my grip on the leashes. I didn't have friends in this neighborhood. Folks didn't come around to chat—they avoided me and Bruno at the dog park, and I generally tried to pretend like they didn't exist. My neighbors were adept at doing the same.

"I do," I said carefully, weighing my words. "How are you today?"

"I'm swell, actually. Hi, Bruno," she said, reaching her hand out tentatively. Huh, that was interesting. I didn't even know she knew his name, though I suppose she could have heard me called Bruno's dad enough to figure it out.

"He's calm. He'll take head rubs from anyone who wants to give them." *Please don't let this be the time he decides he doesn't like someone.*

But my boy was true to my word, his butt shaking like it'd fall off from her pats. Then she pulled back and looked down. "And who's this guy? You get a new dog?"

I'd known where this was going, and somehow I was still surprised. "No. Well, yes, I guess. That's my husband's dog."

She cocked her head to the side. "I didn't know you were married."

I was a little too private to be having this conversation with a perfect stranger, even one I vaguely recognized. I reminded myself it was all part of the game and plastered on my best grin. "You probably haven't met him. DeShawn runs a high-end restaurant downtown."

"DeShawn." Her eyes widened, and if I hadn't known better, I'd think she didn't know. "DeShawn Franklin? That De-Shawn?"

"The one and only."

"Wow." She knelt on the ground. "May I?"

I shrugged. "I don't know how Corey is with visitors, but I can't imagine he'd object."

And he didn't. He was just as happy and excited as Bruno had been.

When she stood, she looked almost apprehensive. Was this going to be my life from now on? Until this trial was over and we went our separate ways again? Which… I didn't want to think about that. At all.

But I took pity on her. "Ask your questions."

Her smile still didn't look sure, probably because she knew it was none of her damn business. But Grandma had told me to prepare for this. I should've done a better job.

"Are you really married to him? Like, how'd that happen?"

I smiled. "Yes, I'm really married to him. I married the De-Shawn who was a sous chef with dreams of being an executive chef, not this version. No way in hell I could've pulled this version." I punctuated the last statement with a chuckle, and her shoulders relaxed as she laughed along with me.

"Is he as nice as he seems on TV?"

No lie, that question took me aback. Because DeShawn was an absolute sweetheart, and one of the many reasons I'd stopped watching him on TV was that I didn't feel that part of him was captured enough. He was always polite but focused, business minded, and not the sweet boy who liked to dance around in the kitchen to Beyoncé while we worked.

I smiled at her. "Sweeter. He's about the kindest guy you'll ever meet. Which is why I'm still surprised he ever looked at me twice."

The boys were getting a little restless, and she noticed and stepped back. "And you, you have a restaurant, too, right?"

Wow, DeShawn's magic was working already. "Yeah, Franklin's. It's in the business district. We've got a great brunch on Sundays." We really didn't. Sunday's menu was the same as any other day; it just happened to be when we were busiest. But an actual brunch menu wasn't a terrible idea. Not by a long shot.

"Really? Then maybe I'll see you tomorrow." She pointed to the boys, who were straining by now. "Sorry for interrupting your walk. I'll see you around." She set off with a wave, and I let Bruno and Corey drag me for a few moments while I got my thoughts in order.

That hadn't been as bad as I feared, but I suspected she—and I hadn't even gotten her name—was just a nosy neighbor. What happened if we got more people like Noah Tippin? I knew we had plans to meet tomorrow to talk about just that, but if tonight was that busy, would tomorrow be even worse? Would we have time to talk?

I hated to say it, but I didn't think we'd have time to wait. Not after that news broadcast, DeShawn's texts to me about how much press was at his restaurant—one I'd never visited, and I was going to have to change that soon, wasn't I?—and the interruption to my nightly walk. Yeah, we were going to have to talk. Tonight.

I finished the walk and fed the boys, then went upstairs to take a shower. There wasn't much left for me to do but get comfortable and wait for my husband to come home.

Things I'd forgotten in the years DeShawn and I had spent apart: how late he came home from a shift at the restaurant. I don't know why I was expecting him home at nine, even ten, but it was pushing on midnight with no sign of him. I'd cooked a meal—not DeShawn's quality or Sheila's, but it was passable—and sat there with my thoughts.

When I heard the garage door open, my heart stuttered. The sound was so...domestic. So easy to get used to, and I pinched myself on the forearm—hard—to shake that fantasy from my mind. Because we weren't going there, even if it was the easiest thing on earth to imagine.

I heard the garage door begin shutting, then the door leading into the mudroom open. Corey and Bruno woke, then scurried off to wait for DeShawn's greeting.

"Hey, boys. Aren't you supposed to be asleep now? Did you wake up just because Daddy came home?"

That was so DeShawn. All dogs were his dogs. I heard from the staccato, super-charged beat of two sets of feet tapping on the hardwood floor, Corey's barks joined by Bruno's deeper ones, that Bruno was just as enthused by DeShawn's greeting as Corey. They ran back toward their dog beds, DeShawn following at a more leisurely pace.

"Hey," he said, his smile tired but genuine.

"Hey there. Had a long day at the restaurant?"

"Yeah. Got a lot of questions. We're going to need to suck it up and have that talk." He looked almost apologetic about it, but I just nodded.

"I got asked about it today, too."

He startled, then tilted his head. "What do you mean?"

"I was taking the boys for a walk, and a neighbor I've seen regularly for years appeared and was suddenly interested in talking to me."

He snorted. "Let me guess—that's not a usual occurrence."

"Not in the least. She's the one who scoops her dog up and runs across the street every time she sees Bruno. Now she suddenly wants to pet him."

He closed his eyes and massaged them with his thumb and forefinger before letting his arm fall to the side. "Did she ask about me?"

"Oh, for sure. I gotta say, she was smooth with it. She asked about Corey, which led to you."

DeShawn paused, like he was considering it, then tilted his head in agreement. "Points for that."

A small snort-laugh escaped. "Yes, but if tomorrow is anything like this, we might not even have time to talk. So I think we either gotta do it tomorrow morning, before we even go into the restaurant, or—"

"Now. I'm wired and desperately need to get the smell of kitchen off me, but now. Because I don't want to wake up tomorrow until it's time for us to leave."

"I know that feeling. Why don't you go upstairs and take a shower, and I'll heat something up for you?"

"You dear man." He started in that direction, but I called out to him. "Yeah?"

I chewed my lower lip for a few moments, unsure if I wanted to make the offer I was about to make. What the hell? "You can use my shower if you want." He raised a brow and waited for me to continue. "I had special showerheads installed. Three of them, and the pressure's great."

His lips rolled into a smile, and he nodded. "Thanks. I'll do that."

He turned and walked up the stairs, and I heaved out a breath, bracing my hands on the island and rocking back and forth.

I'd set rules. Created them, had the best of intentions for them, and had a reason behind them. And yet here I was, throwing them all to the wind for a chance to be with this man. In any capacity, for however long the powers that be allowed it. Sure, I could pretend it was because of what Grandma had said, that it was a necessary part of playing the game, but in the quiet of night, I had to be honest and ask the real question. Was I really ready to set my heart up for failure the way I had so many moons ago?

DeShawn had *hated* the thought of living in the suburbs.

He felt it was too cold, too removed, and I had to say, I understood where he was coming from better now than I had then. It could certainly be more than that, and given his stature, probably would be, but that would be because of his profession, what he did, not who he was.

I sighed and padded to the stove to reheat the meal I'd made for myself. Nothing special, just some baked chicken with a garlic cream sauce over mashed potatoes with some asparagus on the side. I put together a plate and set it in the convection oven to reheat, then plopped on the couch and tried to pretend I was comfortable and not terrified of the upcoming conversation.

DeShawn came down who knows how many minutes later, because lying on the couch at nearly midnight with nothing but snoring dogs and the low hum of whatever was on TV to keep me company meant I'd fallen asleep.

"Hey." DeShawn's touch on my shoulder was soft, gentle, and seared me straight to my bones. "You're exhausted. Why don't you go on to bed, and I'll eat whatever delicious creation you've got going in the oven? We can talk tomorrow."

As tempting as the offer was, I knew we needed to handle this now. I pushed myself up to sitting and ran a hand over my face. "No, I'm good to talk now."

He arched that famous brow at me. "You sure?"

I looked at him, at the care and consideration in his eyes that I'd once been awed by, then had spent nearly a decade convincing myself hadn't been real. But there it was, staring me in the face. "I'm sure."

He smiled and squeezed my shoulder, then straightened. "Okay. Let me grab my food." He walked the few steps to the kitchen to pull the plate out of the oven, then pointed to the small circular table. "There?"

"Sure." We sat, and I let him get a few bites in before starting. "So," I asked, "have you seen the news broadcast?"

DeShawn groaned. "First, this is delicious. The sauce? Top-notch." He took another bite and did a little shoulder shimmy, and I muffled my laugh. That shimmy was the sign he was truly enjoying his meal. Another swallow, and then, "I haven't seen it, but Grandma texted. Practically gloated about how romantic it was, the well wishes for our reunion. All that."

"Noah did the reporting."

That gave him pause. "And it was positive? Gotta say, that surprises me."

"Same." Which explained why I was waiting for the other shoe to drop. I swallowed those doubts and focused. "So what's our story?"

DeShawn took a bite of his asparagus, did the little shimmy again, then sat back. "Honestly, I don't know that we need to have a story. I think truth works really well in our favor for this. We can say that we'd planned to divorced, had filed the paperwork, and had gone on our separate ways under that impression."

"But why do we get back together? I know we don't want to bring Grandma into this."

He furrowed his brows but nodded. "No, you're right about that." He paused, took a few more bites, then, "Well, we would've had to at least get together even if we wanted to refile the complaint, right? Or"—he paused and snapped his fingers—"maybe we *do* use Grandma. In the sense that we had every intention of simply refiling, but she pleaded with us to meet each other in person just one time before we did that. Say she felt terrible for not seeing the paperwork earlier, and brought us to the house together to give us the news."

I nodded. "That could work. It could be that forced reunion, us both on edge, and seeing each other—"

"Sparked something. Sparked something we'd forgotten we had."

"And we decided to give each other another chance."

DeShawn nodded, and I swallowed. Hard. Because this didn't feel like a story we were making up. This felt like something real. An actual reunion. And I was going to have to mollywop myself about the head to remember it wasn't.

DeShawn had finished his plate and hopped up, going straight for my dessert fridge and coming back with two mini tarts. He held one out to me, then clinked his against mine when I accepted.

"So no lying," he said.

I shrugged. "Well, maybe a little, because this isn't real."

He paused with his tart halfway to his mouth. "Right. It's not real."

But the look on his face said he didn't believe that, not any more than I did.

Chapter Thirteen

DeShawn

Malik and I were in the car. Together. On the way to Franklin's to prepare for Sunday brunch. He'd gotten up and walked the dogs this morning, bless him, because between the water pressure of that shower—which was every bit as good as Malik said it was—that excellent meal, and given how long I'd stayed at work, I was done.

Franklin's didn't open for another two hours, not until ten, but when we pulled up at eight, there were already a few reporters out front.

"Jesus Christ," I muttered.

"Is this really going to be our life?"

"At least until they get bored of us."

"How long's that going to take?"

I chuckled and leaned across the console to kiss Malik's cheek. "You find me another Black, gay, starred chef who just reunited with his ex-husband, and I'll shove him in their faces."

Malik searched my eyes, then gripped my chin, just the way I liked it, and pressed his lips to mine. The kiss was short, hard, and clearly for the cameras. And I didn't care, because I loved it. Loved it, and wanted more, and needed it.

We broke away and I pressed my forehead to his. "You have to stop."

"I thought I was following your lead."

"Malik," I said, looking up in his eyes, "right now, I'm pretty sure I'm following yours."

He cleared his throat and we climbed out the car. Or tried to, since the crews had inched perilously close during our interlude. "Chef DeShawn! Are you going to be here all day? Will we have a chance to interview you?"

I held a hand up. "Guys, I would love to talk to you all, but I'm not used to working Sundays, okay?" They all laughed, and almost looked a little chagrined. "But I'm here to help, and I need to talk to the chef inside about what my duties are for today. So I hate to leave you stranded out in this gorgeous weather," I said, then winked, "but it's going to be a few hours."

I walked toward the rear door, Malik's hand landing protectively against the center of my back. God, I remembered how much I loved that. His firm touch, grounding me when I felt a little out of control, keeping me here, on this plane, with him.

We walked in and Sheila poked her head out the kitchen. "Be sure to lock that door. I almost forgot, and had to bully them back out."

I groaned, and Malik shook his head.

"They're impossible," she said. "They absolutely will not go away. One of the crews said they've been here since six this morning."

I looked at Malik and shrugged, but I could tell from his tense jaw that it was a bit much for him, and wished I could do something.

"Well," I said, "let's go to the kitchen and talk. I can help you prep while we're there."

Her eyes lit up. "I'm never going to say no to the help, and definitely not by you." I laughed and followed her to the kitchen, Malik behind me.

"How was last night?" he asked her.

"Amazing. Busiest we've been in probably a year, but everyone was here looking for you. Either one of you. But they enjoyed everything, and they left good tips, so I'll deal with the disappointment of them not being here for the food."

I laughed at that, because I knew the feeling. "I can't tell you the number of times I've wondered if people come to the restaurant for my meals, or just for me." I paused. "That sounds really pretentious, doesn't it?"

Malik squeezed his thumb and forefinger together, and Sheila nodded. "It does," she said, "but I can believe it."

I flipped her off, and she laughed.

"How was James?" Malik asked, and the smile on his face was almost sinister.

Sheila's laugh was joyous. "He was so mad he had to work. It was like that time when he was what, seventeen or eighteen, and had thought he was just going to stop by to show off the place to whatever chick he was seeing? And Dad sat her down and comped her meal, but made him serve for an hour?"

I laughed, remembering the story Malik had told me. James had been supposed to work that evening, but he'd no-showed, as was his usual. Malik had been at community college at the time, and had been called away from his study group to fill in. He'd been pissed even recounting it, because he'd nearly failed that exam, but his father had been furious when James showed up like his shit didn't stink.

"I think that was the last time James ever brought a girl here," Malik said.

Sheila nodded. "Probably. It's probably also made him want to go into ownership rather than actual working."

I snorted but didn't speak, and Malik's grin and wink told me Sheila was spot on.

"But," she said, pushing a sheet of paper at me, "I was thinking about this last night. What do you think?" I held it up, and Malik leaned over my shoulder to review it. It was a dedicated brunch menu, for Saturdays and Sundays. A take on most of the meals I'd seen when we were here last week, with options for individual portions and family style. Talk about great minds thinking alike. Franklin's food was delightfully hearty, but that was going out of favor for brunches. Now people wanted something that plated well, looked picturesque for the inevitable photos, and didn't require the rest of the day to sleep off.

"You and your brother sometimes share a brain." I rolled my eyes and swallowed a moan at Malik's low chuckle against my neck. I scanned the menu and grinned. It was the definition of Southern Classic, and now I had a hankering for biscuits and gravy. But a light hollandaise sauce wouldn't be amiss either, especially if we had multiple Benedict options. A Nashville hot chicken and waffles, maybe with a lavender or elderflower-infused maple syrup, would play well, too. "Do you have a pen?" I asked, my hand out, then winced at my slightly brusque tone. There was nothing like reviewing new menus to put me in solid work mode.

Sheila handed me one, and I started making slight changes, then handed it back to her. "How's this?"

She looked at it again, then smiled, and I blew out a breath of relief; she wasn't offended by my terseness. "Amazing, actually."

I grinned and glanced at Malik. And seeing the look he gave me when Sheila smiled? Man, it did something for me.

I handed it to him, and his review was a bit more perfunctory. "We have everything we need for this today? Anything else we need to get?"

Sheila grabbed a pad and started scribbling, then handed it to him. He checked his watch, and I did the same. Almost nine. "I'll make copies of this," he said, "and call James and give him the ingredients."

Sheila snorted. "He's going to be pissed, having to come in here and work again."

Malik shrugged. "Ask me if I care. This was what he wanted. He doesn't just get to give the orders and walk away while everyone else has to execute them."

He walked out and I turned to Sheila.

"Their sibling rivalry sometimes bleeds into the professional sphere," she said.

"So I see. How can I help?"

Sheila looked around, like she wasn't really sure she could ask me, then shrugged and pointed to the vegetables. "Well, collards need to be cleaned, lettuce needs to be chopped. You know, kitchen stuff."

I smiled at her. "Yeah, I do. Let's get into this."

For the next half hour, Sheila and I prepped in companionable silence. When she realized I wasn't trading on my name, she had no problem putting me to work. When the other cook showed up, stuttering to a stop when he saw me, Sheila was ready. "Mac, meet my brother-in-law, DeShawn. Now close your mouth, stop gaping, and let's get going."

Mac approached me slowly, swallowed hard, and picked up a knife. Side by side, we chopped more vegetables, cleaned more collards, boiled more water for pasta, and grated more cheese than I had in years. It was beyond anything I could have imagined.

And fifteen minutes before the place opened, James showed up, bags of additional groceries in hand.

"I'll add these to our orders going forward," Sheila said, "but for right now, start chopping those."

"Do I look like a line cook? One of your lackeys to boss around? This is not my damn job."

Wow, James was *pissed*. Sheila paused what she was doing and faced him, one hand on her hip. "If the executive chef of one of the biggest restaurants in DC can be here on his day off to help, then pray tell, what's your excuse?"

James whipped his head to me and I smiled. "Morning."

He blinked, then straightened and set the bags on the counter. "Morning," he guttered out. He nodded at Mac, then glared at Sheila, who shrugged.

"Not my fault you didn't see him. He's kind of unmistakable."

Rather than watch James wallow in his frustration, I turned back to my station. Beside me, Mac did the same. We were silent for the next few minutes, not quite as comfortable, but maybe that was because I could feel James's stares on my back.

Then Malik knocked on the frame separating the bar area from the kitchen and smiled. It was tight, and everything in me ached to go to him. He held up a stack of menus. "Thank god we had some thick paper back there." He pointed to the overhead clock, which I hadn't even noticed. "I'm going to set these out, then open the door."

A heavy, breathy pause, and we all looked at each other. Sheila nodded, and I tried for my best smile. It was go time.

Malik

I could count on one hand the number of times in the last year we'd been this swamped when we opened the doors. Any day. When I'd told DeShawn Sundays were our best day, I wasn't lying, but by *best* I meant twenty to thirty couples would show up altogether. Not at the same time.

But that's where we were the minute I opened the doors. And not just the regulars, the ones who'd been here before big business took over. We had faces I'd never seen before, lookie-loos who I'm sure were far more interested in what a celebrity chef was doing in this hole-in-a-wall spot than the food itself. But by god, we'd take it.

I put on my best game face, because I hated serving nearly as much as James did. I just hadn't spent my youth trying to get out of it. But we had two servers on staff for Sundays, a third coming in later, during our busiest hours. We needed three, not now, but *right now.*

And for a while it was fine, because I was the unknown. I heard the whispers as I circulated, about whether DeShawn was actually there, then comments about how, even if he wasn't, the food was really good so it was okay to stay for a while, and I hid my smile. Sheila's motto had always been "You get them in the door, I'll reel 'em in." She'd be thrilled to know just how right she was, especially since DeShawn had prettied up the offerings.

But I knew what the people wanted, and when I went back to load up a few more trays, I said so. "Chef DeShawn, I think they're clamoring for your presence."

He turned and looked at me, his eyes bright with a joy I hadn't seen in way too long. Even on the spots I knew he'd wanted when we were together, the ones I could watch before he became really big and I had to flip the channel. "Yeah? Time for us to make the rounds?"

"Time for *you* to make the rounds," I corrected. "They're not even remotely interested in me."

"They are. Trust me." He stepped back and removed his apron, then walked to the edge of the kitchen before letting his hair down. This was the polar opposite of the DeShawn folks got at the restaurant, the one who, despite his bad-boy persona, still had to maintain some level of professionalism. No, this DeShawn wore no jacket, let his hair fall entirely loose, and looked for all the world like a regular guy. As much as was possible for him.

But when he stepped out the kitchen and onto the main floor, a cheer went up. He laughed and smiled and pulled me by my pants to kiss me. The crowd gasped, and DeShawn pulled back and arched a brow before turning to the crowd. "Did he not tell you who he was? Y'all thought he was just a regular server?"

A chorus of yeses. DeShawn looked at me with mock exasperation, and I shrugged. "I was just trying to do my job."

"He's adorable, Chef!" someone in the back yelled out.

"Today I'm just DeShawn. Chef is in the back putting together all these amazing meals for you guys. And they're great, aren't they?"

He started clapping, and the entire restaurant joined in, then began chanting "Chef! Chef! Chef!"

Sheila came out a few minutes later, looking more flustered than I'd ever seen her. She waved, and everyone broke into applause again. She curtsied awkwardly, then looked at me and mouthed *what the fuck is this?* All I could do was shrug again, because the hell if I knew.

Sheila tucked back into her safe space in the kitchen, and DeShawn grabbed my hand, tugging me to the first table. He bent and took selfies, I took pictures of him with entire tables, and he dragged me into more than one photo. He regaled the tables with stories of our exploits when we were young, and with how he felt seeing me again now.

I stood there, silent, shaking my head at his shenanigans. And that seemed to…endear me to people? I became the silent one to DeShawn's vibrancy, and really, that checked.

That's what we'd been in the days before, me the boring

stalwart who stayed at home as DeShawn's star began to rise. But he'd seemed to like that, too, being able to come home and not have to talk about his day, not have more expectations put on him.

Because the trick to DeShawn? He was as introverted as me. He just actually liked people, and I didn't. He loved being around them, so long as he had time to recharge, and I wondered how much time he'd taken for himself in the past years since he'd become so well-known.

The television crews that had been outside the restaurant when we arrived were inside, too, and one of them cautiously approached me. "You're Malik Franklin?"

I smiled. "I hope he's not out here kissing a doppelganger."

She laughed, and some of the tension I'd seen in her shoulders dissipated as well. "Right, right."

I straightened and ignored the steadily increasing thump of my heart. "What can I do for you?"

She looked around and back at me. "Tell me about your restaurant."

Boy, this was what James should be here for, but he was busy pouting about having to help out in the kitchen. He loved talking about it, about its history and plans for the future, and I was not that guy. But I also knew she was asking me because of my relationship to DeShawn, and I wouldn't let the opportunity to promote the restaurant slip through the cracks just because I wasn't the best candidate to talk about it.

"This is my parents' pride and joy," I said. "They opened Franklin's nearly thirty-five years ago, back when this was a more residential district. It was a mainstay around here, a place to come gather and enjoy each other's company. A place to celebrate, sometimes even a place to mourn. But it's always been a place where love was the center of everything we did."

Huh, that didn't sound too bad. James would probably

approve. The reporter seemed to, because she was nodding rapidly and scribbling notes in her pad. "What's it like in a changing environment?"

I sighed and looked away. "Sometimes I wonder what our new place here is meant to be. I think we still have a place, are still meant to do good in this neighborhood, but carving out our new spot isn't a straight-line process."

"I can imagine. I can also imagine that having someone with the cachet of DeShawn Franklin really helps elevate your profile."

This time I glared at her sharply, enough that she took a discreet step back and I rolled my eyes, turning partly away. I didn't like the insinuation in her tone and I wanted to get back to where I was at least modestly able to avoid in-depth interaction. Maybe it was better to switch places with James and let him serve for a while. It'd be worth it to avoid the growing feeling that I'd stepped in it somehow.

DeShawn caught my eye from across the room and frowned. I shook my head, but he started toward me anyway. And something about that—him cutting off whatever he was doing to make sure I was okay—moved something deep in me that wasn't sure it wanted to be shaken.

He got right next to me and wrapped an arm around my waist, pressing into me. Then he looked at the woman, still standing awkwardly in front of me. "What did you do, Heidi?"

"Nothing! I was just asking him a question."

"Mmmph." A woman at a nearby table coughed loudly, what sounded suspiciously like "bullshit," before smiling sweetly at DeShawn. "She asked him a loaded question and played scared when he didn't take kindly to it."

"What'd she ask you? Did she tell you she was a reporter?" DeShawn's voice was soft in my ear, soothing the riled-up parts of me. I wanted to nuzzle in that sound and let it lull me to sleep.

I grumbled and moved closer. "Nothing. Just said your being here would be good for the restaurant."

DeShawn snorted and pressed a kiss to my chin, leading to a chorus of "awwws" around us. "Somehow I don't think she said it as benignly as all that."

He leaned around me and glared at her. "Heidi, I'm sure you've reviewed our filings with the court, and pulled the SCC paperwork for the restaurant with the state. This restaurant existed the entirety of our marriage and Malik never once asked me to be here. We share the same last name and they've never tried to trade on it, even though I have the name because I married him. Whatever little game you're playing, stop it. And don't pretend to be the demure princess here. It doesn't play like that."

"Wellll," the woman sitting at the table said, smirking at Heidi and even giving a little neck roll, and her table clapped. "Go head, Chef DeShawn."

He smiled and shook his head, burrowing into my neck. I glanced at Heidi, who looked almost apologetic, but not quite, before she disappeared to wherever she'd come from.

I wrapped my arms around him and walked him backward toward the kitchen, aware of more than a few eyes on us, more pictures probably being snapped for the internet gods.

"Thank you," I said when we got the small hallway leading to the bathrooms and my office. "I didn't know how to respond and you stepped right in."

He grinned and palmed my cheek. "I've brought this all on you. The least I can do is be there to back you up. Besides, if I remember correctly, Heidi does a lot of work with Noah, and that means right now she can't be trusted."

"She's right, you know. Having you here does elevate our profile."

"Good." His voice had lowered, his eyes fixated on my lips.

"Unh unh." Sheila had poked her head from the kitchen and was staring us both down. "Y'all get in here and help me out. Stop playing cutesy for the crowd."

I pulled back and laughed, and DeShawn gave her a mock salute as he said, "Chef, yes, chef," then followed her into the kitchen, me trailing behind.

Chapter Fourteen

DeShawn

"That was amazing," I said as we climbed in the car.

"I know, right? We have never been that busy on a Sunday. Not since I started working here."

"Good. I'm glad I could help."

"You did more than help, DeShawn. Hell, you put me in a position where I might have to apologize to my brother."

"No way. Perish the thought." Malik's smile was big and bright and I wanted to capture it just like this forever. A damn shame I had zero drawing capabilities.

I laid my hand on top of his on the gearshift, and he wiggled his fingers until he got his thumb out and rested it against mine.

I looked down at our joined hands and didn't know whether I wanted to laugh or cry. When we'd been married, we used to drive like this all the time. One hand on top of the other, or fingers entwined, or one hand on a leg. And I hadn't even realized how much I missed it, how much I missed the sensation and the memory of someone being that close to me, until now.

We drove the rest of the way home in companionable silence, then parked the car.

"Over under on the dogs making us take them for a walk tonight?"

Malik chuckled. "Lord willing, under. Bruno is not the type of dog who does cold concrete well, and hopefully he's taught Corey the fine art of walking himself in the backyard during his master's late nights."

I nodded, even as I heard the scamper of feet toward the back entrance.

"They're here," Malik said, and winked at me. And my heart, already pounding at its cage to be set free, started actively picking the lock. I followed him and we opened the door, and sure enough, there were our boys, butts nearly wagging off. We dropped to our knees and pet our dogs, but they'd be damned if they didn't get love from both of us before letting us up.

We followed them into the family room, and I toed off my shoes before collapsing on the couch. And immediately sat up. "Do you need me to grab a shower first? I don't want to leave this smell of kitchen on your couch."

Malik's laugh was bright, but he shook his head. "You're fine. I'd rather the smell of kitchen than the smell of Bruno, and he gets up there all the time."

"Praise god for pet vacs," I mumbled.

"Amen." Malik turned the TV on, but I wasn't paying attention. I pulled a foot up and was working my way through my nightly massage, pressing into the pads of my feet, trying to recall the shiatsu technique I learned the best I could.

"You still doing that regularly?"

Damn. I'd totally forgotten. Malik had gifted us a joint shiatsu massage class when we were still dating, because I'd been a sous chef then and constantly on my feet, and those dogs barked loud at the end of the day. It had been so damn thoughtful, I couldn't believe it. And how I could've forgotten it? Beyond me.

To him, I shrugged and gave a sad little headshake. "Not as much now. I'm not on the floor like I used to be."

"Do you miss it?"

I nodded. "Yes. All the time. But I love what I do, and that's the conundrum."

"I bet." He reached over and tapped my leg, then pointed to my feet. "Let's see how much I remember."

I hesitated, not sure I wanted to go there. Because this caring, as much as it meant to me, had almost always been foreplay for us as well. Because I couldn't help the way my body responded to Malik's hands on any part of me, the way his touch loosened my muscles and brought me a sense of peace, calm, desire. Because he'd known exactly what I was doing, and would often finish his massage and go directly into a blowjob, and my dick started to thicken just at the thought of it.

"Are you sure?" My voice was so damn soft I wasn't sure if I'd imagined saying the words.

But Malik heard it, and nodded. "I'm sure." He patted his lap. "C'mere."

So I angled until my back was flat on the couch, then propped up long enough to grab a few cushions before setting my feet tenderly on the very edge of his leg. Malik looked at them, then me, then snorted and scooted closer to me.

He took one foot in hand and began to press, and my eyes nearly rolled in the back of my head. "Dear god, that's amazing."

Malik's chuckle was low, knowing. "I'm glad. Close your eyes and relax. You deserve this."

I wasn't so sure about that, but I let myself sink into the touch. Into the way it felt to have him here, with me, like this. Of his own free will and not because of obligation or necessity.

A little bark from Corey made me open my eyes. "What is it?" I tried to pull my foot away, but Malik stopped me.

"He's just seeing you on the television."

I craned my neck and, sure enough, there I was, a repeat of an old DCFoodie show.

"How do you like it? The shows and appearances and all that?"

I looked at him, not sure if he really wanted the answer to that or if he was just trying to be polite, but his soft smile told me he was genuinely curious.

"It's...okay," I said. "A lot of grunt work, a lot of retakes for something I feel should be more natural. Because for cooking, we don't get retakes in the kitchen. But it is what it is."

I wasn't going to tell him the truth, that I was actively over it. But I guess something in the way I spoke hinted at it, because Malik's next question cut straight to the heart. "You don't want it like you once did?"

"No. I thought I did, but it's a bunch of bureaucratic bullshit that I have no time, no interest in dealing with."

I honestly kind of hated it. When I'd first started, when I'd first been approached as someone who could be a star, someone who could make a living making recipes, being on networks, having my own show, it'd sounded like the most amazing thing possible.

And I'd had ideas. I wanted to do the whole road trip thing, finding small gems that served great food, but I wanted to specialize it. Focus on Black communities, marginalized communities, gay communities. Communities owned by and who actively had marginalized folks on staff, in power positions.

But the executives said there wasn't a market for it. Said that people—read: them—would consider it racist if only marginalized communities were targeted. They'd had no response when I asked whether members of those communities had called in and questioned them about their relative exclusion on other shows. It told me everything I needed to know. But my contract with Criteria specified some level of media presence, so I'd made my national idea local, doing weekly television segments and shouting out marginalized restaurants in the area.

It had been one of the things we'd fought about, my desire to have this big, national presence, warring with Malik's desire to stay home. He wanted me to have the show, but he didn't want to be on the road like that. It wasn't who he was. And he didn't want his husband to be gone for weeks on end the way he anticipated I would be. I'd tried to tell him those fears were overblown, but he was probably right. I just hadn't wanted to admit it.

I decided on complete honesty. "I'm not sure what I gave up was worth what I've gained."

Malik paused, his back going stiff. Then he cleared his throat and continued his massage. "Oh."

I opened my eyes and looked at him. "Malik. I…"

…had no clue what the hell I was going to say, and it didn't matter. Because Malik let my other leg fall and climbed on top of me, fusing our lips together. And I sank into it, because *this* was what I wanted. That feeling of Malik, his weight bearing down, me maneuvering to widen my legs so he could fit himself between them, my hand scrabbling to pull his shirt from out of his pants, to feel his skin against mine for the first time in way too long.

Malik tangled his hands through my locs to hold me in place, squeezing tightly. I hissed, then punched my hips up toward him. "You know how much I love that," I whispered.

He looked down at me and almost tenderly ran a thumb across my forehead. "I know."

He kissed the top of my head and I wanted to melt. Because that was the love kiss. That whatever-it-is-we'll-figure-it-out-together kiss. The one that told me everything was going to be all right. By god, he'd make it all right.

I tilted my neck as much as possible, given Malik's grasp on my hair, and he rewarded me with short, biting nips down my chin and along my jawline, his hands running down to the hem of my T-shirt and pushing it up and off. Could he feel the way my chest heaved? The way my heart beat, its rhythm calling out Malik's name?

My shirt gone, Malik looked at me, a sort of reverence in his eyes, then ran his hands over my pecs. He squeezed the nipples, and my eyes fluttered closed. He knew how much I loved that. And when I gripped his forearm, he chuckled, the sound a little too knowing, before bending down and capturing one nipple in his mouth. A jolt of electricity shot through me at his touch. I thought I'd missed it before, but nothing came close to how good he felt here, with me, wanting this.

With my free hand, I found the top of his belt and held on, and he rolled his hips into me the way I needed him to do in a bed, naked. "God, I want you," he muttered, and I nodded.

"Yes, please."

He pushed off, holding his hands out to help me sit upright.

Then a low, rumbling growl from the left caught our attention and we turned. "What the hell?" Malik asked, then fumbled to turn on the light.

"Dear god," I whispered, then sprinted around the coffee table in the center of the room to grab Corey. Bruno had apparently decided he wanted to sleep in his own bed tonight, and Corey was having none of it. He alternated between nipping at Bruno's foot and on his tail, and *he* was the one growling when Bruno didn't move. Bruno, bless that boy's heart, just looked at us with the long-suffering sigh of a dog resigned to his fate.

Malik's eyes widened, and his shoulders shook for a minute before he bent in half and started laughing. "Looks like Corey has a what's-yours-is-mine mentality." He raised a brow. "Wonder where he got that from?"

"You shut your mouth." I laughed and pulled Corey away, who even now was whining and looking for all the world like he wanted to get back to Bruno. Bless him, Bruno dragged Corey's bed closer and moved to lay half his body on it, leaving space on his own bed, and I let Corey go. He scampered over and climbed into the spot Bruno made—which was smaller than his own bed—settled down, and promptly fell asleep.

"I really am sorry," I said once they'd settled.

And I was. Not just about Corey, but about the fact that whatever that was on the couch? Was over. Broken. Spell gone. Malik would surely go back to his rules. The ones that put very firm guidelines on what we were and were not allowed to do, so I fully expected that by morning, he'd be the worst roommate ever. I'd have to get ready for that, and I was not looking forward to the game face I'd have to put on tomorrow, to keep the words from cutting.

"Don't be. These things happen. Now we can go back to our regularly scheduled programming." The resignation in his voice made me look up, but he'd shoved his hands deep in his pockets, his shoulders stiff, and his expression had morphed back into that cool, unaffected look I was growing to loathe.

Of course. I'd expected it, but hearing the confirmation still stung. I smiled, but it was strained and felt brittle. "That's probably a good idea."

Malik looked at me, and I couldn't tell what I saw in his eyes. Was it relief? Regret? Something else altogether? "You sure?"

I nodded. "Absolutely. Night, Malik."

He paused with one hand on the banister. "Good night, DeShawn."

Malik

It was honestly a little disconcerting how quickly DeShawn and I had fallen into a routine, notwithstanding my paltry attempt at boundaries. I'd let go of the dog-walking issues, but we were still supposed to cook our own meals, handle our own business. But when I woke up the next morning, sometime around seven thirty, I knew DeShawn had already taken both boys for a walk, else Bruno's whines and scratches would've woken me much earlier. And since DeShawn would be at Criteria this evening, I'd return the favor. There might even be breakfast, and I wouldn't argue if there was.

A routine. Like couples made. And I couldn't even be upset about it.

Lord knew I wanted to be. I wanted to march in there and pretend like nothing had happened the night before. Like I hadn't heard DeShawn's words, his musing that maybe what he'd given up wasn't worth what he'd received, and pounced. Just laid myself down on top of him, taken what I'd wanted from the minute he'd walked in the restaurant.

And as I climbed out of bed and handled my business before throwing on a pair of slacks and heading downstairs, the smell of waffles drifting up to greet me and get my taste buds jumping, I knew it was hopeless to pretend there was nothing there.

I reached the bottom step and the boys scampered toward me. In the kitchen, DeShawn glanced over and smiled, a shy, almost apprehensive one. The kind he'd give if he thought I was about to turn into the grumpy ogre again.

I finished petting the boys and walked into the kitchen, setting a slightly shaky hand on his back and leaning in for a kiss to his jaw. "Good morning."

DeShawn stared at me. Stared, then laughed and shook his head. He leaned in to press his lips against mine. "Morning." He rolled his lower lip in and, like always, I wanted to bite it. "How'd you sleep? I hope I didn't wake you when I got Bruno."

"Fine. Did your dog behave himself this morning?"

He arched his brow. "I'll have you know my dog..." He trailed off and laughed. "I got nothing, don't even know how to finish that. My dog is an absolute mess."

I laughed and massaged his shoulder. "At least he's cute about it."

"And he'll be the first to tell you."

We stopped talking then, our conversation having reached its end, and I cleared my throat. DeShawn smiled at me, then pointed to the stool opposite the island. "Go on and sit down. I'll have breakfast ready for you in just a few moments."

"Waffles?"

He peeked at me, then smiled, and I wasn't sure if it was for me or him. "They still your favorite?"

"You know they are."

His eyes twinkled. "I know."

I sighed and ran a hand over my face. I was breaking every rule I'd made, tearing down the boundaries I'd set to keep myself sane. And DeShawn wasn't doing a thing to stop me.

"DeShawn," I said, pulling his attention from the waffle maker he was staring at, "what are we doing? I know we're supposed to be getting comfortable so we can play things up for the cameras, but this?" I gestured to the kitchen. "This is way more than that, and you know it."

To his credit, he didn't try to deny it. "I know. But we've been talking and talking about how we're going to make this work, to pull this off, to fool these people. We were interrupted in public, and it occurred to me that maybe what we need to do is just talk to each other. About where we've been and what we've been up to for these last couple of years.

And I figured the best way to do that, to ease this into it, was breakfast."

It'd be easy to make some excuse about needing to be at the restaurant, which was technically true, James had held up his end of the lunch bargain, and our profits and expenses had both increased. But it was nothing that couldn't wait until I had waffles. And this conversation.

I straightened up and tried to loosen my shoulders. "Okay. Let's do this."

"Coffee first." He pushed a cup across from me, made in the French press I loved but never took the time for, then grabbed a mug of what I assumed was tea, because DeShawn had never drank coffee, and sat down next to me. He'd made us each two waffles, and had set out a bowl of mixed berries, a little container of powdered sugar, and the pure maple syrup I kept on hand.

I cut myself a piece of the waffle and bit into it, then put my fork down and stared at him. "What the fuck is in this?"

His grin was positively sinful. "Bourbon."

I was halfway through my drink and snorted, fumbling with a napkin on the counter to wipe myself. "Are you serious?"

"Would I lie to you about that?"

"No."

"I'm glad you know."

I laughed and took another bite, then smiled at him. The DeShawn I saw on TV was such a big name, someone everyone wanted to be with or near. In his orbit. But since he'd come to stay with me, he hadn't seemed the least bit upset about the quieter lifestyle. About sitting at home, just us and the dogs, enjoying each other's company while the television droned on in the background.

"You look like you've got some serious thinking going on over there."

I tried to shrug, but it felt jerky. "I guess I'm just marveling at how comfortable you seem here."

He snorted. "You mean after saying for years that I wanted no part of living in the suburbs?"

"Well, yeah. That."

He took another bite, chewed longer than I thought was probably necessary, then sighed. "I made that into more than what it was. We were younger, you know, and I thought I knew every damn thing. Thought I knew what I wanted, and I was full steam ahead with it. Turns out I'm maybe not as brilliant as I'd assumed I was."

"What?" I teased. "You saying you made a mistake?"

"Yes." There wasn't even the tiniest bit of hesitation in his voice, and that caught me off guard, but he wasn't done. "I know I said it the other day, but I meant it. I gave up a lot to get this position, this job, this cachet. And it took me away from the people I loved."

My face was going to burst into flames. Surely he didn't mean—

"From you. From Grandma. Hell, sometimes I wondered if I even miss Uncle Robert." I gaped at him. He looked up and winked. "And then I realize, nah."

And then I bust up laughing, and he joined me for a moment before going serious again. "But I stopped seeing Grandma as much as I wanted to. You and I divorced. It was like starting over, and that hadn't been part of my plan."

I swallowed hard and nodded. After I got my associates and left home to finish my bachelors, it'd been to get away and see some of the world before returning. Once I'd finally accepted myself, my sexuality, who and what I wanted, I'd worried my family wouldn't approve. It was unfounded, but twenty-year-old me didn't know that, and I slowly but surely cut them off. Tucking my tail between my legs and going back home had almost felt like going backwards. By that time, my family had written off the idea of me returning, being part of the family business. So when I showed up, sheepish, looking like a puppy that had wandered away and only returned after his disappearance made the nightly news, I'd been stunned at their open welcome. The prodigal son returning, as James had happily, if a bit surly, put it.

They'd told me I had my pick of any position at the restaurant, and I knew James was afraid I'd want his. When I'd told them I wanted to be the accountant, that I had no interest in running the place, he'd been by far the most relieved. And when I told them that before we did anything else, they had to know I was gay, I'd expected them to turn right back around and tell me I could find my own way home. Which wouldn't have done much, since I had a car.

But they hadn't done that. Sure, Mom had burst into tears. When she dried them, she said it was because she was so happy I felt I could finally be open with them. That had gutted me, knowing they knew I'd been hiding something from them.

And I'd continued to hide. I'd hidden DeShawn. Because no matter how open I learned to be, that part of my past was mine to hold on to. To cherish, to take and pull out and run my finger softly across when times got too hard and I needed to remember what it felt like to be loved. So yeah, I'd kept that quiet.

DeShawn reached out and laid a gentle hand on my forearm. "We've grown a lot, haven't we?"

I looked at that hand, then gave in and did what I wanted. I brought it to my lips and I kissed his knuckles. "We have."

"Would you do it again?" he asked me. "Go through everything we did one more time?"

I shook my head. "No. I'd have come out to my parents way earlier, then been by your side for everything else."

He closed his eyes and nodded, and I reached forward to run my thumb underneath them and wipe the tears away. "Hey, no, baby. Don't cry."

He looked up at me, those eyes of his shimmering with wetness, that smile the same one he had when he was twenty-three years old. The one that had melted my heart.

I bent my head and took his lips with mine, then acknowledged the inevitable. I'd fallen back in love with my husband.

Chapter Fifteen

DeShawn

"You are *distressingly* happy."

I whirled at the sound of Maribel's voice, and arched a brow to match the one she wore. "Good morning, Bel."

She shut the door behind her and shook her head. "Don't give me that. What are you so freaking happy about? Are things going well with your old new husband?"

I kind of loved that phrase. Old new. It was true: Malik and I had a level of comfort that I'd never found in any relationship since him, but given the years we'd spent apart, it was like relearning him all over again. Yeah, old new worked for me.

"Things are definitely going better. Not quite so rigid."

She smiled and sank into the chair. "Glad to hear it. So, what's on the agenda for today?"

From the first time I'd been at Malik's house, I had a hankering to create a variation of his ridiculously delicious desserts. Something to highlight what made them so good, but to put my own spin on it. Because that's what I did.

I took my seat and tapped on the desk with a pen. "Dessert," I told her.

"You were talking about that earlier and we were interrupted, weren't we? What's on your mind?"

For the next few hours, she and I went through various

ingredients, discussing what textures would work best with what meals. Something light and crisp as an accompaniment to the fish meals. Something darker, more decadent, to go with the steaks. Something semisweet, with the tiniest bitterness, to offset the sweetness of a port wine. Our pastry chef was either going to have a field day or cuss me out, but he didn't come in until four.

The door opened suddenly, scaring the absolute shit out of us.

Christopher stood in the doorframe, a folder in his hand, and I couldn't tell if he was furious or exuberant. Either way, his cheeks were flushed, almost ruddy, and he was waving a folder in his hand.

"DeShawn," he said, not bothering to close the door. Maribel rolled her eyes, stood to shut the door, and he took her seat.

"No, sir," I said. "You can take the other one."

He cocked his head to the side. "But she got up."

"Not to *leave*. She got up because you didn't have the courtesy to close the door. Just like you didn't have the courtesy to knock before entering. Move to the side."

Christopher looked ready to argue with me over what I'm sure he considered to be a ridiculous conversation, given there was another chair in the room. But whatever was in those folders must have changed his mind, because he grumbled, then stood and shuffled over.

Maribel took the one she'd briefly vacated and gave me a surreptitious wink. "Thank you."

"My pleasure," I told her, then looked at Christopher. "What is it?"

"Criteria's always booked. Booked a few months in advance."

I nodded. This wasn't news.

"I talked to the maître d, and you're booked so far out that

the system can't handle it. They're actually having to tell people to call back in a month or so to make reservations."

I frowned and leaned forward, pulling the folder from
Christopher and flipping through it. Sure enough, we were
booked out for the next four months, top to bottom, and from
the notes, it looked like many of these people were first-time
patrons.

"What the hell is causing this?" I asked.

"You," Christopher said, as though that was obvious. "You
and your new boyfriend, husband, whatever you really are."

"Oh, that's definitely his husband."

I cut my eyes to Maribel and half stuck my tongue out at
her, but she didn't back down.

"Oh," Christopher said, and sank into his seat. "That's interesting."

"What? You thought we were joking?"

"Well, yes." He sat up and waved a hand. "DeShawn, you
have to understand. You have a reputation. You're a bit of a
player." My shoulders stiffened and Maribel put her hand out
and moved it up and down a couple of times, telling me to
pump my brakes. Which I had to do, because Christopher
was right. "But that's what makes this so great. People are
enthralled by the man who's made you settle down. Everyone wants a piece of him, or what have you. It's outstanding."

"Okay, so this is great and all, but what are you telling me
this for? This news is the kind that you could easily utilize
without my participation."

He clicked his fingers at me and pointed. "Under most cir-
cumstances, yes. But this is unique. People want access to you,
and not just to you. To him."

My stomach tightened at the words, and I was transported
back to the conversation Malik and James had had when I'd
first shown up. About Malik protecting me from them, not

using me as a gimmick to increase their stature. That now made a hell of a lot more sense than I'd given credence to before.

Christopher didn't seem to notice a stitch of the turmoil on my face, but if the slightly flared nostrils and tilted head were any indication, Maribel did.

"So," Christopher said, oblivious to my worrying thoughts, "what I'd like to propose is that Malik be here as a special guest a couple of nights a week. On top of the gala this weekend, of course, which…" He paused and his gaze sharpened for a brief moment. "I notice you haven't RSVP'd for. I assume he's going to be your plus one, right?"

Mother of hell. I'd completely forgotten about the gala. Hadn't brought it up, hadn't even remotely considered it. I nodded at Christopher, though. "I'll be there. I need to check with Malik and make sure he's available as well."

Christopher opened his mouth to argue, then seemed to remember at the last minute that most restaurants, including ours, were open Saturday night. This was the rare occasion where we were closed for the event. He nodded. "Well, it's not like you can bring another plus one, right?"

Sometimes I truly wanted to hit that man. "Right."

He hummed, like he was thoroughly pleased with himself. "So convince Malik to come down here a couple nights a week, parade him in front of the guests for a bit, and they'll love it."

I held a hand up. "Wait."

Christopher paused, halfway out his seat, and sat back down.

"One, I'm not giving you any guarantees. Malik's coming here has to be fully of his own volition, and I will not press him. Two, for every night he agrees to come down here, I agree to go up there. His presence boosts our restaurant, and my presence boosts theirs."

Christopher looked like he'd sucked on an entire bag full of freshly zested lemons, but he nodded. "So long as it doesn't interfere with your duties."

"No more than his presence here interferes with his, right?"

Christopher gave me a withering stare that might've made me back down five years ago. I held his gaze, and he rolled his eyes before leaving.

"Jesus fuck," I whispered after Maribel again got up to shut the door.

"He's a real the piece of work, isn't he?" she said.

"For sure." He hadn't always been that way, and he'd been the first to admit my presence had been a game changer for his company. Somewhere along the way, though, he'd forgotten that people were...people, and not just tools to make him more money. It was increasingly obvious, but I wasn't sure what to do about it.

I opened my top desk drawer and pulled out my phone. "Let me text Malik and see if he's willing to come to this dinner right now before I forget."

Me: hey, are you available this Saturday?

Malik: I can be. What's up?

Me: I'm expected to attend a gala at the International Spy Museum. Will you come? Be my plus one?

Malik: is this going to be one of those things where I show up on your arm and you're stuck running laps around the room while I stand in the corner by myself?

Fuck, that sounded miserable. And was also likely the truth of what would happen.

I looked up at Maribel, who seemed to be on the very edge of her seat waiting for a response. "You're going Saturday, right?"

"Yeah. Me and Jesus will be there. Might even get me a new dress for the occasion."

"You mind keeping Malik company in case I'm forced to, you know, entertain?"

"Or cook, since there's supposed to be a little competition going on, too, right?"

Dear god, I'd totally forgotten about that, but I nodded. "Right. That too." They were doing a version of that "basket of ingredients, make something amazing in twenty minutes" competition, live during the banquet. It actually sounded like a ton of fun, one of the few parts I was really looking forward to.

"One hundred percent here for it. I'll take care of him."

The look on her face guaranteed me they'd be trading most-embarrassing-DeShawn moments the minute my back was turned. Why that made me happy, I didn't know, but my grin was broad as I typed out a text to Malik.

Me: there may be a bit of a cooking competition going on, but my head chef Maribel and her husband will be there. She told me she will take very good care of you.

Malik's response was an eyebrow raise emoji, which made total sense to me. Then—

Malik: that sounds like it might be fun. Count me in.

Me: great. There's something else I need to talk to you about, but it can wait till we get home.

Malik: that sounds ominous.

Me: it's not, more logistical than anything. And not pressing.

Malik: in that case, let me get some work done so I can be ready. I'll see you at home.

That word, home? Boy, it did something to my insides, and my fingers weren't nearly as steady as they had been when I responded.

Me: yeah, of course. See you at home.

Malik

"If you tug at that bow tie one more time, I'm going to glue your arm down by your side. I am not retying it for you."

I glared at DeShawn but let my hand fall. "I'm not comfortable with bow ties."

"Bow ties have nothing to do with comfort," he said, smoothing the lapels of his clearly custom-made tuxedo, adjusting the arms so the French cuffs and cufflinks showed through, then straightening his jacket. "But you look outstanding, and I can't wait to show you off."

None of those words felt fake. They felt almost too real, and what the hell had I done to deserve them? I leaned forward and took his lips in a soft kiss, then straightened.

DeShawn looked magnificent tonight. He'd had an early morning appointment to get his locs tightened, and he'd let them hang loose, falling thick and perfectly groomed around his shoulders and down his back. His tuxedo was black, but in the light, there seemed to be hint of…something. Not so much a shimmer, nothing like that, but maybe a texture? A pattern? I couldn't tell, but the effect was stunning. And stirring, if you listened to my dick, which I was trying desperately not to do.

He'd dragged me to his manicurist and forced us both to get a mani-pedi combo, ignoring my protest that no one was looking at my feet. But my nails did look clean as fuck; I had to give him that. He even sat with me at the barber's, laughing and regaling the guys while I listened to conversation swirl around me. By the time we got back to the house to change, I was exhausted. I didn't know how people who wore makeup did this, because I was ready for bed, and the night hadn't even begun. We'd taken naps—in separate bedrooms, which I was nonsensically upset about—and now were headed out the door, Corey and Bruno keeping a safe distance. It was almost like Corey had taught Bruno to stay back when their humans were dressed to the nines like this. Must have some experience with these types of events.

"You ready to go?"

I nodded. "As ready as I'm going to be."

"Good. The town car should be pulling up."

I spun to face him. "Town car? What the hell do we need that for? I can drive, you know."

"Because there's a lot of alcohol at these events. And even though I won't be drinking until after the competition, I don't want you to have to limit yourself. So the town car will be here to take us down, and to pick us up when we're ready to go."

It made sense. It did, yet it still made me feel like a tiny celebrity. Which was exactly what DeShawn was, sans the tiny part. It was a reminder of how real this was. Sure, we were putting on a show for the cameras, but people were genuinely going to be scrutinizing us, how we behaved around one another, how we spoke and touched and kissed.

"Here."

I looked down to find a small tumbler with a shot of what smelled like bourbon in it. "What's this for?"

"Your nerves are sky high. Take it."

No sense in arguing. I took it to the head, and as soon as I finished, DeShawn's phone beeped. "Car's here. Let's go."

The ride to the venue was just under an hour, but I couldn't keep my mouth from falling open as the driver walked around to open the door. On my side. DeShawn cursed under his breath. "Shit, I should have thought about that. We should have switched sides." He winced and gave me a sheepish grin. "Ready to be blinded by the cameras?"

I looked back at him and winked, pulling together all my bravado. "I'm a nobody. Cameras won't flash until they see you. Let's go." I nodded to the driver and stepped out the door.

The first flash of light was overwhelming, but as I expected, it died as quickly as it'd started. I turned and held my hand back in, and I couldn't tell if DeShawn was rolling his eyes or glaring at me. Either way, it made me laugh. He clasped my hand and I held on for dear life as he climbed out of the car, stopping to smooth his jacket down once again.

And if I had thought the yells and flashing were a lot before, they were nothing compared to the reception DeShawn got once they realized it was him.

"Chef DeShawn! Chef DeShawn!"

He leaned into me. "Smile pretty. This could take a while."

A while? We were on a literal red carpet, cordoned off on each side. DeShawn drew me to one side and smiled. I know I looked like a deer in headlights, but DeShawn laid his hand on my back and squeezed.

Focus on him. Don't worry about anything else, just focus on him.

That's what I did. I have no idea how long it took us to get through the line of waiting photographers—the fans would manage to scamper through and seek selfies with him, with me, with us—but eventually we made it to the front and into the museum.

"Stand here for a moment," DeShawn said. "Give your eyes a chance to adjust."

I did as he said, blinking until the white flash of bulbs stopped popping up every time I closed my eyes, then followed him down the hallway into the large gathering.

"There's Maribel," he said, pointing to a woman in an absolutely stunning gold-sequined, spaghetti-strap dress with a scoop neckline and slits up the sides of both legs.

"Goddamn, mamacita, look at you." DeShawn held her at arm's length and then made the twirling motion with his finger.

She laughed and obliged, then shook her hips a little. "I am ready to dance," she said, then popped the man standing next to her. "But this big lug won't dance with me."

"Querida, I would do nearly anything for you, including letting you wear this ridiculous dress in public. But if I dance with you in front of this crowd, it will be a show they won't soon forget, and that is not my particular kink." He held his hands out to both of us, and we shook.

"You guys, this is my husband, Jesus. Jesus, this is DeShawn, who I work with, of course, and you must be Malik," she said, finishing her sentence with me.

"I am, and it is an absolute pleasure to meet you." I shook her hand, but she leaned forward to give me a quick peck on the cheek before stepping back.

"Please tell me we're at the same table," DeShawn said.

"Yes, and thank god for it. These people are so pretentious."

I didn't even have to look around to know she was right. People swanned in as if this place, this museum, was their birthright. This was a place for people to see and be seen. Hell, I didn't even know what the gala was allegedly for, and I'd bet dollars to donuts most of the people here didn't either.

"Let's find our table," Maribel said suddenly. "I am not accustomed to wearing heels anymore."

And I wasn't accustomed to wearing a tux, so I was down to find a seat immediately and blend into the background.

We found our table and had just settled in when the announcer came on to start the first competition. And, of course, DeShawn was called up for it. He stopped with his hands on the back of my chair and gave me an apologetic grin. "Duty calls."

He leaned in and I palmed his cheek. "Go on and kick ass."

His laugh was loud and bright enough to draw more than a few eyes our way. He kissed me, the barest brush of our lips together, before he stood and walked toward the raised mini-kitchen set up at the front of the room.

"Ooh, I think he likes you," Maribel singsonged, and it reminded me so much of something Sheila would do that I didn't try to stop my mock glare, which resulted in her cackling. Just like Sheila.

Someone pulled out a chair on the opposite side of the table and I tensed, trying to remember why the guy looked familiar. Then I groaned. What strings had Noah Tippin pulled to be seated at our table? A hand landed on his arm, and of course it was Heidi. Because heaven forbid DeShawn and I could show up anywhere without having to see these two.

"My, didn't I get lucky, being at this table?" he said, not bothering to introduce himself or Heidi to Maribel and Jesus. If I looked up the definition of bad penny, I'd probably seeing his overly smug, smiling face staring back at me.

Jesus stiffened, and Maribel rolled her eyes. "The way you say that, you're fooling no one."

The guy shrugged and sniffed his drink before taking a sip. "What can I say? I have connections."

I didn't know what their deal was, but I was determined

not to let them sully my evening. I laid a soft hand on Maribel's arm. "Let's watch DeShawn. See if he remembers what to do in the kitchen."

She waggled her brows at me and opened her mouth like she wanted to say something, then glared at Noah and Heidi and shook her head.

Up on stage, DeShawn was with two other chefs at a long table, a basket in front of each of them, cooking stations behind them. At the front of the room, a large screen showed us what was going on, and when I looked behind me, I saw smaller TVs, probably projecting it to people seated farther back. I couldn't tell what ingredients they were cooking with, or maybe it'd been announced and I just hadn't been paying attention. What I saw was that DeShawn had *all* the seasonings, and I smiled. One of the things I'd had to learn to accept was that D seasoned like his life depended on it, but those jars getting back where they belonged? Forget about it.

"So, tell me how playing married is going."

I startled at Noah's voice. I'd been so focused on DeShawn I hadn't noticed him move to the seat next to mine. DeShawn's seat. "Pardon me?"

"Oh, come on. We all know a man like DeShawn Franklin isn't really married to a nobody like you."

"You do realize we're actually married."

"A technicality. Literally. There's no way he stays married to you when whatever charade you're putting on is over. I haven't figured out what it is, but I will. Even though the way he stuck up for you with Heidi here was cute, I'll give you that."

I inhaled deeply. Channeling some of DeShawn's calm wasn't my forte, but I gave it my best shot. "Why do you and Heidi have such a bee in your bonnets about us? We're minding our business, and it's a little creepy."

He flushed, his cheeks going a deep red before he smiled

and smoothed his napkin over his lap. "DeShawn is an exceptional chef and one of the most recognizable faces in the cooking world. His love life, for better or worse, is a matter of public interest. I'm just doing my job."

Which apparently consisted exclusively of irritating me. And he was doing a good job, as my frustration levels ratcheted higher. Maribel nudged me with her knee, a subtle signal to calm down, and I inhaled as deeply as I could through my nose, hoping Noah didn't noticed how rattled I was. He was a smarmy ass, but my heart still tripped and fell over itself. Not just because I hadn't expected to be cornered, especially while DeShawn wasn't there, but because he was right.

No way DeShawn stayed when this was over. We were helping each other in a mutually beneficial relationship, and at the end of it, he got Grandma's home and I got enough funds to help with a chunk of the projects at the restaurant. DeShawn would go back off to gallivanting with whatever man looked gorgeous on his arm, while I faded back to the shadows.

A glance at the projector showed the other contestants were gone, but DeShawn was still up on stage. And the grin he was giving the host was tight, not genuine. He didn't want to be there. And I didn't want to be here.

Next to me, Maribel leaned forward and narrowed her eyes at Noah. "Are you done being an insufferable puta right now?"

"I'm just trying to figure out what's going on."

"It's none of your damn business," I said, my words almost a growl. "What happens between me and my husband is *our* business, and you'd best stay out of it."

He put his hands up and settled deeper in his chair, but I didn't believe for a single second anything was over. I looked up and watched DeShawn work, trying to let his confidence on stage soothe me. Because I was done with this night, and we'd barely begun.

DeShawn

Being up there for one competition was fun. Being up there for three was a pain in my ass, especially since I was the *only* one who was up here for all three rounds. Allegedly, it was a competition to showcase the various chefs who'd come to the gala, but since I was the local, as one judge called it, they'd changed their plans at the last minute and kept me up there the entire time.

From my spot on the raised dais, I searched for Malik and found a white couple I couldn't quite make out also at the table. But Malik didn't look comfortable the way I would have expected with Maribel and her husband running commentary next to him. He was sitting too damn tall, his shoulders stiff, his gaze stony. Not at me, but at the projectors showing us on a larger screen. Whatever the hell was going on, I wanted off this stage and back with him.

"Three minutes," one of the volunteer judges called out, and I looked down at my meal.

I hadn't even been paying attention to the dessert I was creating, a lemon-ginger ice cream confection I was serving with a raspberry-mint brownie. I'd played with the idea for so long—from the moment I'd tasted Malik's brownie—that it apparently had just become its own concoction when I wasn't looking.

I cut the brownies and plated them, grabbed small ramekins for the ice cream, then aerated a lemon zest whipped cream and mint leaf as garnishment. Whatever happened, I was off this goddamn stage as soon as we were done.

The buzzer sounded and I sighed along with the other contestants. One patted my arm. "You were totally in the zone there. Moving like you could make dessert in your sleep or something."

"Felt that way." I glanced at his meal, what looked like a

bread pudding. "Did you really make bread pudding in thirty minutes? Goddamn."

The chef looked almost sheepish. "Yeah. It's my favorite dessert. Had to figure out a short version for my own needs."

I laughed and we waited while the judges ran through their comments. I didn't even hear what they had to say about mine, but I was more than gratified to hoist the overall winner's trophy. One, it was a little silly because I'd been the only one up there for all the rounds, but two, it meant I was done and could get back to Malik immediately.

I paused for the obligatory pictures, my grin growing more strained the longer it went on. When I finally returned to the table, the guy had moved back to his position and I groaned.

"Noah, what are you doing here?" He'd been showing up everywhere we went since that impromptu night at Franklin's, either him or Heidi, who sat there playing innocent next to him. They were birds of a feather, Heidi always playing passive to Noah's aggressive. I wasn't sure if they actually worked together, but their relationship had a level of symbiosis that set my teeth on edge.

"I was assigned to this table, thank you very much. You're always so rude."

Because you're a fuckboy sat on the tip of my tongue, but I kept quiet, instead sinking into my seat and squeezing Malik's hand. "I'm so sorry about that. I didn't think I'd be gone that long."

"One second place and two firsts," he said. "Not bad."

I smiled, the warmth in his voice making me forget everything else for a few moments. "Yeah? Thanks." Malik leaned in and I kissed his chin before straightening. "I'm still upset about the appetizers, though." That was the one I got second place in. "I still contend mine were better."

"I'm sure they are. You make them for me when we get back home, and I'll be the final judge."

His smile was bright, almost eager, and Maribel cleared her throat. "You two are almost too cute," she said.

"Hush your mouth. There's nothing cute about us."

"All evidence to the contrary, of course."

I stuck my tongue out at her, and Malik and Jesus laughed. But then the music started, and Maribel got to jamming. She grabbed Jesus's wrist and shook it lightly. "Please? Just one turn on the dance floor."

"Absolutely not. You know how I get when you dance."

Maribel leaned over him to us, lowering her voice and cupping a hand to her mouth so Heidi and Noah couldn't make out her words. "He gets horny."

Jesus shrugged but didn't deny it. She pouted, and I couldn't stand it. "Bel, dance with me?"

Maribel beamed. "Yes, absolutely." We paused and looked at Malik and Jesus.

"Y'all okay with that?" I asked.

Malik nodded. "Oh, I am. I love watching you move." If I were the blushing type, I'd be red as hell. Instead, I mock glared at him, then turned to Jesus.

"Sí, this is a much better option."

"And you're gay, so he's not worried about you coming on to me."

I threw my head back and laughed. Jesus splayed his hands in the *what can I say* motion.

"Well, he's right. Let's go."

I checked with Malik one more time, but the grin on his face was warm. I hated leaving him again, but we'd only be on the dance floor for a few minutes, and Maribel truly did deserve to show off that dress. The floor quickly crowded with other people, and we shimmied and danced and laughed. And it was an absolute blast, one I couldn't get enough of. One I needed more of. Just not with her.

After we'd been there for who knows how long, she leaned up and whispered, "My feet. The shoes. I'll pay for this tomorrow."

"Then let me get you back to your man."

"And let me help you back to yours."

The music changed, a familiar refrain starting up: Tamia's "Can't Get Enough." I found Malik chatting with Jesus at the table. Malik watched me even as he spoke, and his eyes didn't waver when Jesus laughed next to him.

I kept his gaze. One brow rose, slowly, as if confirming what we wanted. I nodded. That slow brow raise was matched by a slow smile, and an even slower wink.

I escorted Maribel back to Jesus, and held my hand out to Malik. "Wanna show 'em how we do this?"

Malik didn't answer, but he took my hand and we walked back to the dance floor. We maneuvered through the crowd until we stood roughly in the center, and waited. The DJ had played the opening stanzas on a loop, and when she saw us standing side by side, she grinned and gave us a thumbs-up.

The line dance had been one of our favorites when we were married. It looked complicated, with the rocking and three-quarter turn moves, but was fairly basic when it came down to it.

Then Malik took my hand—not part of the dance—and spun me until I was in front of him, and held me around the waist while we moved. Then he turned me again, so we faced each other, and did the dance in reverse so we'd move in the same direction, something I'd never been able to master. But he'd always said there was no point in having a favorite dance if he couldn't hold his husband while he did it.

The world fell away. There was only me, only Malik, only the memories of times when things were *so good* between us. When there was nothing I wanted more than to always be with him, hold him next to me, see the pure joy on his face when we danced.

God, how could I have forgotten this?

I tightened my grip on him. Words garbled around my brain, refusing to create a cohesive sentence, but I opened my mouth to speak anyway. And then the people surrounding us broke into applause, forcing my attention back to the present. The song was over, but from the heated look on Malik's face, the night was far from it.

Chapter Sixteen

Malik

It wasn't fair to want as much as I did. Not for myself, damn sure not from DeShawn. But as the driver—and thank god for the driver—drove us back to my house, all I could think about was how wired I was. How on edge I was. How glorious DeShawn had looked up on that stage, accepting his awards, proving that, once again, he was the best in the business.

And for a brief moment in time, for however long this lasted, he was mine. And I wanted to remember that, not just with words, some pictures, and holding hands and soft kisses for the cameras. But with something real, something pure. Something filthy.

The driver parked in front of my house and we thanked him profusely before I got out and held my hand for De-Shawn to follow.

"We're not at the event anymore," he said, his voice rough. "You don't have to do all that."

"I know. I want to."

Even in the dim light, I could see the way DeShawn's eyes twinkled, but all he did was nod. I let us in through the front door, which made Bruno come running with a soft growl.

"Shh, it's me, boy." He dropped to his butt for pats, and for me to tell him what a good little protector he was, before going back to the dog bed and wrapping himself protectively around Corey.

"Looks like they worked out their issues," DeShawn said wryly.

I just barely muffled my laugh. Then I laid a hand on the center of his back and guided him toward the stairs. He gave me one of those meaningful looks, those *what in the hell do you think you're doing* looks, but didn't say anything. "You were magnificent tonight."

He huffed, a tiny little laugh, then dipped his head. "Thank you. And thank you for being there. I know it was short notice, but—"

I spun him on the landing between the first and second set of steps and pressed into him, silencing whatever he was about to say next with a kiss. He was still for the briefest moment before his hands landed on my stomach and circled around to my waist, pulling me in tight against him.

"You don't need to say anything," I told him. "I'm glad I was there."

His smile was shy, super sweet, and positively sinful.

My thoughts solidified into three words. "I want you."

His eyes widened, and mine fixated on the way his Adam's apple bobbed as he swallowed. "Yeah. I want you, too."

I wanted to respond with something witty, but words failed me. I tangled my hand with his and led him up the short flight of stairs. He started to walk past the master, toward his room, but I caught him around the waist and pulled him in back to chest. "Just where do you think you're going, sir?"

"To the bedroom?" The little hitch in his voice was positively adorable. I wanted more.

"Do you know," I said, running my hand down the front of his stomach, to caress over his waist, "that I have never christened this house?"

"Not at all?"

"Not one single room." I nipped at his ear and reveled in his low groan. "And I'll be damned if I start with the guest suite. Come here." I couldn't keep this man; I knew that. And I had a choice. I could rebuff my own desires and be miserable in the process, or I could revel in knowing Chef DeShawn Franklin wanted *me*, and let myself have this, for however long it lasted. The choice was clear.

I marched him into my bedroom, to the split king bed I had for no good reason other than to have it. "Think this will do?"

"For this time and every one after that," he whispered.

"Excellent."

I spun him to face me and worked his jacket off, then set it gingerly on the small seat nestled in the corner. I let him take off his own cufflinks, then loosened his bow tie. "Much better coming off than going on," I muttered.

"That's what they all say, isn't it?"

I paused midbutton and laughed. That was part of what I'd always liked about DeShawn, and the sex we'd spent years having. It was never overly serious, always teasing, always fun. We enjoyed ourselves and our bodies, and each other. And for an overly serious guy like myself, that meant a lot.

I finished unbuttoning his shirt and removed it, then ran my hands down the chest I'd once known from memory. So much was familiar, the sparse curls on his chest and down his happy trail having grown slightly coarser with age. And grayer, a sign of the growth and—hopefully—maturity we'd experienced. The thing that was really different was the tattoo sleeves. When we'd been married, he'd just started getting them. He hadn't had a plan for what he wanted, but in the time we'd been separated, he'd clearly figured it out.

"One day, I'm going to map each and every one of these."

DeShawn chuckled low, then yanked me forward by the

top of my tuxedo pants and pulled my shirt out from it. "And one day I'll let you. But not right now."

I held still while he removed my bow tie, then removed my shirt with far more alacrity than I had his. He smoothed it off my shoulders and let it fall to the ground, then wound his arms around my neck. "Goddamn, I missed you."

I wouldn't let myself dwell on how much those words meant to me, how absolutely not even a little bit fake they sounded. I just brought him close, let myself memorize again his touch, his taste, the way he always kissed me like he could never get enough. Which was good, because I damn sure couldn't either.

My hand moved from his back to his stomach, and with one hand, I unfastened his tuxedo pants and unzipped them. They fell to the floor and he started to step out of them. Then stopped, because neither of us had remembered to take off our shoes.

He laughed, breaking off the kiss and bumping his forehead against mine, then said, "Move back and let's get naked."

I took a step back and sat on the edge of my bed, removing my socks and shoes. DeShawn turned to balance himself on the chair and removed his own shoes, and I nearly swallowed my tongue.

"What?" he said, looking at me over his shoulder.

"Are you wearing a jock?"

He straightened and gave me a saucy little smile and shrug. "It works better with the suit lines."

"Uh-huh. C'mere and let me take a closer look."

"That is so unoriginal."

But he stepped out of his pants and walked to stand in front of me. I ran my hands down that lovely, thin-but-strong chest again, to those narrow hips he'd complained were bony when we were young but had filled out just the right amount now, over his dick, hard and straining, the tip peeking out from the jock. I pressed my tongue to his slit and used one hand to pull an ass cheek open. His hands found the top of my head and held on, and with my other hand, I gently massaged his hole.

"Malik, goddamn."

I pulled the jock down just enough for the head to pop free, wet my finger, then went back to sucking while I fingered him. My sex life before DeShawn had been sparse, and after him, nonexistent. But no one ever responded to me the way he did, always eager for what I gave, always reaching for more. His unabashed need spurred me on, convinced me I could please him, and all I wanted was to give him more.

His hands dropped from the back of my neck to my shoulders, gripping and squeezing and digging his palms into me for all he was worth.

"Stop," he whispered suddenly, pushing back. "You have to stop, else I'm going to—"

"Me too." I pulled him down to straddle me, then flipped us until he was underneath me on the bed. I climbed up the mattress just enough to pull his jockstrap all the way off, then fumbled in my nightstand for a bottle of lube that had seen more use in the past few weeks than in more months than I cared to admit, and an unopened box of condoms.

DeShawn snatched them off the bed. "Malik, how old are those?"

I coughed and cleared my throat. "I picked them up a few weeks ago."

DeShawn looked way too fucking pleased with himself at that news. "Hope springs eternal, does it?"

"With you? Always."

The smile on his face went from lascivious to tender, and made my heart do funny pitter-pattering things it hadn't done since my wedding day. Aw, the hell with it. I nestled back down on him, popping myself above him on my elbows. "Am I too heavy for you?"

"Never. You never have been."

I gave him all my weight then, reveling in the feel of our dicks, both slick with precome, gliding together. It would be easy to come just like this. It would be glorious really. But I had no idea how much time I'd have with DeShawn, and if this was it, I wanted it all. Every part of him I could get.

I reached over and grabbed the lube, uncapping it and pouring some on my fingers. DeShawn shuffled and planted his feet on the mattress, opening his legs wide.

"Look at you. You're so goddamn pretty like this," I told him.

"Flatterer," he said, but his laugh was hoarse, husky. Beautiful.

We could banter like this all night, and had before, but my dick, my heart, my everything, were desperate to remember him. I pressed a finger against his hole, and he hissed, gripping his knees tight before intentionally relaxing and pushing out. I fingered him for a few seconds before adding a second, and his rumble came from deep inside his belly. Nothing made me feel more powerful than when I reduced this beautiful man to a writhing mass beneath me. It was everything I could do not to come from the sound of his moans alone.

"Enough, Malik. Now."

I rolled a condom down my length, shaking aside the memories of all the times we hadn't had to bother, then lined up and pushed inside. DeShawn released one leg and gripped my bicep instead, letting that leg fall to the side. I hiked it up around my waist as I pressed into him, taking my time, relishing the feel of being inside this man—my husband—one more time.

The word rolled around in my head and I closed my eyes. DeShawn massaged my back, his breaths a caress against me.

We'd made love for the last time the night before DeShawn filed our paperwork at the courthouse, and I'd tucked that night away to hold on to for the next however many decades I lived. To be here again, inside him, overwhelmed me in the best way, and I tangled my fingers in his locs and pushed in.

When I was fully seated, we both paused, our breaths heavy for a moment before DeShawn wrapped his other leg around me and locked his ankles around my waist. He arched his neck up and kissed the bottom of my chin. "Move."

I buried my head in his shoulder and pulled out. I wanted to go slow. Everything in me urged me to go slow, to take my time, to not rush this moment with this man.

"Fuck me, Malik. Like it's our first time. Like you're trying to prove something."

How the hell could I resist that entreaty? I captured his lips and gave him everything I had, his legs wrapped around my waist, spurring me on, my need to bury myself as deep inside him as I possibly could drumming in my ears. I'd never been able to get enough of this man. And I knew after tonight, I never would.

"Malik, so close."

I gripped his shoulder with one hand and reached between us with the other, stripping his length in long strokes, desperate to make him come as hard as I knew I would. My lips found his shoulder and I bit down, and DeShawn went off like a rocket. I followed, milking him through his orgasm as I reached my own, my eyesight going nearly black with the force of my release.

For a few moments, we lay there like that, until our heartbeats began to match. "They're doing it again," DeShawn whispered.

"Syncing."

"Yeah."

I was twenty-three again. Feeling that same wonder of being with a man who felt so perfectly right that it couldn't be real. A figment of my imagination, I'd told myself, until DeShawn had marveled at it, too.

And after our last time, I'd convinced myself it'd been the fantastical musings of a man desperately in love. Now, I wasn't so sure.

Something about that idea warmed me, and I pressed a kiss to the side of his mouth before I pulled out and tied off the condom, then flopped on my back next to him. He looked at me, a silly, sappy grin on his face, then ran the back of his hand over my cheek.

"Beautiful," he whispered. "Always so beautiful."

I didn't know if he was talking about me or the sex, and frankly, it didn't matter. I'd clean us up and get rid of everything in just a minute, but for the time being, all I wanted to do was lie here with my man.

Chapter Seventeen

Malik

I would have loved to wake up the next morning and do nothing more than relax in DeShawn's arms, laze the day away, naked, the only thing that mattered lying in bed with him.

The dogs had other plans. Or maybe they had the same one, but promptly at five-fifty the next morning, while I was working on maybe three good hours of sleep, Bruno trotted into the bedroom, as refreshed as ever, his entire body wagging as he looked at me expectantly.

I reached a hand out and rubbed his head. "Okay, boy," I whispered. "Give me a moment."

He responded with a soft *woof*, then left the bedroom. I heard a second click of nails outside the door, and knew Corey was right there with him.

I might not admit it, but I'd grown to enjoy sharing the dog-walking responsibilities. We hadn't specifically discussed it, but I didn't mind handling the morning shift because I was normally up and ready to go before the dogs woke. But if I could go to bed the way I had last night, these walks were going to become a problem.

I handled my business in the bathroom and came out to find some clothes. DeShawn was sitting up in the bed, rubbing the sleep out of his eyes. He looked impossibly adorable like that.

"Morning," he muttered, like adding the word *good* in front was too much to bear. I understood.

"Morning. What are you doing up so early?"

"That dog of yours is many things. Quiet ain't one of them."

I chuckled. "Sorry about that."

"No worries." He let his hands fall and looked at me, then waggled his brows. "Besides, I thought you might want some company this morning."

I'd gotten used to my walks being a lonely endeavor, enough that I'd never thought about us doing them together. And I figured I'd been an especially good boy to get the offer. "Well, I'm certainly not going to argue with you about it."

DeShawn's laugh was rich. "Somehow, I didn't think you would. Give me a few minutes, and I'll be ready to go."

I waited for him to get dressed, then we walked downstairs. Was this what my life had become? Something so solitary become almost familial. Me, my *husband*, our dogs, meandering down the street, through the neighborhood, just being together. Years ago, this was everything I could have dreamed of, and even as I reveled in the moment now, I was hard pressed to remember this wasn't real. Noah's words from the night before came back, and I realized, as deep as my feelings for DeShawn had always been, as inevitable as my feelings now felt, I'd been holding part of myself back. Just in case.

Just in case…what? What was I so damn scared of?

Intellectually, the answer to that seemed obvious. If DeShawn's feelings didn't match mine, then I was setting myself up for a deep, deep disappointment. The easy way to resolve that, of course, was simply to *talk* to him. See if we were on the same page, and go from there. My heart balked at the idea, insisting that, for the time being, my ignorance was bliss. And I didn't have the heart—no pun intended—to say it was wrong.

DeShawn had taken the lead on leashing the boys, then looked up at me with an expectant grin. "You ready?"

I nodded and tried for my best smile. Walking the boys was the only time I used the front door, largely because Bruno seemed to get a kick of bounding down the front steps. This morning was no exception, and I held on for dear life not to face plant when I hit the sidewalk.

"He do that often?" DeShawn asked as he reached the curb next to me. "It never occurred to me to go out front. I always use the garage door."

"Because you're smarter than me. He does it all the time, and every time I act like I'm surprised," I said, and rolled my eyes.

DeShawn chuckled and grabbed my hand. I looked down at them, then up at him. He arched a brow, like he dared me to object, then tightened his fingers. "Let's walk."

This was dangerous. Walking down the street, holding my husband's hand while Bruno's initial enthusiasm relaxed into our usual moderate pace. Corey was more energetic, but even he calmed down to match our more leisurely stride. We didn't need words, and the silence between us was more comfortable than it had the right to be.

I remembered wanting this, all those times at the beginning of our marriage when we had playful but serious fights over where we would live, what we would do, what life we genuinely wanted to lead. Now, here we were, in the suburbs, walking our dogs, the way I'd always envisioned. And I couldn't help but wonder what DeShawn had given up to be here, with me, like this.

"So," I started, that thought pulsing in my head. "I never asked this, but what's your home like? I assume you live in the city?"

DeShawn chuckled, the sound soft and warm. "Yeah, I

have a condo in DC. It's funny, though—outside of stopping the dog-walking service and forwarding the mail, I haven't even thought about it."

"Do you miss it?"

He glanced at me, then gave a little half shrug. "Not as much as I probably should, to be honest."

And my heart shouldn't have leapt at those words, but it did.

"Before you ask, I still love the city. But..." He stuttered in his walk and huffed. "But maybe you were right."

"Repeat that for the cameras, please. I need to mark this down for posterity."

DeShawn hip-checked me but didn't stop walking. "When I first moved, it truly was everything I wanted. I don't regret that for a moment. But the longer I'd been there, the older I got, and..." He trailed off and shook his head.

"The more it felt like the city stayed the same age and you became the old man yelling at kids to get off your porch?"

"Yes. That. It stayed loud when I wanted quiet. It stayed bustling when I wanted to slow down. The city didn't change. Everything that makes DC great didn't change, but I wanted something else."

I understood that. I knew DeShawn didn't want those big behemoth-style mansions in Northwest, the ones that looked like an entirely different city within the district, or one of the brand-spanking-new condos they'd torn down entire neighborhoods to create. Those wouldn't appeal to him. He loved Grandma's house, the families that had been there for generations, where people knowing your business grated as a teen and young adult and were comforting as you got older.

"So what do you want now?"

Another half shrug. "I don't know. Hell, sometimes I feel too old to make any big changes and need to just suck it up."

"I know you don't really believe that."

His smile twinkled. It literally fucking twinkled. "No. I don't really believe that."

I snorted and he chuckled, and we fell silent again as the boys reached their turning point and started toward the house. The distance back home always felt shorter, and this time was no exception. It was worse now, because I wanted to drag the distance out to spend more time together. But before I knew it, Bruno was whining at the garage. The stairs were for going out only.

I let us in, and DeShawn squeezed my shoulder. "I'll take care of food."

Especially after last night, the memory of which had stayed near the forefront of my mind, I wanted more than food. I wanted everything, but the words stuck like too-sticky taffy in my throat, and all I could do was nod.

I closed the garage and shut the door, then walked to the living space. The boys were busy with their food, and De-Shawn was rummaging in the fridge. I clicked on the remote and turned it to the local news.

"An explosive story by Noah Tippin."

"This asshole again," DeShawn grumbled from the kitchen.

"What the hell is he on now? We ignored him all night." And the fact that his words had run through my head this morning frankly pissed me off.

"Exclusive tonight, my interview with Robert Moore, the son of one Anna Mae Belle Moore. You might not know that name, but I'm sure you know her grandson. DeShawn Frank-lin, the executive chef of uber-chic, starred restaurant Cri-teria. We've all seen Chef DeShawn with his new beau, his *husband*, Malik Franklin. But what you may not know is the real reason behind the reunion, and you're not going to be-lieve what you hear when I talk to Robert Moore tonight."

My ears burned, the small, dull throbbing sound crescendoing into a cacophony of buzzing noise. I felt DeShawn's hand on my shoulder, watched him call out what I assumed was my name, but heard nothing. He held his phone up to me, and my vision blinked in and out as I saw Grandma's name.

I squeezed my eyes shut, covered my ears and tried to drown out the sound. When I released them, I was at least a tiny bit better. I looked up at DeShawn, standing there in front of me, his phone in one hand, his other clenched into a fist.

"We've got to go. Grandma called. Larry's at the house, and we need to get to them. Now."

DeShawn

If I didn't know better, I might think Malik's quiet—his inability to hear me back at the house, the way I had to force him into the car so we could drive—was shock. But I knew him too well. It wasn't shock or a panic attack or anything like that. It was pure, uncut, rage. It shouldn't have warmed me the way it did, but I was who I was. And who I was loved Malik's anger on my behalf.

The fact was, he was appalled that anyone would finish watching the piece and think negatively of me. Because I knew his anger wasn't for himself. Malik had always been able to take care of himself. He couldn't give a shit what folks thought about *him*, but about the people he loved? He was as protective as they came about that.

So while we drove to Grandma's in silence, my heart was a bit lighter than maybe was warranted given Noah's interview. Which probably wasn't smart of me, but honestly, nothing about this experiment had been all that smart. From the outset, we should have found another way to handle this, but I couldn't bring myself to regret where we found ourselves now.

I pulled up to the house and got out, Malik not having said a single word the entire drive. He also didn't get out the car with me, and I had to reopen my door to unlock the passenger side. When he still didn't move, I walked around to his side and yanked it open, then reached across him and unfastened the seatbelt.

"Come on, beautiful," I said. "Let's get this over with."

He shook his head and looked at me, like he didn't know where we were. Then he frowned and took stock of his surroundings, which confirmed that he probably hadn't remembered much of the drive over. I closed my eyes, said fuck it, and dropped in his lap.

His arms came around me immediately and he buried his face in my neck, inhaling deeply. His hand splayed across my back and I nestled into him.

"I don't like this," he admitted, and I stiffened. His grip tightened. "I don't mean you. I mean Robert and Noah and Heidi. What's their deal? Why do they care so much?"

"Noah and Heidi are tabloid reporters dressed as journalists. They're only here for real gossip. And Robert's obviously trying his case in the media. He wants people to second-guess us."

"Will it work?" Malik's voice was muffled against me, his breath on my skin enough to make me want to say the hell with it, go home, and call Grandma and Larry later. Malik's hand moved to my side and squeezed. "D?"

I pulled back and looked at him. His eyes searched mine, then roamed over my face to my lips. He adjusted his grip, straightened, and kissed me.

My eyes closed and I cupped the back of his neck, deepening the pressure and flicking my tongue out to play with his. Malik groaned, then moved his hand from my waist to my lap. I spread my legs as best I could to give him more access.

And a throat cleared behind us. My squeak was not cute; Miss Maxine's laugh was.

"Annie would love to hear about this." I opened my mouth,

but she shook her head. "I won't tell her, don't worry. But why don't you two go on and talk to Larry while I check on her?" She walked in before either of us responded.

I nuzzled Malik's cheek with my own, willing my erection and my heartbeat to calm. "You ready to get in there?" I finally asked, standing and smoothing my hand down my top.

"No," he grumbled, and I chuckled. Still, he took my hand and we walked up the front steps. I walked in and found Larry sitting on the front couch, my favorite little girl resting her head on his lap, a red balloon attached to her wrist.

She looked up when we entered and I smiled. "Hey, Rissa-boo."

She squealed and scrambled off the couch, then launched herself in my arms. "Hey, Uncle Chef D."

I laughed. Larry's kids could never seem to decide whether they wanted to call me Uncle, or Chef, so they'd taken to calling me both. I loved it. Clarissa was the baby, and still liked it when I called her Rissa-boo. We'd see how long that'd last.

She stuck her arm out at me. "Look, Daddy got me a balloon cuz I asked him to. Isn't it beautiful?"

"It is, sweetie. Prettiest balloon I've ever seen."

She nodded, then peered around me and looked at Malik, and it hit me that she probably didn't know him. Or, at least, didn't remember him, because she wasn't even two when we'd divorced. Still, she smiled shyly at him, squeezed me tight, then returned to Larry's side.

He looked down at her with a fond smile. "She's been under the weather, so Claire asked if I could watch her while she took the other kids out. Baby girl wanted a balloon. Seemed like the least I could do."

"Then I'm sorry your plans were ruined by...this," Malik said.

Larry shook his head and sighed. "I just, what the he—heck

is Robert thinking?" He held a hand up before we could respond. "No, I know what he's thinking. I'm just pissed that the man I knew and admired once upon a time is this damn desperate."

Clarissa looked up at her dad, narrowed her eyes, and held a hand out. Larry closed his, sighed, then fumbled until he pulled a five-dollar bill from his wallet. She took it, smiled as sweet as you may, then rested her head again, the balloon bobbing gently as she made herself comfortable.

I muffled my laugh even as I nodded. I felt the same way about this whole situation. Robert was my uncle, one of only three members left in our family, but it'd become more and more clear that, when Grandma was gone, I was alone. And my heart clenched and squeezed and shuddered at the thought of being left in this world with no family. Sure, Larry and Miss Maxine would always be there, but other than them, who did I have left?

I sneaked a peek at Malik, who watched Rissa with a tenderness I'd rarely seen on him. A part of me latched on to the idea of having a new family, a feeling I'd had to squash more than once, especially as I met and came to know Malik's relatives. How easy would it be to grab on to them? To create something new with them? Would they even want me?

I sank onto the couch, Malik next to me, but we hadn't been there for more than a few minutes when Miss Maxine left Grandma's room. Larry stood and headed toward the bedroom, and she took his seat. Clarissa immediately curled up next to her, and she kissed the top of Clarissa's forehead.

"How is she?" I asked.

"Awake. And pi—frustrated. But her strength isn't the greatest, so go in and talk to her while she still has it."

I nodded, but the words pinged around in my head. The past few times I'd spoken to Grandma, she'd sounded as vibrant and as lively as she always had. So to hear that something, *anything*, had changed for the worst, was the reminder I didn't need this morning.

A soft hand on my arm pulled me from my musings, and I found Malik standing in front of me. "Come on," he whispered. "You can do this."

I started to lean against him, then froze. He raised a brow, then pulled me into him. We walked down the hallway and he paused in front of Grandma's door. "We're gonna get through this," he whispered. "I promise."

I squeezed tight, burying my face in his neck, letting his warmth and his presence surround me. We stayed like that for a few minutes, Malik never rushing me, until I felt strong enough to pull back and nod.

Malik ran his thumbs under my eyes, wiping away the tears I hadn't even noticed, then kissed me softly before trailing his hands down to squeeze mine. "Let's do this."

He opened the door. Larry sat in the same seat he'd been in when she'd first broken her news. The only other chair was the threadbare one, and Malik pointed me to it while he sat on the edge of the bed.

"I'm going to kill him," Grandma started, then punched the sheets next to her.

For whatever reason, the dam broke, and I burst out laughing. Malik and Larry just stared. I waved my hand at them, then looked at her. "This whole drive here, I'm worried about how you're going to take your son being such an unmitigated asshole, worried it's going to make you emotional or whatever, and I get here and you're contemplating straight-up murder."

She seemed to think about it for a moment, then shrugged. "Yes. How *dare* he question me? My goals? My plan? My decisions? He's spent decades making his own, and now he doesn't want to sleep in the bed he's made."

"He was always counting on your inheritance to get him out of that bed and change the sheets," Larry said, like it was the most obvious thing in the world.

Grandma pointed at him. "Absolutely, but that's not how it's going to work anymore."

On the bed, Malik cleared his throat. "Now Grandma," he started, "you know I'm first in line to strangle that man. But we have a bigger problem we need to deal with."

At that, she sighed and seemed to lose a little of her fire. "I know," she whispered. "But I don't want, I never wanted, this to become a tit-for-tat for public consumption."

"Never mind that, as counsel, that's not a course of action I'd recommend," Larry added.

Grandma stared at him. "Speak English, would you?"

He laughed, the same indulgent one he'd given before, then looked at us. "You're *not* doing interviews." He turned to her. "How's that sound?"

"At least I understood it."

"Then what do we do?" Malik asked, his voice rough, like the earlier anger and frustration had barreled back to the forefront. "Reality is, we can't let Robert set the narrative."

"But us doing interviews could potentially backfire," I pointed out.

"Not to mention that they'll all be used in the hearing, whether for you or against you." Larry frowned, then a slow smile spread across his face. Almost sharklike, and if that was even a fraction of him in court, I understood how he'd risen to his position as head of his firm.

"I'm not sure I trust the look on your face," Malik said.

Larry laughed. "I was just thinking. *You* don't have to give interviews to set the narrative. Let people see you, let *them* do. Not just for big events, but for the little day-to-day things. Let them draw the conclusions about your relationship. You

guys are on this classic second-chance romance. People love...
love, and they'll do the work for you."

Christopher's words came back to me, and I cleared my
throat and looked at Malik. "As a matter of fact, my publicist said something to me about you coming to Criteria a few
days a week. If that was something you were interested in. As
a reciprocal arrangement, obviously."

Malik stared at me for a beat, then slowly nodded. "You've
met my brother. You know he'd probably shit himself if you
came to Franklin's like that."

I'd been there before, multiple times, but never regularly.
Malik was right. James would be ecstatic. And honestly, it
would more than serve Robert right if both our businesses
thrived while he shouted to the wind and to the two reporters who believed him, ignored by everyone else.

I settled into my seat and grinned at Malik. "So I guess
we're doing this, then?"

The look he gave me nearly melted my insides. "I guess
we are."

Chapter Eighteen

Malik

I walked down the street to Criteria almost two weeks later. That was how long it took DeShawn's agent to square things away with the head honchos at the restaurant. I'd never been there before, and took a moment to examine it. Criteria was one of those deceptively innocuous-looking restaurants. The kind where the facade melded into the surrounding businesses. The way Franklin's used to look, the polar opposite of its appearance now.

A small group of reporters huddled at the front, and I said a quick prayer that I was still anonymous enough that they wouldn't recognize me walking in. I dipped my head, muttered my apologies, and skirted around one of them, who peered at me a little too closely for comfort.

Inside, I took a breath. The space didn't seem that large from the outside, but inside it had a light, almost airy feeling. It was a place where people were meant to sit, gather, enjoy themselves. Not just be there for the show of dining at a prestigious restaurant. I'm not sure what I'd been expecting, but this wasn't it. There was a small bar over in the corner, one there for making drinks, not to congregate around for happy hours or anything like that. There was only one stool, empty, and I sat.

"You look like you could use a drink or three," the bartender said.

I choke-laughed and nodded. He was right. I wasn't an anxious person by nature, but my nerves were definitely going to work. I wanted something neat, maybe one ice cube. But I needed to keep a clear head, especially if I was going to become a regular. DeShawn needed me to be affable and engaging, not sullen or overly quiet. Sadly, that equaled a chaser.

"Can I get a whiskey and ginger ale? And then a separate ginger ale on its own?"

"Pacing yourself. Smart."

The bartender turned and I drew in another breath. A pianist sat in the corner, his fingers flying over the keys. The song was vaguely familiar, and I closed my eyes, listening. Was he playing Silk's "Freak Me"? Did DeShawn know about this? And if he didn't, did I want to tell him? Far be it for me to cost someone his job, but that didn't seem remotely appropriate for a restaurant of this caliber.

A soft hand landed on my back, and I jumped, just a fraction, before sinking into DeShawn's presence behind me. "That man chooses the best music." He chuckled.

"Not exactly suitable for a place like this, is it?"

DeShawn shook his head. "Not even a little bit. That's why I love it." He bent over and kissed my temple, then straightened. A frisson of energy shot through me, but it wasn't all internal. Even without looking, I felt the eyes of the other customers on us.

"They're watching," I whispered.

DeShawn's smile was sinful. "Good. That's why you're here." Another kiss, this time to my cheek. "Let me take you to your table."

"I'm fine right here."

"I'm sure you are. That's why you can't stay." He held out

a hand and I took it, pausing for a moment while I inhaled a deep breath, then stood.

I turned to the bartender and grabbed my two drinks. "Thank you."

He nodded, and DeShawn smiled. That patented, well-practiced one. "On the house, obviously."

"Obviously," the bartender repeated.

DeShawn's hand on my lower back guided me forward, and I forced myself to stare straight ahead and not look into the eyes of the surrounding patrons. I heard the whispers, but they seem to grow fainter and fainter. Maybe because they were being drowned out by the din of my rapidly increasing heartbeat in my ears.

We were both introverts, but DeShawn was in his element in a restaurant. Folks were shocked when he said he needed alone time to recharge before he could go out again. I was the opposite. I didn't make conversation easily, didn't open up easily, and was ignored easily. Pretending to not be that—for Grandma's sake, DeShawn's sake, *my* sake—only made my pulse thud harder.

"Almost there." DeShawn's soft whisper in my ear cut through everything else and I gulped in another breath before nodding. He led me up a short flight of stairs, where the tables were more spaced out. Where people wanted to be noticed and photographed, to lord their money over the other patrons. Or at least that's how it felt in my brain.

DeShawn led me to a table slightly off from the center. "A little more privacy here."

I nodded and muttered, "Thank you." I set my drinks down, wiped my hands down my pants legs, and took a seat.

DeShawn sank in the one next to me, then leaned over and pecked me on the lips. He cupped the back of my neck, and the pressure grounded me. "I know you hate this," he whispered. "I'm going to have my best server take care of you. Maribel will be out to check in, and I'll make a few rounds to see you."

I huffed. DeShawn was pulling out all the stops to make me comfortable. I wasn't alone; he'd made sure of it. I reached behind me and laid my hand over his, and he touched his forehead to mine. "You don't have to do all this," I told him. "I'm a big boy."

"A big boy who hates crowds, and hates snobs. This place is full of both."

"I can do it."

"I have no doubt. But doing this together means looking out for each other."

I'd gone from nervous to impossibly stubborn, when really I was grateful. So goddamn grateful for DeShawn's thoughtfulness. I closed my eyes, took another deep, cleansing breath, then whistled it out and smiled. "Thank you. I appreciate it."

"Always." He ran the back of his hand over my cheek, gave me a quick peck there, then stood. "I'm gonna go do my job for a little bit. If you see a tall, broad, permanently pinch-faced white guy, that's Christopher. This is his little brain child."

"Got it." DeShawn paused for a moment, like he wanted to stay, so I sat back and waved him off. "Go. Go be great."

He smiled again, that genuine one I was starting to believe was reserved just for me. "On it." He trotted down the steps, and I watched his retreating back as he stopped to shake hands with some of the patrons.

A few minutes later a server appeared, two appetizers already in hand. "From Chef DeShawn, on the house. Fried oysters and an endive pear walnut salad." He set them on the table.

I smiled. "Thank you so much." He grinned and walked off, and I took a deep breath before indulging myself in an oyster. I loved fried oysters, and I loved that DeShawn re-membered it.

I made the mistake of getting caught up eating, and star-tled when someone approached the table. "I'm sorry to inter-rupt," the woman began, "but are you Malik Franklin? Chef DeShawn's husband?"

Here we go. I straightened and grinned, hoping nothing was stuck between my teeth, and nodded. "I am."

Her face lit up. "I just think the whole thing with you and Chef is so romantic. You guys finding each other again after all these years."

I'd been prepared for some blistering rebuke, some ques-tioning of me and DeShawn's relationship, maybe someone seeing and believing Robert's interview, that we were only in this because of the will. But maybe Larry was right. Maybe our story was actually romantic.

My smile widened. "Thank you. We never set out to be some great love story, but I'm glad people are enjoying it." I had no idea where the words came from, but they didn't feel fake or forced.

"I followed his career. And I remember Franklin's. When me and my brother were kids, our family had dinner there every Friday night. My parents said it was our reward for mak-ing it through the week."

She said it with such fondness, and I remembered how packed it used to be. Me and Sheila and James would stay in the office I now called mine, alternating between playing and bickering with each other. When we got older, Mom and Dad put us to work as waiters. People who'd eaten there for decades would remind me how small and quiet I'd been as a child, how I'd hide behind Mom the few times I had to leave the office. It'd been embarrassing as hell, even though the memories made me smile now.

I shifted forward in my seat. "What's your name? Next time you drop by, your meal's on the house."

Her face lit up. "Really?"

"Absolutely."

"That would be amazing." She paused, fidgeting with the straps on her purse. "Would you, I mean, can I take a picture with you?"

The part of me that reveled in being alone, hiding from the world, pretending I blended in to the walls, implored me to politely decline. I shoved those thoughts aside and smiled. "Of course."

She walked around the table and crouched next to me, phone in hand. We took a couple pictures, and she looked at them with the small smile on her face. "My parents are really going to love this. They've been sick and aren't able to come out as much. They'll love to hear I met you." Her voice was wistful, and I was glad James had finally come onboard with the to-go and delivery options. While it was still lunch only, people like this were worth making dinnertime and weekend exceptions for.

"We'll make sure there's plenty for you to take home. We've just started to-go and delivery lunches, and may expand that in the future."

"My parents will love that," she said, then glanced at the phone again. "Thank you. This"—she waved to the phone at me—"means everything."

My heart was light when she waved again and walked off. After that, a calm but steady stream of people came to the table. And wouldn't you know it? Every single one of them was nothing but complimentary, about me, about DeShawn, about our relationship. More than a few had heard of Franklin's. Some were surprised it was still in business, and vowed to come by and have a meal there.

As promised, the server was attentive, Maribel checked on me, and DeShawn showed up nearly every hour. I always knew when he was on the floor, because the clicks and flashes of the camera rivaled those from the gala. I didn't know if all prestigious restaurants were like this, but people definitely seemed to be here as much for him as they were for the meals. More than one asked for pictures of us together, and we said yes every time.

But what I knew, what was undeniable every time I saw him, was that DeShawn was there for me. To ensure that I was comfortable, that I was enjoying myself. And by the end of the night, an excellent meal, good conversation, and two drinks in my system, I felt amazing.

DeShawn smiled at me. "This is my last time out here, then we've got to get the kitchen shut down. Wait for me?"

"Of course."

"You are in a surprisingly good mood."

I winked, trying for seductive, but not entirely sure I made it. "And you're going to be the beneficiary."

His eyes darkened, and he leaned into me, his voice deepening. "Is that so? Let's see what you've got then."

"Chef DeShawn, you're on."

DeShawn

Malik's good mood at the end of the night had given way to the effects of alcohol. My boy had the itis, big time.

I drove home, Malik in the passenger seat, leaning against the window with his eyes closed. I knew he hadn't had much to drink, but I also know how exhausting severe nerves could be, especially when he'd been so far out of his comfort zone. So worried about what people would think, that they'd believe Robert's story instead of the one we were trying to paint. I understood, but at Criteria, I was working and could push those thoughts down. My only concern outside of service and quality was Malik's comfort. I'd have plenty of time to stress about Robert when I went to Franklin's.

I pulled into the garage and nudged his shoulder. He rolled his head over and gave me a sleepy, satisfied grin. "Tonight was awesome," he said.

I laughed. "I'm glad, baby."

He pointed at me. "I like it when you call me baby."

"Then I'll be sure to do it more often."

"You better." He unfastened his seatbelt, looking far more awake now than he had just a few moments ago, and climbed out the car, stretching his arms high overhead. Quite frankly, he looked like a human version of Bruno first thing in the morning.

He held a hand out and I chuckled but took it, and we walked inside. The boys were at the door, probably having woken up when they heard the garage. We gave them their obligatory head pats, and they trotted back off toward their beds. We followed them toward the kitchen.

"You need anything?" I asked. I'd decided to basically feed Malik appetizers all night, assuming he would be interrupted often enough that a full meal would go to waste. Since he'd never been alone when I came out, I'd made the right call.

He shook his head. "I'm good. Just some water, then I've got plans for you."

Whatever plans Malik fancied himself having were probably going to come face-to-face with the reality of being slightly tipsy and in need of a solid seven hours of sleep. Still, I grabbed two bottles of water and followed him up the stairs.

I made a quick pit stop at the bedroom I'd kept my clothes in but hadn't slept in for a few weeks now. I used the bathroom and washed my face, and wondered how we'd gotten here. We'd never talked about it, but after the first time we'd had sex, it had gone without saying that I would sleep with him. There hadn't even been a moment's hesitation, apprehension, or question in my mind that in his bed was where I was meant to be.

And Malik, for all his early protests about keeping our distance, never objected. Every time I climbed in next to him, he wrapped his arm around me, kissed my forehead, and we nestled into sleep. The same way we'd always done when we were married.

I brushed my teeth and walked down the hall. Malik was sitting up in bed, the TV on, an old episode of *Murder, She Wrote* playing in the background.

"You did well tonight," I told him as I pulled my shirt over my head.

"Yeah?" He looked like a little boy who'd just aced his exam. "Thanks. It wasn't too bad. Everyone was really nice."

"Good." I pushed out of my pants and his eyes fixated on the sight. "See something you like?"

Malik looked up at me. "Not yet. One more layer to go."

I pointed at him. "You, sir, are drunk."

"Not even a little. I had two drinks and more ginger ale, water, and coffee than I can count. I'm very sober. And you"— he smiled and nestled down in the covers until he was on one side, his head propped on his hand—"are the beneficiary. Like I said. Now get naked."

I rolled my eyes but got out of those boxer briefs at warp speed. His words at the restaurant had gotten me half hard, and his insistence now took me the rest of the way.

I stroked my dick, and Malik reached over to wrap a hand around mine. "That's for me. Come here."

I climbed on the bed and shuffled until we were face-to-face. Malik trailed a hand down my cheek and cupped the back of my neck, bringing me forward. "Tonight was good. Thank you for taking care of me."

A whole host of words filtered through me, but I finally settled on, "You're welcome." Which didn't come close to describing how I felt.

He tightened his grip on my neck and brought me forward for a kiss. I'd known from the moment I'd laid eyes on Malik again that this was what I'd wanted. Even now, though, I tried not to read too much into anything, and I hovered on the edge, waiting for him to reject me—us—again.

But Malik's lips were so insistent, his tongue licking across the seam of mine, his fingers massaging my neck, that I could do nothing but sink into his touch. I opened, and he groaned, rolling us until I was beneath him. He felt like the best weighted blanket, calm and steady, a protection from the outside world. I never wanted to let him go.

Malik gripped my chin and turned my head to the side, trailing kisses along my jaw and down my neck, while his hand traveled across my collarbone and arm, until he was able to twine his fingers with mine. His dick, hard and jutting against my thigh, nudged right up against my balls. I wanted to raise my legs, wrap them around Malik's waist, feel him inside me again. I shifted, trying to make that space, but Malik chuckled and broke away from me instead. I didn't try to hide my whimper, and I blew a raspberry at Malik's gentle laugh.

He moved down the bed, trailing kisses on me as he went, until he reached the jut of my thighs. He licked a long stripe up one side, then the other, then along the underside of my dick. It was only the strongest force of wills that kept me from coming immediately.

I groaned out his name, my need ratcheting up to unbearable levels. "Malik. Stop teasing."

He peered up at me, somehow managing to make himself

look innocent, even while licking around the tip of my dick. "I thought you liked when I teased you." He punctuated his words by sucking just the head in his mouth, and tightened his grip on my hips when I tried to push farther.

I grunted, which sounded more like a whine. "Not right now."

His laugh was light, not in volume but...just, he sounded like he didn't have a care in the world. It had been over a decade since I last heard him so carefree. Long before our marriage dissolved.

I looked down at him, sure there was some schmoopy look on my face, and he paused his torment. He pulled off and his eyes softened. We stayed like that for a moment before I stretched a hand down and palmed his cheek. He pressed into it, then glanced at me and winked.

"Well, I don't want to tease my baby, now do I? So I guess I better get this over with."

That was all the warning I got before he took me straight to the root. I yelped, gripping his head, the sheets, anything I could get my hands on. I'd forgotten about his absolute lack of a gag reflex, and I was on the edge again immediately.

"Malik, wait," I panted.

He hummed, the sensation shooting through me, before pulling away. "Oh, would you like me to slow down? Take my time? I thought you didn't want me to tease." I flipped him off, and he burst out laughing again. "That's my boy."

At least he slowed down, though. He sucked on my length, using his hand like a cock ring around my base. He alternated between sucking just on the head, his tongue swirling around the frenulum, dipping inside my slit, and going all the way down. Holding himself, pressing as deep as he could while I pumped helplessly against him.

"You feel so good." I could barely get the words out. "Why do you always feel so good?"

Malik answered with a groan, his hands tightening on my hips. I was so close, balancing on the precipice, and that tipped me over.

"Gonna come," I muttered, and felt his hum as I came in a rush, my entire body tightening around him, holding his head like it was the only thing tethering me to this earth.

Malik held on to me until I loosened my grip, then released me and crawled up the bed to straddle my chest. He jerked himself like a train was barreling down on him.

"Yes," I whispered, "come on me."

Malik's groan was nearly guttural, as strips of come splattered across my chest. "So good, baby." His dick pulsed again with the praise. "That's so good."

He collapsed to the side and leaned his head on my shoulder. "I don't know where that came from, but it was amazing." Malik's smile was calm, sated. "With you, it always is."

I couldn't argue with him there.

Chapter Nineteen

Malik

I was beyond ready to leave by the time the dinner rush at Franklin's started. Normally I stayed for the beginning of it, but accounting had actually taken all my energy today, and I was looking forward to going home, grabbing a bite to eat, and then passing out on the couch until DeShawn returned.

That thought brought me up short. In the past, I'd walk Bruno, grab myself something to eat, and quite frankly, go upstairs. The only noise in my house past seven thirty or eight? Was Bruno, walking up and down the stairs, doing whatever it is dogs do when left to their own devices. But now, I had a reason to try to stay awake, someone I wanted to see when he walked in. I smiled at the thought, then shook my head to clear it.

I parked in the garage and frowned. DeShawn's car was here, which was odd because he was usually at work by this time. My heartbeat increasing a fraction, I walked in to find him and the dogs passed out on the couch, the same way I'd planned to be. God, he was beautiful like this. The stress of being the big man on campus had fallen away, the furrows between his brows softening, those faint lines around his eyes relaxing in sleep. He'd always been lovely, but right now, like this? Absolutely stunning.

I knelt next to him and ran a hand over his face, then leaned forward to kiss him. "Hey, sleepyhead."

He hummed, a slow grin spreading, then opened his eyes. "Hey there."

I smiled. "What are you doing here?"

DeShawn rolled his eyes. "I went in early, and Mondays are our slowest night. Maribel told me to come home, and here I am."

The word *home* made my heart pitter-patter in contentment. "I'm glad." I swallowed the *I miss you* that wanted to come out, straightened and stretched my back, because being too long in the crouched position wasn't good for me anymore. "You rest, and I'll walk the dogs."

"I can come with you."

"No." I shook my head and pointed to the staircase. "You go on, take a hot shower, then climb in the bed and relax. I'll whip something up when I get back and feed you."

He sat up and swung his legs off the couch. "You're going to feed me in bed?"

"I damn sure am. Now get."

DeShawn stood, squeezed my hip, and pressed in for a kiss. He didn't say anything, just walked over to the boys and crouched down. "You guys be good with Malik, okay?"

Corey woofed softly, like he understood exactly what De-Shawn was saying, while Bruno just reveled in being petted. DeShawn leaned in and pressed a quick kiss to the side of my mouth, then walked past and darted up the stairs.

I grabbed a yogurt out the fridge and scarfed it down, then leashed up the boys and headed out. I needed to talk to someone.

I dialed Grandma, hoping she was awake and feeling up to talking, and was lucky she answered on the first ring. "It's mighty early for you to be calling. Tell me my grandson isn't breaking some new arbitrary rule."

I snorted. "We're past that, but D taking the night walks has thrown my schedule. What makes you think I'm not calling just to hear your lovely voice?"

"Because you know better than to call at this time for that."

I couldn't even muster up a retort. "I'm calling because you were right."

"Well, that's not surprising. What exactly am I right about this time?"

I laughed, pausing when Corey stopped to do his business on a patch of grass. "I want him back," I said simply.

"It's about time. What finally gave it away?"

I laughed. "I came home, ready to eat, crash on the couch, and wait for DeShawn to get off." I ran a hand over my face and let it fall, even though she couldn't see me, and the boys were anxious to get going again. "That was my first clue, that I wanted to stay up for him."

"That's a pretty good one."

"And then I come home and he's there."

"He's there? Not at work?"

"Took the night off. Was there, sleeping on the couch, waiting for me."

"You two have always been disgustingly romantic."

I couldn't even argue with her. It *was* romantic, that we were on the same wavelength, the same page, without ever saying the words. Our relationship had begun that way, us reading each other's body language and cues and not talking about what we wanted until we'd already fallen in bed together and had stopped messing around with anyone else. In many ways, the exact same as what we were doing now.

"No lie, I *really* liked coming home and seeing him that way. Sprawled out on the couch, waking up happy to see me.

It's everything I never knew I wanted, what I didn't know I was missing."

Grandma laughed, and I frowned at the phone. "What's so funny?"

"You say you never knew you wanted that, but I sure did. You bought that big old house when you moved home, like you were trying to prove something to somebody, and I told you then it was for him."

Her words brought me to a complete standstill. "Say that again."

"I don't need to. You heard me, and you know I'm right. You fobbed me off, tried to play pretend that it was nothing but an old woman's fantasies, and I let it go. DeShawn's the one you've always wanted in this space, and now you have him. Now your vision of what home should be is complete, and it's on you to make sure it stays that way."

I blew out a noisy breath, then turned the dogs around and started our return. It's not that what she said didn't make sense. It's that it made *too* much sense. Had I subconsciously been building a home for us, waiting for him to return to me? To touch me, kiss me, make love to me?

"You're deep in thought. And I'm only awake because the meds hadn't kicked in yet. I'm going back to sleep now."

I laughed. "Sounds good. And Grandma?"

"Yeah?"

"Thanks you, for being there for me."

"Anything for my favorite grandson-in-law."

I snorted. "I'm your only grandson-in-law."

"Tomato tomah-to." She hung up with a laugh, and I walked the boys back inside.

I got them situated with food and water, then busied myself in the kitchen. Part of me wanted to go upstairs and check on DeShawn, but I'd be loath to come back down here if I did that.

After looking at my fridge, I realized I wasn't all that hungry. Right now, soup and sandwiches sounded amazing. I pulled out the ingredients and plugged in the panini press to heat up. I always kept the ingredients for broccoli cheese soup on hand, and normally kept broccoli and broth in the freezer. I pulled it out and got to work, grating cheeses while I waited for the broth to boil. I tossed the broccoli in just enough to thaw, then turned off the heat, added the cheese, cream, and spices. Two roast beef and caramelized red onion panini sandwiches later, I plated everything and headed up to my bedroom.

I paused at the door, and if I hadn't been holding the increasingly heavy tray, I would've covered my mouth with my hands. DeShawn was asleep, his locs falling over his shoulders and down his chest, his eyes closed in that same quiet repose he'd been in on the couch. I moved in closer and set the tray on the nightstand next to him. Just like before, I ran the back of my hand over his cheek and waited until he opened his eyes.

"Hey, Sleeping Beauty. You up for some food?"

He blinked, then sniffed. "That broccoli cheddar?"

"Is there any other kind?"

His smile? The sweetest thing I'd seen in years. I waited for him to sit up, picked up the tray, and set it over his legs. "Broccoli cheddar soup and roast beef sandwiches."

DeShawn hummed. "Dinner of champions." I sat next to him, and we toasted our spoons together before digging in. He took a few bites and groaned. "This is amazing, Malik. I wasn't super hungry and this hits the spot."

"I'm glad," I ground out. DeShawn looked so *right* in my bed, and Grandma's words filtered back to me. We needed to stop bullshitting and decide if this reunion was real or not, if we wanted it to continue once the trial was over. But it wasn't a conversation to be had now. Not when DeShawn was just waking up. Not when we were both tired, had worked all day, and needed the rest.

You're full of shit. I ignored the voice in my head, even though it spoke truth. Every day was going to be some variation of this one, and we couldn't wait forever to have this talk. But, as I looked over at DeShawn, his meal finished, his eyes starting to close again, I decided another day or two wouldn't hurt.

I moved the tray to the nightstand again and literally helped tuck him in, then pressed a kiss to his forehead. "You get some good rest, okay, baby?"

He smiled. "Yes, hubby. I'll get some good rest."

He was asleep before I could process his words, and after staring at his figure again, I grabbed the tray and went downstairs.

DeShawn

I could wake up snuggled next to Malik every morning. He was warm beneath me, his arm holding me tight against him. Memories of how we used to start our mornings, with sex or blowjobs or just holding each other and quietly watching TV, ran through my head.

I nosed his jaw, pressing light kisses as I went. Malik stirred, groaned, and tightened his grip, then blinked open his eyes. "Good morning, husband."

I closed my eyes. He'd said that every morning of our marriage, always reaffirming our connection. One of those things I'd missed without realizing it, and had given up hope of ever hearing again. I hadn't even thought Malik remembered it.

Now, a jumble of words flew in my head, but nothing sounded quite right, so I stayed silent. I snaked my arm around his waist and squeezed, then smiled into his chest when Malik kissed my forehead. We lay like that, the only sounds the hum of the television and, eventually, Corey and Bruno's claws on the floor.

"Guess we gotta get up," Malik whispered.

"Don't wanna."

He laughed at my faux-petulance, just as I'd hoped. It'd been a running joke when we were younger. "Stay here. I've got this."

I shook my head and threw the covers off me, grateful for the temperature control that kept the room from being frigid. "I bailed last night. Let's do this."

Malik climbed out the bed and yawned, and god, he was adorable. Which absolutely had to be the rose-tinted glasses of me being in love talking, because we were both objectively frumpy, in need of showers, and had morning breath. He grabbed a pair of track pants from the floor, and I followed suit, slipping my feet into a pair of sneakers.

The boys were waiting patiently in the foyer, tails and butts just wagging. We were heading out the door when I snagged his wrist.

"You okay?" Malik asked, the tiniest frown forming.

I nodded. "Yeah. I was just thinking, would you mind taking them again? I wanna cook for you, treat you the way you did me last night."

He looked at me, something in his eyes softening. Almost like we were on the same page, and I wanted so much to believe it. But I needed some time alone with my thoughts, because I wanted more than anything to turn this playacting into something real.

Malik held me by the hem of my shirt and leaned in for a kiss. "We'll be back soon."

I smiled and waited by the front door until they were out of sight, and even that felt disgustingly domestic.

Alone, I ran to the kitchen and rummaged around for ingredients for bananas foster waffles. They were Malik's favorite, and when we were together, he always kept them on hand. I doubted that had changed, and I was right. I set to work getting the meal together, wondering how to start the conversation.

Hey, so, despite the fact we haven't talked about it at all, wanna make a go of it again?

How would you feel if I said I'm still in love with you and want you back?

So, it turns out Grandma had an ulterior motive to her will, which was getting us back together, and we wouldn't want to disappoint her, now would we?

All those sounded trite, and the silence now was as overwhelming as it had previously been comforting. I found the remote and clicked on the TV, needing some background noise. And stared at myself on the screen. That would never not feel weird.

I vaguely remembered taping this episode for DCFoodie a few years ago. Sheesh. I'd become disenchanted with TV, even though Christopher was booking me left and right, and the weight of playing nice was starting to wear on me. What could I have possibly had to say? I turned the volume up.

"I've had to deal with a lot of loss, and I've made a lot of mistakes. I live with the regret of that every day, and I like to think it's made me stronger."

The host smiled. "Are there any things you'd do over?"

I'd looked away then, like my mind had gone deep into a flashback, before turning on that practiced grin of mine and pumping it up to full volume. "There are always things I'd do over. Make better decisions, maybe not as selfish ones. Tell the people I love that I loved them. Not let them go."

Jesus Christ. Grandpa had just died when I'd given that interview, and I'd been open about that. Anyone listening would think it was about him, and in many ways, it was. But I could just have easily been talking about Malik, and in retrospect, I probably was. Come to think of it, that's when Grandma would've gotten the notice that our case was closed for inactivity. Would I have done things differently had I known we were still married? I couldn't say for sure, but I think I had a starting point for this conversation.

I got the boys' dog food and water together, and just in time. The garage door opened, then Corey and Bruno trotted in, ready to eat now that they'd had their exercise. "You have a good walk?" I asked Malik as he trudged in after them.

"I just don't understand how people have that much energy first thing in the morning."

"Meet someone too exuberant for their own good while you were out?"

Malik got a glass of water from the fridge door and guzzled it before looking at me. "I was talking about the dogs."

I fell out laughing, causing Bruno to half glance from his bowl. Corey was not so moved. Malik grinned and poured himself another, swallowing it down before setting the glass in the sink. He frowned and took in his surroundings, then glanced at me. "What is all this?"

I couldn't help my smile. "What does it look like?"

"Bananas foster?" At my nod, he clasped his hands to his chest. "You dear man, you do love me."

He stiffened immediately at the words, and even though my brain screamed out *I do!*, the words stuck in my throat. Did he mean it the way I meant it, or would he run away if I made his statement serious?

My phone rang then, breaking the…what? Increasingly awkward moment in the kitchen? We were like a reality show gone bad.

It was tempting to ignore the phone and be serious with him the way I'd planned. That was the whole reason I hadn't gone on the walk with him, right?

The ringing stopped, and started again immediately. I snatched it up and my heart skipped. Because Christopher was the kind of guy who liked to talk in person. He only called if it was urgent. I winced, giving Malik an apologetic look, and accepted the call.

"Hello?"

"DeShawn, I have some amazing news!"

I had never in my life heard Christopher this excited about anything. Honestly, I didn't know he had it in him. "What is it, Christopher?"

Malik approached from the kitchen island and laid a hand on my back. I let myself lean into him, his touch. Even if he hadn't meant what he said, I needed to pretend, if only for a few moments.

"I just got off with a Perfect Palate rep." I sucked in a breath. They were the station I'd met with early in my career that'd rebuffed my ideas. "They saw clips of you from the gala, and they loved it. They want to do a program special of prestigious and starred chefs doing a cook-off for a grand prize that goes to charity."

That…actually sounded pretty cool. Malik must have heard enough through the phone to get the gist of it, because he gave me the biggest, cheesiest smile and two thumbs up. I smiled back at him and put the phone on speaker.

"And DeShawn, this is the kicker." Whatever Christopher had just said, I'd totally missed. Oops. "There's some serious, and I mean serious, interest in you spotlighting minority-owned restaurants. There's a real market for it now, more than there was before."

I'd ignore the reality of what it took to create such a market, because these were words I'd never thought I'd hear. My disenchantment with TV had started after the miserable pitch I'd made on this topic years ago. That executives were reaching out to *me* now, and actively wanted to pursue that kind of show? This was a bucket list item, the cherry on top of the sundae I'd always wanted to create.

"What do I need to do?" I was practically vibrating, the only thing keeping me grounded being Malik's arm snaked around my waist. I could feel his smile against my cheek. He was really and truly excited for me.

"We're shooting a pilot in New York in a few weeks. Can you make it?"

"Of course. Give me the time and date, and I'm there."

"Will do, and DeShawn? Congratulations."

Christopher hung up and Malik barely let me pocket the phone before turning me around and kissing me. His lips were insistent and I opened for him, gripping his shirt to try to get closer. He rocked into me, his dick hard and long inside his pants, and I knew exactly how I wanted to celebrate.

Of course, he pulled back as soon as I got my hand in position. "I'm so goddamn happy for you."

I closed my eyes and touched my forehead to his. I felt the sincerity in his voice and thrilled in it. Because this opportunity? Wasn't a *me* thing. It wouldn't have happened had we not had to play house, had people not been so damn curious about our relationship.

Malik tugged me close, and for a few moments, we just stood like that. Corey pushed himself between us, determined to share in the hugging. My phone rang again and I fished it out. "Hey Christopher, what's up?"

"They've scheduled the pilot date, apparently the only one that works for everyone's schedule. It's the eighteenth."

Malik pulled away, and I opened my calendar app. "The eighteenth? That works. I'll go up there a day or two in advance." I needed to talk to Maribel, make sure she had everything in control while I was gone.

"Of course. Let me know what you need and I'm on it."

We hung up and I fist-pumped the air, which earned me a laugh. But it was harsh, an almost strangled sound. Malik's face had gone stony, far from the exuberance I expected.

"Malik, what is it? What's wrong?"

"The eighteenth?"

"Yeah, what about it?"

"That's the trial date."

Chapter Twenty

DeShawn

Christopher looked like a goddamn bouncing puppy. Seriously, Corey and Bruno would probably tell him to calm the hell down already. Next to him, though, Maribel was just as excited. At least that, I could understand, because she would be stepping into my role big time while I was gone. But the enthusiasm I'd had barely twenty-four hours ago? Gone. Completely obliterated with the reality that I needed to be somewhere on a date when Malik needed me most. And we were here because I'd nutted up and been unable to call Christopher back yesterday, instead retreating to the couch and lying on Malik's lap, Corey and Bruno curled up in front of the couch.

"I need to reschedule the pilot date."

Christopher cocked his head, like he understood the words but couldn't quite make them make sense. "What do you mean? We have a date."

"You said the eighteenth worked for everyone else. It doesn't work for me. So we need to find a new day that works."

"I can't. We can't. We need to strike while this iron is hot. I checked before I called yesterday, and the next day that works isn't for like another three or four months. By that time, the gala will be out of people's minds. They won't remember what happened, and Perfect Palate might move on. Not just from the special, but from a series for you, too."

That was a low blow, but I hadn't hired Christopher because he played nice. I squeezed my eyes shut. The part that I hated most? Was that I could see Christopher's point. "How long have they been planning this?"

He took a deep breath, like he was trying to regain some of that all business, all the time persona. "They'd been playing around with the idea of doing a special with starred chefs for a while. Watching you at the gala really solidified it for them. So basically, you're the genesis of this entire thing."

Fucking hell. The words out of his mouth were literally everything I'd wanted—dreamed of—when I launched this career. And I'd scraped and clawed, and hadn't gotten anywhere near the success on that level that I'd envisioned. And now, here it was, a carrot dangling in front of me, beckoning me to it. And all I had to say was yes.

Maribel leaned forward, her brows creased with concern. "DeShawn, what's the problem? This is what you always wanted, and as of yesterday, I thought it was a done deal. What's happened?"

I looked at her, then Christopher, then back to her. "That's the trial date."

"Oh." She drew out the word, sighed, and sat back.

"What? What trial date?"

Christopher's confusion brought home just how much I'd withheld the key elements of what Malik and I were doing. Not that I regretted it. Christopher was interested in my professional life, and my personal life only to the extent it impacted the professional one. He'd needed to know I was married so he could stop getting me dates for events, and so he could deal with the press fallout. The hows and whys had been irrelevant, and he hadn't asked.

"Here's the thing. I don't know if you saw the interview my uncle Robert did with Noah Tippin?"

Maribel and Christopher both nodded, Maribel's face creasing in disgust. I could only imagine how he'd behaved at the table while I'd been on display.

"The thing is, Robert sued Malik. He's accused him of trying to con my grandmother into cutting Robert out of the will. His trial is on the eighteenth."

"So you're not really married?"

I chuckled mirthlessly. "Oh no. The whole thing came up because we really *are* married. We were married before I starting cooking seriously, when I was just a sous chef trying to make ends meet, and we divorced—or tried to—when our goals diverged." That was all he needed to know.

Christopher shifted in his seat, frowning. "So all that talk about the divorce not going through?"

"Was true. We didn't find out until my grandmother called me to the house. And she *is* dying." God, I wanted to scrub my mouth out with soap after saying that. "And she *did* change her will, and left everything to me and Malik."

"So your uncle really is suing you to keep you from getting the money."

At that, I shook my head. "Not me—Malik. He's suing Malik to keep him from inheriting." Semantics, as far as I was concerned, but I was trying to be precise.

Christopher whistled, and I almost thought he got it. Then he opened his mouth. "So, pardon me for sounding dumb about this, but I guess I'm not seeing what the problem is."

"What do you mean?"

"Well..." He shrugged, like whatever he was about to say was obvious. "You're not part of this case. You just said you're not the one being sued. Are you a witness or something?"

I looked away, which was as good as an answer, but I spoke

anyway. "No, I'm not a witness." I'd wanted to be, but I didn't have firsthand knowledge about Malik and Grandma's relationship after we separated, so according to Larry anything I said was hearsay. Whatever the hell that meant.

Christopher shrugged again, and I was tired of that damn movement quick. "Then honestly, I don't see why we can't go forward. I mean, if it's between you missing a trial that isn't really about you and waiting another three or four months to get everyone back together, it kind of feels like an obvious choice, don't you think?"

I stared. Blinked, once, and once more for good measure. "Have you always been this much of an asshole?"

Christopher had the nerve to roll his eyes at me. "Look," he started, "you're all hearts and flowers over this guy, and I can't even say I don't get it. Hell, I'm the first to say his appearances at Criteria have been a great boon for us. But let's be real. This special, and the potential of getting your own show? Is beyond anything we've been able to do. This gives you a national spotlight, international if we play our cards right. And I have to look at this from a business perspective. That's literally my job."

I knew that. It was why I'd gotten an agent, because someone had to focus on business so I could focus on doing what I loved. Not that I'd forgotten about my responsibilities to Criteria; it was still my baby. But leaving Malik now felt *wrong*, like I was choosing something else over him. Again. I didn't want to have to make a decision. I hadn't wanted to make one when Malik and I were failing, and ultimately I'd forced him to do it. Seven years later, it was Malik versus something else, and once again, I was paralyzed by indecision.

Christopher stood and walked to the door. "Look, De-Shawn, I need an answer here. If you're not in, they'll find someone else. But if you *are* in—and your work was the catalyst of this brainchild—then you need to suck it up, and you need to be there. I'll give you tonight, but I need to know first thing in the morning."

"He's such a douche," Maribel grumbled when the door clicked shut.

"But he's not wrong."

"Which only makes him douchier."

That drew a startled laugh out of me, and she smiled at me sympathetically. "I'm sorry," she said. "I know how much you've always wanted this. And I know how much you want him. I wouldn't want to be in your position."

"I need to talk to him."

"I think you already know what he'll say."

I sighed, because I did. "He'll tell me to do it. He'll tell me I've worked this hard, and he'll be damned if I don't go for it."

"So what is it you really want him to tell you?"

I felt the side of my cheek tip up into a half grin, but I couldn't look at her. "I want him to tell me to stay."

Malik

I'd been to Larry's office before, but had been so mentally preoccupied the first time I hadn't paid close attention to my surroundings. Now I was looking at the space again and had to say, it was a little ridiculous. What office needed to be large enough for a full-size executive desk, sofa, coffee table, circular desk, and a full bookshelf and hutch combo? I mean, really. It wouldn't take much to just sleep there, and I had no doubt Larry had spent more than a few nights on that couch instead of in a bed.

"Mr. Franklin? We seem to have lost you a bit?"

I looked at Collin, Larry's secretary. I was here to prepare for trial, but Larry wasn't there. He was, as his protégé Gwen said, charging somebody for something because, goddammit, he wasn't a pro bono attorney and didn't do family law or trusts and estates. She and Collin seemed to find the entire thing hilarious, but it kind of flew over my head.

And there I was, lost in my own little world again. I closed my eyes and massaged them with my thumb and forefinger, then focused on Collin. His gaze was sympathetic.

"I'm sorry," I said, and let my hand fall. "What was the question again?"

"How long after you filed your divorce papers did you renew your connection with Mrs. Moore?"

I shrugged. "I never lost the connection. Even when we were separated and I moved, there was never a time I didn't speak to Grandma."

Collin hummed and scribbled on his pad. "How frequently did you speak with her, either on the phone or in person?"

"We had a weekly phone call set up for Thursday evening at 7:30 p.m. I'd get home, walk my dog, come back in, and call her."

"And for how long did you have these weekly phone calls?"

"From the time DeShawn and I separated."

"What about seeing her in person?" Gwen cut in.

"Not as much," I said, and the remorse punched me in the face. In the beginning, it'd been because the house held too many memories, and I'd needed the distance. Then I'd gotten complacent. I should've seen her more often. I should've sucked it up and made the trip up to Baltimore, instead of always finding excuses why it was too long a drive. "Probably once a quarter," I admitted, shame burning through me at the admission. "Four or five times a year, a little bit more during the holidays."

"In any time that you saw her in person, did you ever see her son Robert there?" Collin asked.

"Once. In seven years, I saw him once, and he was storming out of the house, mad as hell, and was furious when he saw me."

"Did he say anything?" Gwen's face softened, and she went from hard-ass attorney to juicy gossiper.

The gleam in her eyes gave me a chuckle. "He pointed at me and said, 'You think you can replace me? You're not fucking replacing me.'"

"Did you say anything?"

"I knew there was nothing to say. I'd seen him when he was like that before, and there's no getting through to him like that. I wasn't even going to try."

Collin nodded and sat back, dropping his pen to the table. "I'll be honest, I'm listening to all this and wondering why in the hell he's even trying to fight."

Gwen nodded. "Same. He has to know he's going to lose, right?"

Somehow it only hit me then how much we'd protected Robert. No one, not even Larry apparently, had talked about Robert's background. I sighed. "Robert has a gambling problem. Where they live, it's right next to Pimlico. He got sucked in young."

"Pimlico?" Gwen asked.

"Preakness Stakes. The second leg of the horse racing Triple Crown."

She frowned for a moment, then her eyes widened. "Oh. Well, no wonder Mrs. Moore wants you to have the cash."

"I...what?"

Gwen stared at me, like I, an accountant, should have put the pieces together already. And maybe being too close to the case meant I'd missed something obvious.

I closed my eyes, blocking out Gwen's stare and Collin's curious gaze, and thought. About Robert, his vices, and the one thing he was always short of, and my eyes popped open. "Motherfucker."

"What?" Now Collin, who'd tried until then to maintain some semblance of professionalism, dropped pretenses and leaned in, his elbows on the table.

I groaned. Grandma's plan finally made sense, and I wanted to bang my head for not figuring it out before. "You know, I couldn't figure out why Grandma would give me the cash and DeShawn the house. Or, hell, given it all to DeShawn. I'll be honest, we wouldn't be here if she'd switched it. Which was the entire idea."

"Back up, and tell us what you're thinking." Gwen shifted forward, the gleam in her eyes replaced by a stone-cold attorney. A little frightening, but I think I liked it.

"The house doesn't do Robert any good. It does need work. We'd have to put some major money into it if we wanted to sell it, money Robert doesn't have. I'm not even sure I'd sell, and I know DeShawn won't. Robert doesn't get what he needs financially if it's sold as is, and who knows how long it'd be on the market. But cash lets him wild out a bit."

Me too, I wanted to add. I could do a bunch of things, personally and for the restaurant, which Grandma had basically said had been part of her decision.

"There's still something I'm missing here," Collin said, and I shifted to explain.

"DeShawn doesn't have much family. His mom passed when he was an infant, he was raised by his grandmother, and Larry is the closest thing he has to a brother. In terms of blood, Robert's really all he's got left. And that means he'll take care of his uncle, even against his better judgment."

"Exactly where my head was." Gwen sat back in her chair and drummed her fingers against the steel arms of it. "If De-

Shawn gets the money, Robert gets what he needs from *him*, even if he couldn't get it through Grandma."

"Exactly. Because DeShawn's a big old softy and would have a hard time saying no."

"I take it you don't feel the same way about Robert?"

I screwed up my nose and shook my head. "Nah. I don't have that issue. But DeShawn, even if he did want to help, wouldn't mortgage the house just to do it."

"So Grandma knows you better than you think."

I smiled at Collin. "Grandma was playing the long game."

"She didn't count on you guys being legally still married, though," a voice said from behind us, and I turned to see Larry lounging in the doorframe. "She actually had a bit of a fit when we found the paperwork, afraid you guys would think she'd been hiding it."

"Never. That never occurred to me."

"Good." His nod was sharp, and he pushed off the frame to walk in. "But everything you said, about your personality, about DeShawn's and the way Grandma's mind worked as she was doing this, is spot on. These are literally the conversations I had with her when she told me what she wanted."

Larry's eyes bore into me, and I shifted in my seat. Like I'd said, Larry was functionally DeShawn's big brother, and he was protective of him. Which meant I was never quite sure how Larry really felt about me. He put up with me, sure, but that didn't mean he liked my ass, especially post-divorce. He had a remarkable poker face, though, so I couldn't tell how he felt about Grandma's wishes.

He handed me a sheet of paper. "Our official witness list."

I looked down at it and saw there were only three names on it: mine, Robert's, and Grandma's. But next to her name was the parenthetical *de bene esse* deposition. "What's this mean?"

Larry squeezed himself into the last remaining chair and

placed his forearms on the table. "That means she isn't going to testify in person for trial. We'll take her deposition like we were at court, then submit it to the judge."

"I would've thought Grandma would be thrilled to stare Robert down."

He snorted. "She would. But Mom called and told me she couldn't do it. She'd try, but she's gotten too weak."

When Grandma had called and told me her decision about her cancer and ongoing treatment, I'd honestly expected the end to come quickly. I had nothing but imagined worst-case scenarios to draw on, but I'd seen her more in the past few months than I normally did in a year, and she looked and sounded good the entire time. It was only the last time De-Shawn and I had seen her that I'd even had a hint she was starting to decline.

But to hear this? That she wasn't well enough to get up, get dressed, and get to the courthouse? That her testimony—her decades of failed attempts to help a son who didn't want it, and who expected as much or more in her death as he had in her life—would be reducible to nothing but words on a page? It was almost too much, and I choked out a sob.

Larry sighed and wrapped an arm around me, tugging me close. "It's okay, Malik. We're going to do this for her, and then we're going to spend whatever time we have left annoying the shit out of her. Do you hear me?"

A hoarse laugh escaped and I nodded, sniffed, then tried to sit up. He wouldn't let me. "That sounds like a plan." I pulled away again and he let me go. Gwen offered me a tissue and I gave her a trembly smile. I'd forgotten she and Collin were there, but all I saw was compassion, and maybe a hint of tears, from them. I blew my nose and took a deep breath. "I need to see her."

"You do. She needs to see you and DeShawn together again."

I'd managed to go this entire afternoon without thinking about DeShawn. About how much I needed him to be there, and how unfair it was of me to ask. But now I was faced with the reality that, once again, as much as I loved DeShawn, and thought he loved me, even if we hadn't said the words, it still might not be enough to make him stay.

Chapter Twenty-One

Malik

"I can't get the dates moved." DeShawn sounded so forlorn, so desolate, that I had to reach out and squeeze his hand.

It wasn't a surprise. I'd known that from the moment I walked in the house and found him sitting on the couch, his head in his hands. He'd been quiet on the drive over, responding to my attempts at conversation with grunts and one-word answers, like he'd been psyching himself up to give me the bad news and couldn't wait a minute more. "It's okay. We knew it was a long shot. You go and be great, and Larry and I will take care of things here."

His laugh was harsh, grief stricken. "Maybe I should just pull out."

I turned in the car and laced our fingers together, then brought our joined hands to my lips for a kiss. "You will do no such thing. You're going to go, you're going to kick ass on that show, and then you're going to do what you've always dreamt of."

"It means leaving you again."

I closed my eyes, tightened my grip on the steering wheel with my free hand, and smiled even as my heart seized and my throat tried to swallow my words. "We knew this was temporary. We were playing for the cameras, for the courts."

"I wasn't."

And there it was. At some point along the way, our initial ruse had turned into something so much more, so much stronger, and now we were throwing it away. Again.

"I wasn't either." It was as close to *I love you* as I could get, but if I said those words, I'd break down. Completely lose it, beg him not to let me push him away, and I couldn't let that happen. Not for him, and not for me.

DeShawn swallowed hard and closed his eyes, then leaned in and pressed a kiss to my jaw. "Thank you."

"For what?"

"I'd been afraid I was the only one who felt anything. Afraid I'd created a scenario in my mind that didn't match in yours."

I trailed my thumb over his bottom lip and tugged gently. "No. You weren't alone." The kiss was soft, sweet, a recognition of what we had. I could lose myself in him forever, and pulled back almost reluctantly. "We need to get in there."

DeShawn nodded, sucked in a deep breath, and shook his arms out. "Yeah. Let's do this."

We climbed out the car and walked up the front steps to Grandma's house. DeShawn rolled his neck from side to side and paused, his hand on the door handle. There was the faintest tremble in it, and I laid a hand on his back. He didn't turn his head, but I saw his grin before he walked in.

"Grandma, I'm home," he called out.

"I'm—" A cough, just one, then it rolled into a hacking fit. "I'm here."

DeShawn's eyes widened and his legs wobbled. I gripped him by his elbow and pressed into him, letting him lean on me, use my strength. "It's okay. We're going to make it okay."

Nearly the same words Larry had said to me, and I was relieved—grateful, blessed—we all had someone to lean on. Between us, we'd get through this.

"What's taking you so long?"

That sounded more like the Grandma we knew and loved,

and DeShawn let out a watery chuckle. I followed him down the hall and into the room. Grandma was rooting around in the bed for something, and I slipped from behind him and hurried over.

"I got both my boys here," she said, the smile on her face bright. I found the remote to the bed, probably what she was looking for, and held it out to her with my brow up. She sighed and nodded, and I gently raised the bed, stopping every so often to help adjust her against it, until she was in a comfortable seated position. Even that seemed to wear on her, as her eyes closed and chest heaved from the mild exertion.

On the other side of the bed, DeShawn sat in his chair, his hands covering his mouth. I understood. Grandma was visibly weaker, her hair thinning at the top, her skin darkening. All things we'd known would happen but were still hard to see.

She looked over at DeShawn. "Oh, don't look like that. You know how this goes."

He huffed and ran a hand over his face. "Doesn't mean I have to like it."

"I'm not ready to go yet. I got a little while left in me."

"You better. You—" He tugged at a handful of his locs before letting his arm fall to the side. "I don't know how I can do this without you."

Her smile was sweet, a little sad, and she patted the bed next to her. We both sat, and I wrapped my arm around DeShawn's waist, kissing the top of his head when he leaned into my touch. Tears sprang to Grandma's eyes even as she smiled.

"Baby, we all know our times are going to come. That's part of life. I didn't plan to lose your mama the same day I got you, but that was God's will. But I wanted to make sure that my boys"—she broke off and stared at each of us individually for a few short hard seconds—" were taken care of. That meant both of you. I needed to know you were going to be okay."

"Are you sure you didn't do all this to try to get us back together?" DeShawn asked.

She laughed. "I wish. Lord knows I didn't think Robert would sue while I was still alive and halfway kicking. But I'm grateful to him, though."

I couldn't have kept the frown off my face if I tried. "Why, Grandma? What could you *possibly* have to be grateful to Robert for?"

She chuckled and pointed at me. "Always so protective. No, I'm grateful to him because, if he'd waited until I was dead, I wouldn't get to see you two together the way I do now. It's been a blessing, an old woman's answered prayers."

Dear god. Maybe, in the back of my mind, I'd known that. That this ruse wasn't just for the courts, wasn't just for the crowd, but was also for her. So she saw us the way she'd always dreamed, and had that to hold on to. DeShawn shuddered next to me, and I pulled him in even tighter.

I didn't know if he'd planned to tell Grandma about the television opportunity or not, but I couldn't bear the thought of ruining the image she'd created for us. DeShawn was still shaking, though, so I leaned in and kissed the back of his neck. He calmed, and I heard the whistle of air as he breathed out.

"Beautiful. You guys are absolutely beautiful together."

"We love you, Grandma." DeShawn's voice broke and he sounded almost resigned, which matched my feelings.

"I love you, too." She nodded at me, then focused on him. "I want you to fix up this place and make it into a getaway. When the city becomes too much, when you need a retreat, a place you can escape to and pound out new ideas, I want you to bring that dog of yours and come here. You hear me?"

He laughed. "Sure thing, Grandma, but I'm not sure the kitchen is quite up to testing new culinary creations."

She shrugged. "I always wanted a new kitchen. Gut it and

make it live up to its potential. It needs it." At his laugh, she patted his forearm and turned to me. "Now Malik."

I straightened and angled toward her, putting on my best smile. DeShawn squeezed my knee, and god, I loved him. "Yes, ma'am?"

"Don't you sass me." DeShawn and I both laughed, and she shook her head before continuing. "I don't want you givin' all that money to the restaurant. I know you. I know how you are, and I know that'd be the first thing you do. At least half of it is for *you*. Not Franklin's, but Malik. Put it in a savings account, let it grow, toss it in the air for all I care. But no more than half for business."

She knew me too well, and I couldn't even argue with her, because I'd fully intended to spend a hefty chunk on Franklin's. I didn't even know how much *it* was, but now I could at least comfort myself by saying I was simply following Grandma's wishes.

I cleared my throat. "Yes, ma'am. Consider it done."

"Good. You boys go on home. I know that hearing is coming up soon, and I want to hear all the juicy gossip about it when it's over."

"At least you're admitting it's gossip and not your well-meaning concern." DeShawn laughed, even through Grandma's hard stare.

"I won't have you sassing me either. Now you both come on over here and give me my kisses, then get out of here."

We did exactly that, holding hands the entire time, and I didn't miss the smile on her face as her eyes closed and she drifted off to sleep.

DeShawn

I sat on Grandma's words for almost a week. Not about making sure Malik and I were taken care of, or anything like that. I had to sit and reflect on the fact that, for forty years, I'd never really considered what Grandma had gone through when my mom passed.

I'd known she died in childbirth—that'd never been hidden from me. But I'd never sat and reflected on what it must be like for Grandma to lose her daughter that way. She'd probably assumed that being a grandmother would be spoiling me rotten, laughing at my mother's frustration when she tried to discipline me and Grandma went behind her back. She couldn't have expected that she'd have to take on the role of mother again. But she'd taken on the role with a ton of gusto. Even when we fought and argued and I swore she didn't understand me, she wanted nothing but the best for me, even if she didn't always agree on what that was. That had been true about my original career goals, and definitely about Malik and I separating.

That's why I hadn't told her about the pilot. She'd known that was my dream decades ago, and had always cheered me on in pursuing it. But when I married Malik, she pulled me aside and told me that sometimes dreams changed, and I needed to make sure those young dreams matched who and where I was in the moment. I'd listened with half an ear then. I was listening with a full one now.

But damn. After turning it in my head every which way, I was in the same position. It was *still* my dream, and as I finished plating the Cajun shrimp and andouille sausage pasta I'd made for dinner, I couldn't ignore that reality. After all these years, I still wanted this opportunity.

"You're thinking way too hard." Malik pressed into me from behind and rubbed my shoulders. "You know you need to do this."

"I don't know that Grandma would agree."

"She's worried about your personal life. But that's not the

only part of who you are. And the professional opportunities you might get from this show? You can't in good conscience turn them down."

I nodded. Tried to, at least, even as bile threatened to close my throat. He was being so damn self-sacrificing, and I honestly kinda hated it. "So you're cool with letting me go again?"

Malik spun me toward him and pressed close against my body. He rubbed his forehead against mine and gripped the back of my neck. "You know that's not what this is, DeShawn. We're not the same people we were before. We'll figure out a way to make this work, especially when you're this close to finally getting what you dreamed of."

"And if what I dreamed of is you?"

The puff of air against my temple was warm, the faintest hint of stubble scratchy on the side of my face. He squeezed my waist. "I mean, you can always turn it down." I pulled back, and the cheesy grin on his face proved he was joking. "But if you do that, you'll resent me. I can't stand the thought of you resenting me."

He'd said that once before. And he might have been right then. It pained me to think he could be right now, but...truth was, I wanted it all. Malik, the show, the restaurant. Everything. I'd spent seven years without the man I loved by my side, wondering what I could have done differently. To make him stay.

"Do you love me?" I finally asked, and held my breath. I knew the answer. Malik had shown it a thousand different ways over the course of our lives, but that little niggle of doubt pressed against me, whispering that maybe the reason it seemed so easy for Malik to let me go was because he didn't feel the same.

He pulled back and gripped my face. "You know I do. Always have, never stopped. And I want you to have everything you've ever dreamed of. I never want you to regret a choice you made."

I closed my eyes, gripped his shirt. It was close enough. "I love you," I breathed, relief washing over me as I said the words I'd bottled up for so long.

"I know, baby. And you're going to go up there, and you're going to kick ass, and you're going to have the show that you've always dreamed of."

I looked up. "And us?"

He huffed and shrugged, looking around the kitchen and living room. "You know, I talked to Grandma a few weeks ago. She reminded me of how excited I'd been when I bought this place. Everyone thought it was too much for one person, but she didn't. She told me I'd bought it for us. For when you came home. I'd just laughed and let her talk, but she didn't mention it again until recently. And I think she was right." The side of his face tipped up, and he ran the back of his hand down my arm. "I'm not going anywhere."

I barked out a laugh and scrubbed a hand over my face. "Malik, it could be years. If I'm lucky, it *will* be years."

"It's been seven already. What's another decade?"

This time, I shook my head. "You're incorrigible."

"Guilty as charged. Besides, it'll be a few weeks, a couple months at a time, at worst. Me and the boys will muddle along till then." He turned off the stove and took my hands, leading me away from the kitchen and toward the stairs.

"What are you doing?"

He stopped and angled his head back. "You're really asking that question?"

No, not really. We climbed the steps in silence, and when we reached the bedroom, I squeezed his hand. "Stop."

"What is it?"

"I don't want slow and gentle."

Malik's brow flew up. "Pardon?"

"That slow, romantic, this-is-our-last-time-until-the-next-time sex?"

He snickered at the description but nodded. "Yes?"

"I don't want it. I have to leave for this pilot episode, and I want to feel you every day I'm gone." I stuttered out a breath. "I want you ravenous. Like you can't get enough of me. Like you'll always want more."

Malik grinned and walked me backwards. "We're going to be so sore tomorrow."

"Wha—"

Before I could get the word out of my mouth, Malik picked me up and bodily tossed me on the bed, then stepped back and began unbuttoning his shirt. "Strip."

Holy fuck, yes. I got naked as quickly as possible and scooted to the center of the bed. Malik stood there, nude, his long, hard dick straining up. He ran one hand slowly up and down his length, massaging his balls with the other. I wanted to do that for him.

I lay flat on the bed and glanced at him. "Come here."

We didn't have any lights on, but as dusk settled on the day, I still saw how his eyes darkened when he looked me over. I'd never get enough, and warmth spread through me at the thought that I didn't have to.

He climbed on the bed and straddled my face in the classic sixty-nine position. Before I could take his length into my mouth, he'd swallowed my dick to the root. A shudder ripped through me, and I grabbed on to anything I could. Which, in this case, was Malik's ass.

He shifted, and I held him steady while I sucked his balls into my mouth. He groaned around my length, and tremors shot through my system again. Our initially ravenous consumption slowed, me taking the time to indulge myself in the silky feel of him against my lips, the veins running underneath his head, his super-sensitive tip. I could do this for the rest of my life and never tire of it.

But apparently, he could. With one last suck, he popped off me and rolled over. "Hands and knees."

I flipped to my stomach and brought my knees under me, burying my face in the pillow so he wouldn't see the way I laughed at the hoarseness in his throat.

He smacked my ass. "Your shoulders are shaking. I know you're laughing at me."

I looked at him over my shoulder. "My dick made you hoarse."

He pushed up behind me, rubbing his dick through my crease. "It did. Let's see if I can return the favor."

Without warning, he pushed me forward until I face-planted the pillows, then spread my cheeks wide and licked a line from my balls to my hole.

My brain blinked out and I gripped the sheets, rocking back against him while he rimmed me. He snuck a hand beneath my thighs, jerking me off in long strokes while his tongue probed me. I wanted to scream. I wanted to cry. My body didn't know which way was up, but I never wanted to come down.

I won't lie, I did wail when Malik let me go. No warning, just air ghosting against my crease, and no friction on my dick. "Please."

Malik's rumble was mean. All satisfied and smug that he'd reduced me to this, and I smothered my laugh in the pillows. Perfect. I heard him open the bottle of lube, then the squishing sound of him coating the condom, and I curled my toes when I felt that coolness against my hole. He pushed in one finger, worked me quickly, then added another. Just enough to loosen me up, then pressed his dick at my entrance and pushed in.

"Holy mother," I whispered, then widened my stance and

breathed out, rocking back slightly against him. We worked like that until he was all the way in, then he gripped a handful of my locs and pulled my head back.

"Yes," I hissed.

Malik draped himself over my back. "I fucking love you. Tomorrow, you go up there and you do great things. Then you bring yourself back to me, you hear?"

I moaned my assent, since his grip on my scalp kept me from nodding. He'd said it. I wasn't even sure if he knew, but I felt those words as keenly in the middle of sex as I would have anywhere else. Malik loved me, and this wasn't goodbye.

He pulled me upright enough to bite the side of my neck and my thoughts shattered with how good he felt. My dick jumped, I shuddered again, and he let go of my scalp to wrap his arm across my collarbone. I dug into his forearms as he fucked me to within an absolute inch of my life. Normally I tried to be an active participant, but not tonight. I closed my eyes and let him have me. And it was perfect. Everything about him, about *this*, was perfect.

Malik's free hand never stopped moving over me, up and down, roaming over my increasingly sweaty body even as he pumped into me like a mad man. "I love you, D."

I nodded furiously. Tried to say the words back, but wasn't sure I made it, and with a hoarse yell, Malik tightened his hands on my hips almost to the point of pain as he came.

I wanted to collapse with him, but Malik wrapped a hand under me and grabbed my dick, stripping it in hard, sure strokes until I found my own release. My legs wobbled and I thought I'd face-plant, but Malik gentled me onto the bed, turning us to the side before pulling out.

"Be right back." He climbed off the bed and I heard him in the bathroom, before he returned with a warm cloth to wipe me down. "I need to change the sheets."

I waved a hand at him. "Leave it. It'll dry soon enough."

I imagined the crinkled face Malik gave me, but he didn't argue, instead climbing in next to me. "I can't wait to see you on TV."

I blinked open sleepy eyes and stared at him. "You see me on TV all the time now."

He huffed and shook his head. "No, I don't. I haven't been able to watch you at all. Now I can watch you and know you're mine."

I reached up and cupped his jaw, then pressed my lips to his for a kiss. "Goddamn right I am."

Chapter Twenty-Two

DeShawn

Well, Malik was right about one thing: I was sore. Lesson learned: be careful what I wished for.

I looked around the set I was on. Similar to what I was already used to with the local station, but larger and grander, with way more people involved. I closed my eyes and tried to remember this was what I wanted. Me, here with three other famous chefs with world-class cuisine, getting ready for a competition that was supposedly a mix of surprise basket items and "creative" ways of preparing them, such as with razors instead of knives or without stoves. I wasn't sure my stomach was strong enough to handle it.

"You have any idea what we're getting into?"

I turned at the sound of one of the contestants standing next to me, looking at people creating makeshift stages and shaking her head. She reminded me of Maribel with the dark brown hair and golden highlights, but where Bel laughed at the slightest provocation no matter who was around, this woman had a severity about her. One that looked like a facade used to get where she was today. I recognized it all too well.

"Seriously, what is all this?" she repeated when no one responded.

A snort escaped before I could stop it. "I have no idea."

She turned, reached a hand out, and I shook. "Paola Qui-
ñones. A pleasure."

"I know you. You own Las Virtudes."

She beamed, her expression softening. "Indeed. And you're
the EC of Criteria. I've been meaning to get down there for
years."

"We'd be honored to have you."

Her shoulders relaxed even more, and she leaned into me.
"I admit, I've followed the stories of your reunion. That's part
of why I agreed to this. Your love story is epic. I can't wait
to meet him."

I wasn't sure it was all that, but I laughed anyway. "Unfortunately, he couldn't be here today. We have a thing back home."

"A thing?"

"Trial. His trial is today." We'd texted this morning, and
he hadn't seemed overly nervous. More resigned than anything, although optimistic about the outcome.

Paola stared down at me like she could peer into my soul,
and I wouldn't be surprised if she could. She frowned and
looked off into space for a moment before clicking her fingers. "The interview that gossip hound Tippin did. It was
with your uncle, right? He sued your man? And you're here?"

"I hate it," I told her honestly, hoping it didn't come back
to bite me in the ass during the actual competition, since that
shit was as much psychological as it was skill based. "I want
to be with him, but I'm not a witness and I couldn't get the
pilot date changed."

"Bullshit." The venom in her voice gave me pause and I
blinked at her. "You're a bigger name than the other three of
us combined. If you needed a new day, they'd give it to you.
And it's not like they can't do something else for a day or two
while you're gone."

I wasn't sure I believed all that. I knew I was popular locally, but I couldn't imagine that translated on even a regional level. But Paola was nothing if not determined, and she'd already marched over to someone and was pointing at me. I didn't know if I wanted to sit up straighter or hide somewhere I couldn't be found.

Paola returned a few minutes later with an older white man, clipboard in tow. "He needs to leave."

The man looked unimpressed. "He's already here."

The look on Paola's face would have felled a lesser man. "He has an emergency. Today. We can surely go a day without him, right?"

"Why? No sense in making changes unnecessarily."

I couldn't even say I disagreed. Fact was, we were all there, and there was no reason to move the date when everyone was already available.

I opened my mouth to say that, then paused. Just for a moment, I watched the other chefs. All surrounded by family. By kids and maybe even friends. And here I was, alone because Malik couldn't be here with me. Calling Grandma and letting her calm me down wasn't even an option, because I hadn't mentioned this to her. For something that was supposed to be my dream, I was lonely as hell.

"You stay here," Paola said, then walked away.

"She's totally going to win," I muttered, and the guy laughed.

"Probably so. She's like a puppeteer, putting people where she wants them."

"Yeah. I like her."

There was a small commotion, then Paola was on her way back, her hands on the arms of the other two contestants. "I've already talked to them. They've agreed to stick around, film some of the other stuff, and we can officially start the competition when you return."

"We're already here," I protested, but it was weak. Mentally, I'd left and was on my way back.

"Look," one of the other chefs said, "there is no one in this industry who hasn't heard about you and your guy. We all saw you at the gala, if not cooking then doing that line dance with him."

I grinned at the reminder. Jesus had recorded us dancing and sent it to us, and Malik had actually authorized James to use it as the first post on Franklin's brand-spanking-new Instagram page. When I'd asked him about it, he'd just grinned and said he liked the video.

But the guy's words hit home in a different way. No matter what Christopher thought, this show wasn't just about me and *my* star. People were invested in me *and* Malik. Even if Malik wasn't on the show, folks were curious about us. They were following our relationship. Larry's plan—to let others create the narrative—had worked. What would it do for me to be absent when my husband needed me? Especially when there was nowhere else I'd rather be?

Hope sprung in my chest and I grabbed on to it. "Why would you do this for me?"

The guy Paola had originally snagged just shrugged. "Look, I'm about ratings. Having your guy here improves ours."

"Everyone's heard your story," the other chef added. "I was kinda bummed he wasn't here. I was looking forward to getting some tips on how to beat your ass from him."

I laughed. Malik would earnestly give him tips to make sure he lost, if anything. But my "competitors" thought so highly of Malik they were willing to let me go home and get him.

I closed my eyes. Malik'd used the word *home*. Where he was, that was home. Always had been, which was why I'd felt so adrift for so long, even as my professional life had taken off.

"You guys sure about this?" I forced myself to look each of them in the eyes, and they all nodded in turn.

Then I checked my watch and bolted. "Shit, I have to get back to him. Trial starts in three hours."

I thanked them all again, then one more time as I shoved my shit together, then darted out the studio. A cab actually stopped for me, and we were off to LaGuardia.

"No luggage?" the driver asked. He'd popped the trunk when I gave him my destination.

I looked down at myself. "Shit." At his raised brow, I tried to nod. "Nope. No luggage." It was all still back at the hotel. Thankfully I was booked for another few days, but I needed to make sure I got back up here to get my stuff.

I didn't have time to worry about that now. The cabbie hopped out long enough to close the trunk, then we sped off. I pulled out my phone and, praise Jesus for commuter flights that ran every half hour. I was able to grab one, even though I wouldn't be there for the start of trial. The point was, I'd be there, where I was supposed to be, with the man I loved, who'd actually said he loved me, giving him the support he'd always given me.

My phone rang, and I wasn't surprised to see Christopher's name. "What?"

"Did I seriously just hear you left the set? What the hell were you thinking?"

"That I had somewhere more important to be, and you know what, Christopher? Everyone agreed with me."

He sputtered for a minute, like the thought of people being on my side had never occurred to him.

When he didn't respond after a few seconds, I sighed and kept talking. "It doesn't matter. I'm going back to Malik. Once everything is more settled, I'll have you reschedule."

"We're going to have a serious talk about this when you return."

I huffed and shook my head. "No, we're not. Goodbye, Christopher."

I hung up and thunked my head against the seat, and the cabbie glanced at me from the rearview mirror. "You that famous chef?"

I looked up at him and tried to smile. "Some days, yes. Today, I'm just going home to my husband."

I closed my eyes and let that word seep into my veins. We'd said the I love yous, I heard his promises, the reincarnation of the vows we'd said to each other all those years ago. What could I accomplish with Malik by my side, cheering me on, whether lying on the couch next to me or from thousands of miles away?

The thought came to me and I grabbed my phone to call my irritant of an agent. No matter how pissed Christopher might be with me, he wouldn't ignore my call, and wouldn't you know, I needed him. After this, if I never did a thing with TV again, it'd be worth it. Because these past few months with Malik had been better than anything I could have dreamed of, and I wouldn't jeopardize it again.

I huffed. How about that? Grandma was right.

Malik

I don't know why I'd thought Robert Moore, Professional Hustler, would have had the foresight to hire an attorney, especially once he knew Larry was representing me. Apparently, I'd given the man too much credit. The longer I sat in that courtroom and listened to him drone on, the more I wondered what the hell he was doing. Attorneys were expensive as hell, and I guess I couldn't say shit since I wasn't paying Larry. But seriously, Larry was doodling and listening with half an ear, and the judge looked about to fall asleep.

"Imagine how I felt, your honor, being replaced in my mother's heart, first by my nephew, and then again by that man over there. He was trying to separate us, to make her choose him over me, and you can't let him get away with it."

Robert paused then, and the judge took that as her moment to strike. "Is that all you have for me?"

He frowned, looked down at his papers, and shrugged. "I guess."

"Mr. Jackson, any cross?"

"Yes, your honor." Larry stood, took the time to fasten his suit jacket, then strolled to the podium. I was pretty sure he didn't need to be so formal, since Robert had talked from the desk, but informal and Larry didn't seem to go together.

I tuned it all out, secure in knowing Larry had this in the bag. I tried to mentally review my own list of questions, but my mind kept going back to DeShawn. To the way he'd felt that last time, to the anxiety emanating from him the next morning when I dropped him off at the airport. Our texts had been short, the bare minimum to ensure we were both okay. More and I'd beg him to return. Yes, yes, I knew he'd be back in just a few days. But given how new this commitment was, how recently we moved on from pretending this was fake, I wasn't handling even the small separation well.

He didn't need that kind of pressure before the trial, and definitely not while he was filming, but the second it was over, I was calling. To check in, give him the results, hear his voice and reassure myself he was still with me, location be damned.

The heavy courtroom doors opened and Larry's secretary, Collin, slipped in. He motioned to the deputy, whispered something, then sat down behind us. I couldn't tell if Larry even noticed, but his questioning didn't miss a beat.

"Excuse me, Mr. Jackson," the judge said, and pointed. "Someone from your office is here."

Larry turned with a frown, which deepened when he saw Collin. Collin winced but walked up to him. They spoke low, probably about some emergency at the office, then Larry nodded and Collin wiggled his fingers at me before leaving.

"Your honor," Larry started, addressing the judge, "I know we're nearing lunchtime, but I don't have any further questions. Since Mr. Moore didn't designate any more witnesses, would you like to hear my motion to dismiss now or when we return?"

"Now, if you're ready."

Larry launched into his argument, and while I tried to pay attention, I took the time to look—really look—at Robert. He'd been cool when DeShawn first introduced us, only becoming antagonistic as our relationship strengthened. Grandma had hinted obliquely about his gambling issues then, but it hadn't seemed to be a serious issue.

Looking at him now, though, I could see the way the years had worn on him. His face was drawn, his eyes tight, his hands gripping the edge of the table like he was barely hanging on. As angry as I was with him, with the way he'd whittled away Grandma's money now and wanted carte blanche to keep doing so, he was still her son. DeShawn's uncle. My... something. I'd told everyone saying no to him was easy for me, but I knew I'd try to help, at least a little, if this went our way. I managed to hold in a chuckle, because I'm pretty sure Grandma knew that, too.

Larry sat down next to me and nodded, then Robert stood and said whatever he had to say. As the defendant, I knew I should care more, but I honestly didn't have it in me.

Apparently I'd zoned out too much, because Larry nudged me as the judge began speaking. "I've listened to the testimony today, and I've thoroughly read the deposition of Mrs. Anna Mae Belle Moore. Based on all of the above, I find that Mrs. Moore was in her right mind at the time she created the will in question, and furthermore, find no evidence of undue persuasion from Mr. Malik Franklin. If anything, I see a loving relationship, one that I'm sure Mrs. Moore wishes she had with you as well."

Robert looked up and scowled at that, but the judge was unmoved. "Based on the evidence presented, I'm going to grant the defendant's motion to strike. This case is dismissed."

I felt relief, sure, but not for me. For Grandma, absolutely. For me, I felt empty. This case was the whole reason I'd gotten DeShawn back, and even though I'd originally sworn we'd end when the case did, now that I understood what we could be, what we could have, I wanted to celebrate. To hop on a plane and fly to New York and follow him around the country while he wowed audiences, if necessary. Hell, it wasn't a bad idea.

Larry laid a hand over mine and leaned in toward me. "Let's leave and give Robert some space."

I nodded. "Yeah, good idea." I gathered my things and stuck my hand out. "Thank you for everything."

He smiled and gripped the back of my neck, shaking me gently. "DeShawn's my brother, which basically makes you my brother, too. And that means I have to look out for both your asses."

"Please. You're just glad it's over so you can get back to charging someone."

"You goddamn right. I'm a securities attorney. I don't know how I get stuck with pro bono family law and estate cases."

I laughed maybe a little too loud. "We'll try to keep out of your hair for the next little while. Like the rest of our lives."

"Sounds like a plan to me."

We walked out, Robert sitting sullenly in his chair as we passed. He looked the tiniest bit like DeShawn's grandfather then, and that hit of remorse shot through me one more time.

Larry opened the door of the courtroom and I followed him out, only to be greeted by flashing bulbs and a horde of reporters.

"What the hell?" A bulb flashed in my face, and I instinctively stepped back and covered my eyes. I hadn't expected reporters, not when DeShawn was out of town. There'd been none when I arrived, and this should've been a lunch break only. But as I looked at the crowd, Noah and Heidi conspicuously absent among them, I saw smiles and anticipation. I didn't know what to do with it.

Next to me, Larry chuckled and pointed to a figure barely visible with the cameras and mics in the way. "Your boy doesn't go halfway." He clasped my shoulder and stepped to the side. "Neither should you."

I heard the words, but couldn't respond, my eyes fixed on DeShawn walking through the crowd. It wasn't until he stopped a foot away that I convinced myself it wasn't a mirage. Even then, I was afraid to reach out and touch.

"What are you doing here?" My voice was barely a whisper, like I was afraid of the answer.

"You're more important than the pilot. You didn't make me choose between you and the show, and I still made the wrong choice. I should've been here with you from jump, and I'm sorry it took me too long to see it."

It took me a moment to realize what he was saying, but when I did, the weight of the world fell off me like chains being unshackled. I snagged his wrist, tugging him close and tipping his chin up. "I love you."

His smile was a beacon of light straight through me. "God, I love you, Malik. More than the career, more than the restaurant, more than the dream of having my own show. This dream, being with you like we have been? Nothing comes close."

I pressed my forehead to his, much like I had a few nights ago. "I don't want you to regret staying."

"The only regret I've had in the past decade is losing you."

And I believed that. If he was here, with me, now? I'm sure Christopher had barked in his ear the whole way over.

"What about the pilot?"

De Shawn snorted. "Turns out you're more popular than me. The other contestants were more than willing to let me leave for a few days, especially if they have a chance to meet you."

I huffed. As long as I didn't have to be on screen, I'd be fine. "Sure thing." I leaned into him. "You get the press?"

"Nah. Apparently they'd tried to watch the trial, and said the judge decided to prohibit cameras, so they've been waiting outside."

I vaguely remembered Larry asking for that, but had long ago forgotten.

DeShawn pulled back and ran his thumbs down the sides of my face. "Marry me."

His words rang loud and clear, and I stared at him. His eyes shone, full of that boyish joy and enthusiasm he'd had the first time he proposed all those years ago.

I tightened my grip and pressed a kiss to his lips. "Last I checked, we're already married."

His smile would light me up for the rest of my life. "We are, aren't we? Then marry me again."

To that, there was only one response. "Yes, I will."

Chapter Twenty-Three

Malik

"What are you feeling?" DeShawn's voice was a touch too high, a sign he was more anxious than he appeared.

I pulled to a light and looked at him. We'd left the courthouse and were on the way to Grandma's. Even though she'd expected this outcome, it was almost an unwritten agreement we'd tell her in person rather than over the phone. "I'm glad it's over, that it's one less thing we have to worry about. What about you?"

He leaned against the headrest, his eyes closed. "Too many things."

"Name them."

He laughed, then reached out and grabbed my hand, twining it with his own. "Relief. Joy. Sadness."

All of which made perfect sense. There was always a chance Robert would contest the will itself, but I doubted it. I worried, though, about how DeShawn and Grandma would feel when I said I planned to help. Not a lot. I damn sure wasn't going to be an ATM spitting out money, but I wasn't as heartless as I'd played at Larry's office.

We pulled up to the house and DeShawn reached across the console to pull me in for a kiss. "I love you."

Those words would never get old. And after I said them once, I could seem to shut up about it. "Love you, too."

We climbed out the car and walked up the front steps. Miss Maxine's car was already there, but Larry said he had some work to do before he came. DeShawn opened the door and we walked in to find her bustling in the kitchen. She beamed when she saw us. "My boy take care of you guys?"

I snorted and shook my head. "Your boy is amazing."

"He does good work, doesn't he?"

Understatement of the year, no doubt. She came into the living room, wiping her hands off with a towel, then threw it over her shoulder and pulled us into her embrace. "I'm proud of you guys. For putting up with Robert's bullshit, for holding on to each other and making this happen."

DeShawn grabbed my hand and tangled our fingers together again, and I couldn't stop what I'm sure was the dopiest of grins at him.

"How is she?" DeShawn asked, inclining his head toward the bedroom.

"Worried. I had to give her a mild sedative so she'd sleep, but she should be awake now. Go on and check on her."

We nodded, and I followed DeShawn down the hallway and into Grandma's room. She was just starting to wake, fumbling for her remote in the sheets. She grinned when she saw us, and slowly raised the bed up. "Hey, boys. How did things go?"

Her voice dropped off at the end, but I could tell it was from fear and not weakness. I sat on the other side of the bed, as close to her as possible, DeShawn at my back. "We won, Grandma. Everything's going to be okay."

"Good. Serves him right, thinking he could just come in and change what I wanted like that."

DeShawn didn't try to hide his grin. "Yeah. From what I heard, preparation wasn't his strong suit."

She huffed. "Boy thinks he can get through life on bluster, and is surprised when it doesn't work." Her eyes grew softer then, as she looked over to the side. "I'd hoped after his dad died that he'd come around, but it never happened."

DeShawn pressed his face against my back and wrapped an arm around me, then reached out with his free arm to lay a hand on top of Grandma's as well. "You can't blame yourself for that. Uncle Robert had problems before Grandpa passed. I think grief made them worse, but Papa didn't cause, and couldn't solve, his problems."

She closed her eyes and her shoulders sagged. "I know."

That look was all it took for me to firm up my decision. "Grandma, I'm going to give him some money."

A tiny smile graced her face. "I knew you would."

DeShawn's shoulders shook, and he pressed a kiss between my blades. "Malik, we all knew you would."

"Is that so?" I tried to sound offended that they knew me so well, but my own laughter was bubbling up.

"Yes, you can be a hardass and everything, but you're not the type to leave someone high and dry. No matter how much they deserve it."

And I was glad. They understood me, better than I wanted to give them credit for, and didn't object. It was all I could ask for.

Grandma cleared her throat, which turned into a small fit, and I rubbed her shoulder gently. When she finished, she looked over at us and pointed between us. "What does all this mean?"

"What do you mean?" I asked.

"I'm too old for games, Malik. This. The two of you. The trial's over now. You don't have to pretend."

"Now, Grandma," I started. "You know darn good and well we weren't pretending."

She smiled. "I'd hoped not. I saw the love in your eyes, saw you guys wanted more, and I hoped it would last. But I always feared y'all would be too stubborn to see what you had."

DeShawn tightened his grip on me and leaned to the side. "That's because you know us too well. But we got our heads out our butts."

I placed my hand over his on my stomach and smiled at him. For the first time, we weren't letting our fears, our worries about what we should be doing, get in the way of what we had.

"I'm glad I got to see it. Now go on and get out of here." She shooed us to the door, and after we both reached down to give her a kiss, I grabbed DeShawn's hand and led him to the front.

Larry had arrived and was sitting on the couch with his mom, sharing a small pot of tea. "How is she?" he asked without preamble.

I gave a half shrug. "She's good. Sad about Robert, but good."

Larry nodded. "I get it. Robert was like an honorary uncle to me, too. It was hard to see him like that today."

My sentiments exactly. DeShawn perched on the arm next to the chair I'd sat in and, at Miss Maxine's muffled gasp, rolled his eyes and slid into my lap instead. I kissed his shoulder and sat back.

"So, now what?" Larry reclined and ran a hand over his head. "You guys have plans for what you're going to do?"

DeShawn went quiet, so I answered. "We'd like to do a renewal of our vows. Here, if it's possible."

DeShawn whipped his head around and stared at me, like he needed to confirm I knew what I was saying. I gave him a small nod and continued. "We want Grandma to be here for the commitment ceremony, and we know she can't travel. So we'll do it here, and would like to do it fast."

A soft sniffle made me turn my head. "Mama, don't cry." Larry pulled Miss Maxine against him and kissed the top of her head, even while shaking his own. "We'll get it set up ASAP. Will this weekend work?"

DeShawn looked up, and the smile on his face was more beautiful than any I'd seen since the day we were married. "To make sure we can do this for her? This weekend isn't soon enough."

I wholeheartedly agreed.

DeShawn

I had maybe been a little hasty about wanting to renew our vows so quickly. Not that I regretted it, not even a little, but dear god, the amount of work that went into that was out of control. Not just getting the celebrant, which was honestly the least of our worries, but the food, the decorations, cleaning up the inside of the house enough so that Grandma wouldn't fret. I'd put Christopher to work and made him handle rescheduling my scenes for the show. He'd also put my name to good use with the hotel and extended my stay, and would arrange to have my luggage held until I got back to the set.

All things considered, it was a *lot*. Next to me, Malik grumbled. "Why is this so elaborate? Did you think it was going to be this much? It's like the wedding all over again."

"Tell me about it."

But they were celebrating us. And fighting in the kitchen. Or something. Maribel and Sheila had created some elaborate fusion of Criteria and Franklin's food, and Lord only knew how that was going. I wanted to jump in there and add my own touch to it, but I had been forced from the kitchen. Literally.

Miss Maxine had insisted on getting a new dress for Grandma, an event that Maribel and Sheila dropped everything to assist with. The result was her sitting in the front of a small row of chairs, James protectively holding her arm, looking as elegant as I'd ever seen. The celebrant stood by the fireplace mantel, with just enough space for me and Malik to walk down the hallway and the grand total of four steps to reach them. Larry and Miss Maxine had done outstanding work turning the inside of Grandma's living room into a chapel.

"You ready?" Malik asked. We sat in my childhood bedroom, in matching tuxedos that clashed with the peeling dinosaur wallpaper, waiting until it was time to go.

"I've wanted this for a long time."

He smiled and leaned in for a kiss. "Me too. I was scared, you know."

I gasped, placed a hand over my heart, and fluttered my lashes. "Of what? Little old me?"

"You're impossible." Malik rolled his eyes, trailed his finger over my cheek, then gripped the back of my neck before letting his hand fall. "I was terrified I wouldn't be able to stop myself from falling in love with you again."

I thought about it. "Not going to say I'm mad you failed."

"I didn't fail. I realized I didn't have to fall in love with you again. I never fell out of it. No matter what, you had always been a part of what I wanted for myself. I have loved you since the day I laid eyes on you."

"That is really romantic and demonstrably false."

He snorted and stared at me in mock consternation. "Just what is that supposed to mean?"

"You fought me so hard from the time I met you."

"Because I knew you'd be dangerous. I knew if I ever had you, I'd never want anyone else."

I closed my eyes at his words, and remembered. Remembered his wide-eyed stare when I asked him out, remembered him fighting off tears when I proposed, remembered his resignation when he asked for a divorce. Remembered that kiss at Franklin's, remembered dancing at the gala, remembered the love on his face at the courthouse.

I shrugged. "I can't much get upset at that."

He chuckled, then bussed a kiss against my jaw. "You ready to get this show on the road?"

I took a deep breath, nodded, then stood and held my hand out. "Yeah. I'm ready."

There was a soft knock on the door before Sheila, who somehow found time in all the madness to grab a shower, change, and look absolutely lovely in her emerald-green sheath dress, poked her head in. "We're ready when you are."

Malik smiled at her. "Be right out, sis."

She walked away, and Malik stood, pulling me up and tangling his fingers with mine. "Thank you for not giving up on me. On us."

I squeezed, then looped an arm around his neck. "Thank you for giving us a chance."

Hand in hand, we left the bedroom and walked down the hallway. Three rows of seats, the celebrant, and Corey and Bruno, of course. They'd both refused the doggy tuxes we'd purchased, but still managed to look regal as they sat side by side at the front of the living room.

I smiled at the people as we passed, Sheila and her husband Bryan, James, Maribel and Jesus, Larry, Miss Maxine, Malik's parents, and Grandma. We reached the front and a shiver ripped through me. We were really doing this.

Malik tightened his grip and I glanced at him with a small smile. He winked at me, then grinned at the celebrant, who returned it full force.

"There is little I love more than a renewal of vows," they said, their smile broad and bright. "People who, after looking at their life, their history, the ups and downs that come from marriage, decide, not to let each other go, but to cement their commitment and move forward. We all know how infrequently that happens. We all know how easy it is to take the other way out." They speared us with a look, and I coughed into my hand.

They chuckled and looked at the crowd. Grandma was already sniffling, and from the corner of my eye, I saw both James and Larry hand her tissues. The celebrant waited until Grandma waved at them to continue. "There are many times when parties need that out. I won't stand here and tell you that every marriage can be saved. Some can't, and some should not be. But it is a true blessing when people find their love can be saved, and they want to give themselves that chance.

"I'd be lying if I said I didn't know DeShawn and Malik's story. It's been like reality TV for the past few months." The room laughed, but none so deep and as heartfelt as me and Malik. "But this is the best ending. Those happy-ever-afters that seem unrealistic to the masses, but are the only possible outcome of a love like this."

They faced us head on. "Malik, DeShawn, I am so happy for you. So honored to be part of this today, and to see you stand here, before your loved ones, and renew your commitment to each other."

They turned to Malik. "Malik Franklin, do you with these words renew your vows to DeShawn Franklin, promising to love him always, for richer or poorer, in sickness and in health, for better or worse, even if Corey throws up all over your wood floors once a week for the rest of your lives, until death do you part?"

Malik started laughing so hard he almost cried, and was nearly bent over with it.

They fluttered their lashes. "Was it something I said?"

The entire room laughed again, then Malik straightened. "Yes. I do so renew my vows."

They turned to me, and I took a deep breath. This wasn't a dream turned nightmare turned fantasy. I'd taken one look at Malik when I walked into Franklin's and thought, *This is all I want.* And I'd known, from the minute Malik looked at me, that I had a snowball's chance in hell of it happening, but here we were.

"DeShawn Franklin, do you hereby renew your vows to Malik, and promise to love him for richer or poorer, in sickness and health, for better or worse, even if Bruno makes any new piece of furniture his personal nemesis and tears it all to pieces, till death do you part?"

I closed my eyes. I would not laugh. And we all knew that was a lie, because I had to break away from Malik to get myself under control, enough that the boys came over to me to check what was wrong.

Corey whined and rubbed up against me, Bruno standing strong behind him. I knelt down and rubbed the tops of their heads. "I love you both," I said, petting them again before standing up and taking Malik's hands. His expression was so full of love I couldn't look away as I answered, "Yes. I do so renew my vows."

"Excellent. Then by the power vested in me, I hereby renew your commitment as husband and husband. You may kiss your spouse."

Malik tugged me into him, his lips hard and unyielding, and didn't let up until Grandma whistled. He broke away and shook his head, then pointed a finger at her. "Behave, young lady."

Grandma popped his hand. "Never."

He smiled and pulled me close, and I let myself sink into

his embrace. Fully, wholly, and unreservedly. For the first time in too long, I knew we were going to make it, and as I looked out among my friends—my family—I was certain we'd all find a way.

Epilogue

Malik

"So how's the show going?"

DeShawn curled up on the bed and rolled his eyes. I wanted to be there with him, in part because that hotel bed looked like it was bigger than our king, and in part because DeShawn absolutely knew what he was doing with his locs down like that, falling over his shoulder on his bare chest. I was a simple man, and I wanted my husband.

"I love it, honestly, but I can't wait to finish up this stop and come home. We have a lot of work to do."

I smiled. Just seeing his face brightened my day, but he was right. He'd finished the cooking competition, coming in second to Paola, but it wouldn't air for a few months yet. That was good, because we needed the time to come to grips with our new normal.

We'd lost Grandma just after he finished taping. Miss Maxine had found her sleeping peacefully in her bed, holding a picture of the three of us from the renewal ceremony—and a list of instructions for her funeral, which was so like her that DeShawn had spent more time laughing than crying. Tamala Mann at the service, Janet Jackson at the burial, and more love than we could imagine surrounding us.

"She'd love to see you doing so well," I told him. "She'd be so proud." I didn't need to say who. We both knew.

"She would. And she'd probably caution me to make sure my goals don't clash."

"They don't, baby. That, you don't need to worry about."

DeShawn nestled in the bed and closed his eyes briefly, before looking at me with a soft smile and nodding. He needed the reinforcement. I was more than happy to provide it. "How're renovations coming?" he asked.

"Good. Got another three weeks on the kitchen, so you know that means five. But you should see the yard. The landscapers did a fantastic job."

His smile was breathtaking. We were doing what Grandma wanted, turning her home into a getaway retreat for us. I'd taken on the bulk of it, since DeShawn was pulled from all sides. He was leaving Criteria, turning the reins over to Maribel, to work at Franklin's. We'd done another revamp of the brunch menu, which was based on the fusion cuisine Maribel and Sheila had created for our ceremony. Turns out that having a famous husband *did* help, not that I'd ever admit it to James. But so did my suggestions, and we'd added more staff and longer hours. James was beyond thrilled, and so was I. We'd kept the homey charm, because even in the heart of the business district, people looked to us for that warm, welcoming feeling. We were determined to give it to them.

And I had my husband. My. Husband. I'd wanted him to do the pilot, then the show, and come home to me as much as possible. I hated being apart from him, and when I could find someone to watch the dogs, I took time off and traveled with him. We were minor celebrities, it seemed, and it would never stop being weird to me.

"Where're my boys?"

I whistled. "Corey, Bruno, come here and say hi to Papa."

They scampered along the hardwood floor, Bruno skidding to a stop and nearly knocking into the table. I caught the laptop just in time.

I picked Corey up so he could see DeShawn and the dog nearly lost himself with joy. "He misses you."

"I miss him back. And my big boy. And you. Can't wait till I'm home."

"Just another week."

DeShawn smiled. "Just another week. I love you."

"Love you more."

"You try."

"And succeed."

"If it helps you sleep better at night, I'll allow it."

I broke into a loud laugh. "As a matter of fact, it does."

"Good."

DeShawn's eyes were starting to droop. I checked the time. "It's getting late. Go to sleep, baby. I'll talk to you in the morning."

"Love you, Malik."

"Love you, too. Night."

We hung up and I shut everything down, secure in my house, now a home, with my husband never far from my thoughts. After everything we'd been through, somehow we'd found our way to the other side, and back to each other.

I huffed. Would you look at that? Grandma was right.

Acknowledgments

A very special thanks to my dear friend, Adele Buck, who, even though she had her own book releasing in less than two weeks, took time to read the very first version of this and offer invaluable insights on how to make it tighter and stronger. I'm so glad to have met you on this journey, and wish you all the absolute best going forward!

To my crew, who keeps me sane and mostly sober: Maarika Sterling, Jacinda Sable, GiGi Thomas, Lisa Lin, and Irette Patterson, thanks for holding it down on another one.

Mackenzie, what started as a Twitter conversation turned into a real-life book, which wouldn't have happened without your encouragement. Thanks for always believing in my stories, even when I'm not so sure.

To J, I know we always joke about who loves who more, but the way you've hustled so I could live this dream is more than I ever expected. Thank you isn't enough, but I do, from the bottom of my heart.

About The Author

Jayce Ellis started writing as a child (just ask the poor sixth-graders forced to listen to her handwritten cozy mystery), then made the tragic mistake of letting the real world interfere for the next two decades. When she finally returned to her first love (her husband and two turtles, Chompers and Desi, remain locked in an eternal battle for second), she'd transitioned from mystery to romance, and there she's found her true passion.

Jayce writes about people a bit like her, Black and queer and striving to find the good in a world fixated on the bad. She prefers her angst low and her characters hot—a term encompassing all shapes, sizes, and complexions.

There may be a hint of irony in Jayce's day job as a family law attorney, but she soothes herself in worlds where people communicate and find a way to work things out, even if there's rarely a neat, tidy little bow wrapping things up. Because really, where's the fun in that?

www.authorjayceellis.com/newsletter
www.twitter.com/authorjaycellis
www.facebook.com/authorjayceellis
www.instagram.com/authorjayceellis

*D'Vaughn and Kris have six weeks to plan their dream wedding.
Their whole relationship is fake.*

Keep reading for an excerpt from
D'Vaughn and Kris Plan a Wedding *by Chencia C. Higgins!*

Chapter One

D'Vaughn

The Real Deal

"Are you just going to stare at it?"

Blinking out of my reverie, I looked up from the hefty, legal-sized, manila envelope that had been delivered directly into my hands not even an hour earlier, and stared at my best friend, my lips turned down pitifully. Pushing an obviously annoyed breath out through her nose, Cinta stomped across the living room and snatched up the envelope from where I'd placed it on the coffee table. Spinning on her heels, she stomped back across the room and leaned against the round bistro table that made up the dining area of the tiny apartment that we shared. Shooting a quick glare at me, she ran her fingernail underneath the seam, opening the envelope and pulling out its contents.

My heart lurched in my chest at the thick stack of papers now in her hands. *That had to be a good sign, right?* They wouldn't send me a ton of paperwork just to tell me that I hadn't been selected...right? Instead of voicing my thoughts, I stared anxiously at the woman who knew me better than anyone, watching her eyes rove the first page.

"What does it say?"

Ignoring me, Cinta pulled the first page off of the stack and tucked it on bottom, continuing to read in silence.

"Cinta," I called, getting annoyed that she was reading on while I was still in the dark.

She continued reading, moving the second page to the bottom. That was the last straw for me, because there was no way in hell she'd read the second page that damn fast.

"*Cinta!*" I screeched, shooting onto my feet.

Brows lifted, she swung her gaze over to me. "Girl, why are you yelling?"

I just stared at her, my face scrunched into a pout. Taking pity on me, she giggled and waved the papers at me.

"If you wanted to know, you could just read them yourself."

I took a single step toward her, lifting my hand to reach for the papers before pausing and shaking my head.

"I can't, Cinta," I whined, fear causing my voice to tremble. "I'm scared. Just tell me if it says yes or no."

Pursing her lips, she shuffled the first page back on top of the stack. "Well..." she drawled, her lips drooping with remorse, "I'm sorry to say...but both of those words appear on the page."

Releasing an indignant shriek, I flew across the room and snatched the stack of papers out of her hand. As my eyes flew across the first paragraph, my heart skipped at least three beats and my brain felt a little fuzzy.

Congratulations, D'Vaughn! We received your audition and believe you would be a wonderful addition to season three of Instant I Do.

The papers shook as my hands began trembling and the words blurred as my eyes watered. I looked up to find Cinta beaming at me.

"You're in, boo!"

I was in?

I couldn't believe it and wasn't sure if I should jump for joy or crumble onto the couch and cry.

Auditioning to be a part of *Instant I Do* had been a long shot. I wasn't a particularly outgoing woman and, although I was attractive, it was no secret that reality shows tended to put a certain style and shape of woman in front of the camera. Petite, with flawless skin. Dazzling smiles and relaxed hair. Skin so fair it was almost translucent. So aggressively heterosexual they were willing to fight another woman over a man offering community dick that was mediocre at best. In the more than twenty years that I'd been watching reality TV, it was clear what was the norm, and I was none of those things.

Well, I did have a dazzling smile thanks to three awkward years of orthodontia in junior high, and I was known to rock a bone-straight wig every now and then. That's where the similarities between me and the "norm" ended. Beyond that, I didn't tick any of the other boxes.

Yet, I held papers in my hands that said they'd chosen me. Far too often, even the calls for queer representation tended to leave out people who looked like me, but not this time. They'd accepted me in all of my cocoa-brown-skinned, plus-sized, and lesbian glory, so I suppose they were doing something different for season three. Brushing away the warm trails of tears from my cheeks, I read on. The first page informed me that I was to be a contestant on the show and then listed the contract, nondisclosure agreement, filming schedule, and terms and conditions that made up the rest of the stack. There was also a party I was required to attend where I would meet the other contestants. Moving back over to the couch, I sat down and spent the next hour silently reading through every page.

When I finished, I turned to Cinta with a wide smile on my face.

"Is this really happening?" I asked in a dazed voice.

Nodding, Cinta grabbed my forearm. She'd read everything just as I had, and knew the minute details of what I'd been tasked with for the next six weeks.

"Not only is it really happening, Vaughn, it's happening right now!"

"I can't believe this."

"You'd *better* believe it. I told you that you'd be great for that show."

"Yeah, but I don't—"

"It's not about how you look, D'Vaughn, even though you're gorgeous. I have no doubt that you could go all the way with this thing because you *never* bring anyone home. *Instant I Do* is all about convincing your family that you're marrying a stranger, right? Well, you're perfect for that because your family has no idea what your type is, so they'll believe whatever you tell them."

I gave her a skeptical look. In theory, what Cinta was saying might be true, but she was forgetting one crucial detail.

"Except…"

Cinta waved me off. "That's a small detail."

Furrowing my brows, I gave her a disbelieving look, only to have her raise her eyebrows. After a moment we both burst out laughing. I shook my head.

"A small detail, huh?"

She held her index and thumb an inch apart. "I might've went a tad overboard, trying to downplay it."

Snorting, I shot her another glance before straightening the papers in my lap. I had to sign them all and then have them notarized. "You think?"

Cinta sighed and leaned back against the couch. "It's likely to be a shit show."

Pushing a heavy breath out of my nose, I nodded. My hands shook with nerves at the knowledge that my deepest struggle was coming to an abrupt end. Placing them on my bouncing thighs, I dug my fingers into the flesh, grounding myself as I swallowed that anxiety down. This was necessary. It was past time for my family to know everything about me so that I could lose the stress on my shoulders and breathe easier. I hadn't possessed the ability to do it on my own, and now I was getting the backing of an entire network.

"Yep. It's probably the main reason they selected me. I mentioned it in my audition and their eyes probably lit up when they heard that. It's guaranteed drama."

"And that's what makes up these shows."

"It's what gets them millions of viewers every week," I corrected. I wasn't naive enough to think that my particular situation didn't have a hand in securing my spot on the show. In fact, I'd used it as bait, knowing that my personality was otherwise too plain to be given a shot and that I needed a hook. It wasn't in any of my paperwork, but I was sure that it had worked like a charm.

It got me in; now I just needed to make sure that it didn't get me kicked off the show.

♥♥♥♥

Party Time, Excellent

The party was at a mid-rise condo on the outskirts of downtown, within walking distance of both Minute Maid Park and BBVA Stadium. I parked on the street and used the code from my paperwork to get inside of the gated building. There were two men already on the elevator when I stepped on, probably coming up from the parking garage one level down, and after nodding their way, I moved into the back corner and fiddled with my phone as a distraction. Inside of the canvas bag hanging from my shoulder was the signed sheaf of papers. Per instructions, I'd had them notarized before sealing them in the tamper-evident envelope that was also included in the box. It was all incredibly official and very, *very* real.

My stomach rumbled with nerves and I hoped that the men couldn't hear it. I stepped off the elevator and onto the eighth floor, taking my time as I walked down the eerily quiet hallway until I reached the right door. I knocked twice and stood back, willing my knees to stop knocking and my heart to stop racing. When the door opened, the sound of music and laughter reached me, and my nerves escalated. While I preferred to avoid large gatherings of people I didn't know, I wasn't the most awkward person in social situations. I knew how to hold my own.

Dropping my head back, I stared up at the giant of a man who stood on the other side of the door. He smiled and moved back, gesturing for me to enter. Clad in boot-cut jeans and a clingy, scoop-necked shirt, he looked significantly more casual than I assumed everyone would be.

"Hi there. D'Vaughn, right?"

Nodding, I stepped inside of the posh apartment and promptly froze when I caught sight of the camera pointed right at me. A second man, this one dressed in soft khakis and a white shirt that blended in with the wall behind him, stood in the corner of the foyer holding the large piece of equipment on his shoulder and motioned for me to keep going. I'd been expecting this, of course—today's event had been at the top of the list on the film schedule—but it still caught me a little off guard. Releasing a breath, I dipped my chin once, shooting the man who'd opened the door a quick glance before I continued into the apartment and observed the bright, inviting decor in the foyer. There was a chandelier overhead that highlighted the art on the walls and the two large plants in attractive, glazed ceramic pots on stands.

"That's me," I confirmed with a close-lipped smile.

The man behind me closed the door. "Welcome, D'Vaughn. We're glad you could make it. I'm Kevin Henderson, one of the executive producers of *Instant I Do*."

Relief gripped me. No wonder he was dressed down; he was staff. Turning around, I held out my hand which he shook with a firm grip. "Pleasure to meet you, Kevin."

Smiling, he nodded. "Did you bring your paperwork?"

I reached into my bag and pulled out the sealed envelope, handing it over. His smile widened.

"Ah, excellent!" After tucking the envelope under his arm, he showed me the closet where I could hang my coat and bag, and then pointed me straight ahead, down the short hall of the foyer. "You'll find everyone else in there. Go on in, grab a drink, and mingle."

Facing the direction from which the noise level came, I hesitated, causing Kevin to chuckle.

"I promise you that no one in there will bite you."

Lifting a brow, I turned to him with pursed lips. "How can you be so sure?"

"We ran extensive background checks on each of you," he informed me, a somber look on his face. "No one was a biter back in elementary school."

Throwing my head back, I busted out laughing and he shot me a wink. In five short minutes, Kevin had managed to eradicate more than half of the nerves plaguing me, and I suddenly felt more at ease than I had all day. It was almost enough for me to forget about the man standing seven feet away, capturing our entire exchange.

"Okay," I conceded with a nod of my head. "I'll take your word for it."

He nodded toward the hall and, without saying another word, I took a deep breath, smoothed my hands down the front of my dress, and headed toward the noise. The sound of laughter erupted just before I entered the living room of the condo and I was grateful that just about everyone's attention was focused on the teller of the joke instead of the doorway that I had walked through.

The great room of the condo was divided in half, with a sleek, chrome-filled kitchen to the left, and a sunken living room decorated with a stylish leather sectional on the right. Cameras on tripods sat beneath boxed lights in each corner of the room, and two people dressed in all black circled the space while carrying cameras with furry microphones mounted on top on their shoulders. In the living room were six people standing in a semicircle, deep in conversation. They stood against one side of the room, next to one of the three large windows that overlooked the busy streets below, with the lit baseball stadium towering over residential and commercial buildings just a few blocks away. Nearly everyone in the group held a glass in their hands, and I decided that was a smart move. Holding a drink would not only occupy my hands, but it would give me a reason to speak as little as possible.

There was an island in the kitchen with an under-mount sink and an eye-catching graphite countertop that currently doubled as a wet bar. It was covered with a cluster of glassware, an assortment of alcohol, a bucket full of ice, and several mixers and accompaniments. Shooting a cursory glance at the group of people on my right, I noticed one of the cameras swing toward me and hooked a mean left, heading straight for the island, and filled a ten-ounce tumbler with Jameson, chilled ginger ale, and a couple cubes of ice. I forced myself not to look up.

"Remember to act natural," Cinta had reminded me as she helped me get ready for tonight. It was so much easier said than done.

Clutching the edge of the counter, I took a fortifying sip

from my lowball glass, allowing the crisp bubbles from the soda to coat my throat before I deigned to face the other people in the room. According to the paperwork I'd received, there would be a total of five couples this season, so it was likely that one of the six people already present would be my fiancée for the next six weeks. It probably wouldn't do me any good for my first impression to be that of a wallflower. Taking a breath, I girded my loins and moved across the room, being careful when descending the short flight of stairs into the living room. The absolute last thing I needed was to face-plant onto the gorgeous cherrywood floors.

I approached the group at a snail's pace, feigning as if I didn't want to spill my drink, but stalling until the last possible second. With my eyes over the rim of my glass, I observed the group. All eyes seemed to be on one woman who looked to be thriving under the attention. She was tall, with long pink hair that looked like it grew out of her scalp as it framed her mahogany-toned face and hung down to her waist. Cinta would have drooled over a wig so beautiful. A white bodycon dress molded to her substantial curves, curves that put mine to shame and made my heart flutter with joy at the same time. I'd fully expected to be the biggest person on the show this year, but whoever this woman was blew that theory into the stratosphere. Seeing another undeniably fat woman warmed my soul and made me tip an invisible hat to this season's producers.

The woman tossed her hair over her shoulder and lifted the wine goblet she held into the air. "We need to toast to *Instant I Do finally* gaying up the show!"

The group burst out laughing, and everyone raised their drinks into the air, knocking their glasses against one another in a ripple of clinks. Lifting my glass to my mouth, I giggled softly. I agreed wholeheartedly with her sentiment, and had said as much in my audition video. To my surprise, her eyes flitted over to me and she pursed her artfully painted lips, a playful look in her brown eyes, which were framed by thick lashes.

"Oh, no, ma'am! There is no way you're going to hide your gorgeous self over there, honey." Breaking the circle, she crossed the living room, her six-inch heels clacking elegantly against the hardwood floors as she made a beeline for me. Wrapping a hand around my wrist, she tugged me over into the circle.

All eyes were on me, and I knew without looking that at least one camera was likely zooming in on my face which was quickly growing hot with embarrassment. The last thing I'd expected was to have the attention of everyone present. In fact, it was something I had planned to actively avoid.

"Everyone," the woman announced to the small crowd, "we have a new arrival."

Lifting my drink in lieu of waving, I smiled and offered a lame "Hi."

The pink-haired woman turned to me. "What's your name, honey?"

"D'Vaughn."

"Nice to meet you, D'Vaughn. I'm Diamond."

"Hi, Diamond," I responded, a smile creeping onto my face. Diamond's energy was so infectious that it seemed impossible to not smile when around her.

Glancing around the circle, I found nothing but friendly faces smiling back at me. I received waves and greetings in return, continuing the job of putting me at ease that Kevin's friendliness had started. By the time we were all introduced, I felt immensely more relaxed.

"Miss D'Vaughn," Diamond began, stepping back to eye

me from head to toe. "I gotta say, you are wearing this mint-green dress, honey!"

Smiling, I dipped my head and murmured, "Thank you."

A couple of people chimed in to agree, and my face warmed all over again. The short-sleeved, A-line dress with sweetheart neckline cinched at my waist before flaring out down to my knees. Cinta had made it for me as a celebration gift after I submitted my audition video, and when I'd tried it on there hadn't been a doubt in either of our minds that it accentuated my best assets. I took a sip of my drink, trying to think of a way to shift the conversation away from me, but before I finished my thought, loud speaking interrupted me.

"Aye! Party over here!"

Following the shout, we all turned toward the entryway as two people appeared. As I laid eyes on them, I involuntarily sucked in a breath, swallowing liquid down the wrong hole. Of course, I began coughing, bringing everyone's attention right back to me. I could have melted into the floorboards.

"I'm fine," I wheezed, waving everyone off as I tottered back into the kitchen to grab a handful of napkins.

Turning my back on the rest of the room, I tried—and failed—to clear my throat as quietly as possible. I was wondering how much worse things could get when a hand came to my back just as a cold bottle of water was pressed against my left palm. Gratefully, I closed my eyes and sipped from the bottle, sighing with relief when my cough slowly ebbed away. When I felt like I could breathe without choking, I sighed and turned to the kind soul who'd helped me, thanks already forming on my lips. The words died, however, when I found the very person who'd caused me to start choking in the first place.

The finest person I'd seen in a stone's age stood directly at my elbow, with her hand on my back and her face mere inches from mine as she bent to get a good look at me. We were the same height, which meant she was just a few inches taller than my five-five when I wasn't wearing heels, with smooth tawny skin that was dusted with light brown freckles across her face. Her hair was a mass of dark brown locs that hung around her face in crinkly waves. Her arms and neck, exposed by the short-sleeved button-down that she wore, were covered in colorful tattoos, and I counted at least six piercings just on her face and ears.

"You alright, beautiful?"

Her voice was as rich and smooth as the Jameson I'd been sipping on, and my tongue felt heavy in my mouth. I tried to say something so that I wouldn't just be standing there, staring at her stupidly, but nothing came out. Defeated and even more embarrassed, I nodded.

Offering me a small smile that made my heart flutter a bit, she tilted her head to the side. "Are you sure?"

I nodded again, wondering why the previously loud room suddenly seemed so quiet.

"I won't believe you unless you say something," she teased, her eyes crinkling at the corners.

"I'm fine," I croaked before taking another sip from the bottle in my hand. It wasn't clear if the water was now for my throat or my thirst, but it got my eyes off of whoever she was, and I considered that a victory. In my peripheral I watched her subtly lean away from me and drag her warm, brown eyes down and up my frame. I couldn't tell if she liked what she saw, and I quickly averted my gaze when she brought her attention back up my face.

"Alright, beautiful. I'mma get out of your face, then."

Allowing myself to look her way, my eyes immediately fell to her mouth and I saw her smile widen in real time before she stepped back, putting a few extra inches of space in between us. She shot a glance over her shoulder before turning back to me and nodding slowly.

"I'll see you around, yeah?"

Again unable to formulate a response, I nodded and watched her walk away. Once she was out of the kitchen, it was as if the volume in the room had been raised back to normal levels, and I turned around to see that conversations had continued on in my absence. After getting myself together, I rejoined the group just in time to witness another round of introductions go up for the benefit of the two new arrivals. Unsurprisingly, Diamond took the honors, pointing out everyone and giving a quirky little tidbit about the person based off of what she had observed over the night.

There was Margo, the pansexual princess who was a little uptight, but had a great ass; Kirk, the bisexual boy-next-door with thick black curls streaked with blond highlights and a megawatt smile; and Tanisha, the lesbian femme who only dated other femmes and was obsessed with matte lipstick. Beside Tanisha was Nicolas, an unassuming guy who had declared with a shrug that he had no preferences "as long as the hole is wet." Finally was Bryce who looked like a graduate of the Diamond School of Fashion. He wore a shiny bandeau top and miniskirt combination that matched both the sky-high stiletto heels on his feet and his robin's-egg-blue razor-cut bob. His beat was a level of perfection that made me want to burst into tears, and the bag he carried was from a line that was famous for its limited pieces. It was clear from first glance that Bryce didn't follow the culture, he *was* the culture.

Diamond went person-to-person in the small circle until she made her way to me.

"This is D'Vaughn. She's adorable and likes to hide from the spotlight."

"OMG!" I gushed. "How did you know?"

"I have a sixth sense about these things, honey," she declared, winking at me before turning her attention to the newcomers, the cause of my coughing fit and the person whose words had caught my attention in the first place.

"Now," Diamond continued, "since I haven't had a chance to suss you out, why don't you two introduce yourself to the class." She pointed at the gorgeous butch. "How about you go first, handsome."

The tattooed woman chuckled. "Thanks for the compliment, beautiful." She winked at Diamond before continuing. "I'm Kris. I was born and raised in Spring, but I live in the Montrose area now." She tapped a finger against her chin as she looked up at the ceiling. "Hmm, what's something interesting about me?"

Diamond propped a hand on her hip. "This humility has got to be an act."

Kris chuckled and my heart did that fluttering thing again when her cheeks lifted. I shot a quick glance around the circle, certain that I couldn't be the only one affected by her.

"It's no act. I'm incredibly boring on most days. Oh! Here's something interesting about me. I auditioned for *Instant I Do* because I want to find the love of my life."

My eyes widened to saucers, as did almost everyone else's. The group fell silent with varying looks of disbelief on our faces. After taking a look around, Kris laughed and nodded.

"I guess I don't have to ask if anyone thinks that's crazy. Come on, y'all, it's a love show."

"It's a marriage show," Margo corrected.

"Right," agreed Nicolas. "Love and marriage are not mutually inclusive."

Kris shrugged. "In my opinion, they should be."

Nodding, I observed her for a moment before adding, "It's a popular sentiment."

Kris met my eyes. "Indeed it is, beautiful. And it's probably what got me selected this season."

"Aside from the pure perfection that is your face, I'm almost certain that's the case, honey," Diamond mused, before moving on to the other person who'd arrived at the same time as Kris.

They were a burly individual who towered over everyone else, wearing boot-cut jeans and a plaid button-down that was rolled up at the sleeves. Their face was beat with a crisp cat-eye liner, and an eyeshadow and blush that matched their shirt. They introduced themselves as "Jerri with an *i*" and instructed us to use they and them pronouns when referring to them.

After introductions, the conversation shifted to expectations for the upcoming season. A few people wanted to hear more about Kris's quest for love, but I needed to avoid her for my sanity's sake. It was bad enough that I almost choked to death at the sight of her, I didn't need to add "perpetually struck mute whenever she's around" to my contestant profile on the season opener. Somehow, I was dragged into a conversation with Kirk and Jerri, but quickly begged off to refill my drink. To my dismay, they followed me, grabbing drinks of their own as they talked over my head about gender roles and what was expected of us during the season. Since I hadn't been familiar with the show prior to auditioning, I was genuinely curious, but had nothing to add to the conversation so I kept quiet. The tenth contestant arrived, and with them came a final round of introductions. This one was quick and dirty, with Diamond calling out names and folks waving from wherever they were in the room.

About an hour into the night, my feet started to protest my upright position. Although the dark green platform heels were usually comfortable, that was mostly when I was moving around. Standing in one place and allowing my weight to settle made the shoes near torturous. Fully capable of appearing to be engaged in the conversation while sitting, I made my way over to the couch and eased down on the end, leaning my knees to the right and crossing my feet at the ankles. Almost immediately after I sat down, three other people joined me on the sectional, with Tanisha sitting next to me.

"Hey, Dee!" she chirped, pleasantly.

Dee wasn't a nickname that I went by, but I figured I'd let it slide for the night. If Tanisha ended up being my fiancée for the next six weeks, I'd correct her when we discussed strategy.

As if she had heard my thoughts, Tanisha sighed and leaned into me.

"You know, you are exactly my type."

My brows rose and an uncontrollable smile lit my face.

"Really?"

She nodded, brushing her microbraids over her shoulder and twisting in her seat until she was facing me. Her ombré lips pursed as she eyed me from head to toe, the undeniable interest in her eyes warming me from the inside and making me blush.

"Yep. To a T." She gestured at me. "All this pretty brown skin and those dimples? I love it. Then, to top it off, you're thick *and* know how to dress? Perfection."

Bringing a hand to my face, I covered my eyes, my cheeks hurting from how hard I was grinning. "Please stop."

Tanisha grabbed my hand and lowered it from my face. "Don't do that. Don't cover up that gorgeous face."

Dropping my eyes to my lap, I stared at the glass in my hand. I was on my second and final drink of the night, but I might be tempted to have another if Tanisha didn't let up.

Scooting closer to me so that our thighs pressed together, Tanisha bent her head to look at my face. "You're either not used to being complimented, or you're shy as hell and my attention is embarrassing you. Which is it?"

Lifting my eyes to her face, I tried to suppress my smile. "You are embarrassing the hell out of me right now."

With a nod, she scooted away from me just enough so that we were no longer flush against each other. "Alright. I'll ease up; but you should know that if you were my fiancée, I wouldn't."

"Well," I began, lifting one of my shoulders, "it's a possibility."

She shook her head. "Making you my fiancée would be too easy. When I said you're my type, I meant that you're the kind of girl I could fall in love with. This show is about convincing our family and friends that we are doing something unbelievable. Nothing about me and you together would be unbelievable."

I stared at her, lips parted, as I took in what she'd said. Tanisha's words made my heart beat a little faster. I could see her point, though. Although I didn't have a "type" in the traditional sense, my dating history tended to trend toward women who looked like Tanisha. With her caramel skin, pouty lips, and curvy shape, it wouldn't be hard to convince those who truly knew me that we were a thing, and from the attraction I felt toward her, and her flirtatious nature, I wouldn't even have to pretend that I was into her. But truthfully, my aim wasn't to convince my loved ones I was into a stranger—not exactly. I was here to do something that I'd been unable to do, but was wholly necessary. It mattered not if my match didn't make sense.

After I agreed with her, we moved on to a different topic, and she did as she said she would, easing up off of me. Able to breathe, I was in the middle of listening to Tanisha describe her perfect date, when I felt someone tap on my shoulder. Looking up, I saw a dark-skinned woman with a pixie cut smiling down at me.

"Hi, D'Vaughn. I'm Bethany, one of the executive producers for the show. Can you come with me?"

Nodding, I stood from the couch and sat my empty glass on the coffee table atop a coaster, before smoothing my hands down my dress and following Bethany across the living room. When we reached the foyer, she made a right down a hall of closed doors before stopping at the last one on the right. She turned to me, a bright smile on her impish face, and spread her arms on either side of her.

"Are you ready?"

Cringing, I hesitated. "Uh…ready for what?"

Sensing my unease, Bethany shook her head and touched my arm. "No worries, D'Vaughn. It's just a little chat."

"Um, okay then. Let's go."

Bethany pushed open the door, entering the room first. I followed behind her, stepping inside of the bedroom and casting an assessing glance around. There was a full-sized bed bracketed by two nightstands against one wall, and a round, plush rug in the center of the floor. In the space between the bed and the door was a chair with one of those professional light umbrellas trained on it and a microphone dangling above it. A few feet in front of the chair was a huge camera mounted on a tripod. The lens of the camera was aimed at the chair.

Bethany gestured for me to have a seat and I did so gingerly, pressing my knees together and crossing my ankles demurely as I eased down into the chair, my palms sweating more than a little bit. It was a bit nerve-wracking sitting directly in front of a camera, but it was something I was going to have to get used to, at least for the next six weeks. Standing off to the side of the camera, Bethany smiled at me.

"Thanks for giving me a moment, D'Vaughn. This won't take long."

I nodded, curious about what I'd be doing. "No problem," I offered as if I'd really had a choice.

"This little setup here—" she waved at the camera and microphone "—is for what we at *Instant I Do* like to call the Jitter Cam."

That didn't sound promising. "Jitter? Like…wedding jitters?"

Nodding, her smile widened as she winked at me. "Exactly like that! And just like wedding jitters are a natural and normal part of the wedding process, we want your interactions with the Jitter Cam to be as natural as possible. You'll see different variations of this setup over the next six weeks. At random intervals each week, you'll take fifteen to thirty minutes to talk about what's going on, how the wedding planning is progressing, how you feel about your fiancée, et cetera, et cetera. Sometimes it will just be you and the camera, and you'll have the opportunity to speak your mind. Other times, it'll be interview style, with your executive producer asking you questions off camera."

"I'll be doing this several times a week?" That didn't sound too bad. I'd grown up watching *The Real World*, so the concept of a "confessional" was something I was familiar with.

"Generally, you'll only do one Jitter Cam per week, but it isn't unheard of to be pulled into a second or even third session after completing certain tasks during the week."

I nodded. "That sounds pretty painless. What's the catch?"

Tossing her head back, Bethany let off a short bark of laughter. "There isn't a catch. I promise."

Narrowing my eyes, I tilted my head to the side. "Well, we just met, so I have no idea if that promise is worth anything."

Still laughing, she shook her head. "You have a point. The good news is that you can talk about that as soon as I'm out of the room."

My eyes widened. "Wait, like…right now?"

Grinning, Bethany nodded. "Yep. There's no time like the present."

I pursed my lips. "That's the catch."

Her shoulders shook as she laughed again. "Nope. Still not a catch. We need to capture your reaction to the party."

"But the party isn't over."

"Which means everything is fresh. Don't think about it too hard; just give your initial reaction to what you've experienced thus far, and your first impressions of everyone. When the timer goes off, you can come on out."

I nodded and watched as she left the room, then I turned my attention to the camera in front of me. Taking a deep breath, I squared my shoulders and folded my hands in my lap.

Here goes nothing.

Don't miss D'Vaughn and Kris Plan a Wedding
by Chencia C. Higgins, available wherever books are sold.

www.CarinaPress.com

Discover another great contemporary romance from Carina Adores

Instant I Do could be Kris Zavala's big break. She's right on the cusp of really making it as an influencer, so a stint on reality TV is the perfect chance to elevate her brand. And $100,000 wouldn't hurt, either.

D'Vaughn Miller is just trying to break out of her shell. She's sort of neglected to come out to her mom for years, so a big splashy fake wedding is just the excuse she needs.

All they have to do is convince their friends and family they're getting married in six weeks. Selling their chemistry on camera is surprisingly easy…but each week of the competition brings new challenges, and soon the prize money's not the only thing at stake.

Don't miss
D'Vaughn and Kris Plan a Wedding by Chencia C. Higgins, available wherever Carina Press books are sold.

CarinaAdores.com

CARCH0222TR